'Who are you doing in my bed

'I could ask you the same thing,' Amanda registered a deep, cultured voice with a hint of mockery. 'Are you sure it is your bed?'

'No, I am not. In fact I'm sure it is not,' she replied honestly. She saw a mirror hanging over the washstand and inspected her face in it. 'Oh, my goodness! I look a complete fright!'

'I think you look delightful,' the man observed dispassionately. 'Although I must say you do appear to have been dragged through a hedge backwards.'

'Hedge…hedge backwards. It's coming back now!' Amanda drew a breath of relief. 'It was the stagecoach, a few miles after you got on at Felthorpe. You caught hold of me and the stage crashed down the bank and into the hedge. That's the last thing I remember.'

'Then it is no wonder we are covered in bruises. But that does not answer the question of why—although, believe me, I am not complaining—why we find ourselves in bed together…'

Louise Allen has been immersing herself in history, real and fictional, for as long as she can remember, and finds landscapes and places evoke powerful images of the past. She also writes for Mills & Boon® as one half of the Historical Romance™ writing partnership Francesca Shaw, and enjoys the contrast between the fun and stimulus of writing with a friend and the different, but equally satisfying experience of conjuring stories entirely out of her own imagination. Louise lives in Bedfordshire and works as a property manager, but spends as much time as possible with her husband at the cottage they are renovating on the North Norfolk coast, or travelling abroad. Venice, Burgundy and the Greek islands are favourite atmospheric destinations.

ONE NIGHT
WITH A RAKE

Louise Allen

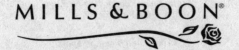

MILLS & BOON®

All the characters in this book have no existence outside the imagination of the author, and have no relation whatsoever to anyone bearing the same name or names. They are not even distantly inspired by any individual known or unknown to the author, and all the incidents are pure invention.

*First published in Great Britain 2003
Harlequin Mills & Boon Limited,
Eton House, 18-24 Paradise Road, Richmond, Surrey TW9 1SR*

© Louise Allen 2003

ISBN 0 263 83527 8

*Set in Times Roman 10½ on 12 pt.
04-1003-79387*

*Printed and bound in Spain
by Litografía Rosés S.A., Barcelona*

For AJH with love and thanks
for the constant inspiration

Chapter One

Mrs Clare floated gently up into a delicious state of half-sleep, half-waking and hovered there for a few moments, comfortably aware that there was no light from the window on her closed lids and that therefore there was no need to wake and get up from the deep and enveloping feather mattress. She snuggled down warmly and drifted back into slumber, lulled by the reassuring sound of deep, regular, male breathing from the other side of the bed.

Perhaps an hour later the sounds of the household rising intruded into her dreams without waking her. Faint riddling noises signified that grates were being readied for the day's fires, a cockerel crowed in the yard and a door downstairs banged. Mrs Clare frowned in her sleep, turned over and burrowed into the pillow. It seemed that the other sleeper had turned too, for her unconscious hand touched body-warmed linen and her body sank into the central dip of the bed, to touch his lightly.

Her dream turned from a pleasant scene in a draper's shop where multicoloured piles of silks and taffetas heaped from floor to ceiling, every one of them so dag-

ger-cheap that it would be a sin not to buy them all, to
a confused image of herself, tangled both in the silks
and in the arms of a man whose face she could not see.
She struggled, but half-heartedly, for his hands were
caressing her body and his mouth…

Amanda Clare moaned gently, wriggling closer to the
long form beside her, then sighed as a strong arm gathered her close in a comforting, sleepy embrace. She
began to wake again, to become conscious of his nearness and her own pleasurable anticipation. Her lids flut-
tered against the light and with wakefulness came an
awareness of a number of disturbing facts.

She had a headache. Indeed, as she turned her head
on the pillow she found that it was very sore indeed.
And this was not her bed, for her stretching feet encountered an unfamiliar solid bed board at the foot. Nor
was it her bedroom, or even, she realised as she stiff-
ened into full awareness, her eyes still tight shut in
alarm, her house. The noises were all wrong, the light
was coming from the wrong side of the window and
the singing voice coming up faintly from the yard below
belonged to none of her servants.

But most frightening of all was the indisputable fact
that Mrs Clare was a widow and had been for two years.
And in those two years she had lived a life of blameless
respectability, which did not involve the slightest intimacy with men.

Very cautiously Amanda opened her eyes and found
herself looking into the sleepy green gaze of her bedmate. He was so close that their noses were almost
touching. At that range it was difficult to tell much
about him, but it was very obvious that he was a complete stranger. Amanda realised that she was holding

her breath and that her heart was banging so hard against her ribs that they felt bruised.

The man's eyes widened slightly, then crinkled into a smile as he leaned forward and kissed her firmly on the lips.

'Aagh!' Amanda shot backwards in a tangle of limbs and bedding and landed on her knees on the floor on the far side of the bed. 'Ouch!' She peered cautiously over the edge of the bed, easing her bruised knees and tugging at the sheet which was round her feet, ready to run for the door the moment the stranger made a move.

He made no threatening gestures however, merely easing himself upright against the pillows with a muffled oath. Her scramble for freedom had dragged all the bedding off, but he was quite decently clad in a somewhat voluminous linen nightshirt. She saw his right cheek was badly grazed and bruised and he was favouring his right arm. Dark brown, almost black hair, tumbled across his forehead and she was very aware that not only was he tall and long-limbed, but powerfully built.

'Who are you and what are you doing in my bed?' she demanded. She thought about getting to her feet, but the high side of the bed was a useful shield and although she was covered from head to foot in a nightgown, the amused green eyes were making her feel decidedly exposed.

'I could ask the same thing,' he remarked. Amanda registered a deep, cultured voice with a hint of mockery. 'Are you sure it *is* your bed?'

'No, I am not. In fact, I am sure it is not,' she replied honestly, cautiously getting to her feet and dragging the faded chintz bedcover around her shoulders. She lifted the rest of the bedding off the floor and tossed it towards him before making a strategic retreat to the far end of the room where a planked door stood under the eaves.

Her hurried steps were painfully jarring. 'Oh, my aching head! What on earth has happened, and where *am* I?'

'I haven't the slightest idea,' the man said unhelpfully. 'But you have the most magnificent black eye, I appear to have dislocated my shoulder although it is back in place now, and my jaw—' He broke off, wincing as he explored it with careful fingers. 'Do you think we have can have been throwing the furniture at each other?'

'I very much doubt it,' Amanda replied tartly, 'although at this moment I am most tempted.' She saw a mirror hanging over the washstand and inspected her face in it. 'Oh, my goodness! I look a complete fright!'

'I think you look delightful,' the man observed dispassionately, 'although I must say you do appear to have been dragged through a hedge backwards.'

'Hedge…hedge backwards… It is coming back now!' Amanda drew a deep breath of relief. 'It was the stagecoach, a few miles after you got on at Felthorpe. It seemed to be going rather fast and then it lurched and I fell across the seat, and you—' She broke off at the memory of him gathering her tightly in his arms as the coach tipped terrifyingly off the road and down the bank. 'You caught hold of me and the stage crashed down the bank and into the hedge and someone was pulling me out—through the quickthorn—and that is the last thing I remember.'

'Then it is no wonder the pair of us seem to be covered in bruises. We should count ourselves lucky nothing is broken. But that does not answer the question of why—although, believe me, I am not complaining—why we find ourselves in bed together.'

'We were the only people on the coach,' Amanda said, thinking hard, too preoccupied to be embarrassed at his blunt speaking. 'But surely the guard or the driver remembered that we did not get on together?'

She had been pleasantly surprised to find she had the coach to herself as they left Norwich, for although it was not a market day at any of the towns along the route she had expected to have to share with several people. Finding herself alone when the coach took up a handsome man with a decided air of rakish elegance was also not what she had bargained for. Amanda's experience of stagecoaches was limited to this one, eventful, journey and her fears had been of finding herself crowded in less than genteel company rather than hoping for the speedy arrival of several stout farmers' wives to act as chaperons.

The man had, however, behaved with perfect propriety, doffing his hat as he entered. He had wished her 'Good morning,' in civil, but indifferent tones, politely taken the seat in the corner diagonally across from her and had settled back against the somewhat worn and grubby upholstery with the air of a man expecting to find the experience entertaining.

Amanda, whilst apparently keeping her gaze firmly on the Norfolk countryside rolling past, watched him from the corner of her eye. He was an intriguing puzzle and there was nothing Amanda enjoyed more than a puzzle. And, as her friends and well-wishers said, the opportunity to helpfully set things to rights. Those who were not so fond of the young widow, including her late husband's cousin and heir Humphrey, called it being 'intolerably managing and far too self-assured for a young woman in her position'.

Why should a fashionably dressed man of…what… twenty-seven or eight…be doing on the common stage? He was too old to be coming home in disgrace from a university or town scrape, and far too well dressed to be too hard up to travel any other way, unless the financial embarrassment was of very recent date. And for some reason, he did appear to be enjoying himself, which would hardly be the case if destitution was forcing him to make the journey in this style.

He was in riding clothes: Amanda shot a glance at exquisitely made boots, smartly cut breeches and a riding coat that fitted to perfection. His linen showed the attention of a superior servant and there was a heavy gold signet on his finger. Clothes were an abiding, if reprehensibly frivolous, interest for Amanda and although her experience of men's outfitting was by now rather out of date, her mental arithmetic arrived at a sum that made her raise her eyebrows.

He was sitting back, legs crossed, arms negligently folded, also gazing out of the window beside him. Amanda felt very sure that he was perfectly well aware of her and could have described her just as accurately as she could describe him, from the lazily amused expression in his green eyes, to the long calves clad in expensive leather. She was itching to start a conversation and find out who he was and what he was doing, but even Amanda blanched at the impropriety of striking up a dialogue with a complete stranger in these circumstances.

The coach had lurched and abruptly speeded up, she recalled, remembering the stranger's sudden alertness and the way he had turned on the seat to try and look up at the box and the driver. The coach had gone out of control very fast and her memory became confused. He had reached across and taken her very firmly in his arms, she did know, realising now how that firm hold and the shield of his body had saved her from the worst of the jarring, cushioning her away from the door as the stage had finally hit the ground on its side. No wonder his injuries seemed more severe than hers.

'I must thank you, sir—' she was beginning to say, when there was a brisk knock on the door and it opened to reveal a cheerful-looking woman in a stuff gown of comfortable cut, a large white apron and a mob cap over greying curls.

'Well, and there you are up and about already, ma'am,' she said, beaming at them. 'I said to Clay—that's my husband, ma'am—that poor lady and her husband will be knocked to flinders and doubtless won't be able to stir from their bed all morning. I'll go right up and see if they can fancy a nice cup of tea, I said, and just look at you, ma'am, with your poor head and all.'

'Yes, well, thank you, Mrs Clay,' Amanda cut in on the flow. 'I am sure a cup of tea will be delightful in a minute. But can you please tell us where we are and how we came to be here? I can recall the stagecoach overturning…'

'Oh, ma'am! What a tragedy!' Mrs Clay twisted her hands in her apron at the thought of it. 'It looks as though Jenkins the driver had a seizure and died right there and then on the box, for his face was all swollen up and red when Clay found him. And poor young Johnson the guard has a broken leg, his head all cut open and he is wandering in his wits, though doctor says he'll be all right given a day or two in bed, Heavens be praised.'

'And my wife and I?' the stranger in the bed asked.

'Oh, sir, you were quite unconscious—and a good thing too, the doctor said, when he saw your arm. Your poor lady seemed to come to her senses when Clay and Bill pulled her out of the stage, but she soon went off into a swoon again.' She drew a deep breath and plunged on with her tale, which Amanda strongly suspected had already been told over and again to whoever was to hand to listen.

'It was a terrible scene, sir! There was poor old Jenkins, lying there dead as though the Almighty had struck him down, and young Johnson, bleeding like a stuck pig and making such a snorting noises I thought he'd lost his mind. And you, sir, with your shoulder all out of joint and your lady, lying there in the dust on the verge! Clay said he didn't know which way to turn what with the horses plunging about in their traces, half in the ditch and half out—'

'You have all done very well, it seems,' Amanda cut the saga short firmly. 'But where are we? Is this your house, Mrs Clay?'

'Why, in Saxthorpe, ma'am, and this is the Lamb and Flag inn, of which Clay has been the landlord these past twenty years. And a better flagon of ale you won't find north of Norwich,' she added, proudly.

'I'm sure not,' Amanda interrupted again. It appeared that the man on the bed was quite content to listen all morning to Mrs Clay's exciting tale, but she was far too anxious to discover just how she had ended up in bed with him. 'And you very kindly called the doctor to us?'

'Oh, yes, ma'am. Dr Pauling and his young dispenser

as well, seeing as there was the three of you in such a state and poor old Jenkins lying there like—'

'Yes, quite, it must have been terrible.' Amanda felt she had heard more than enough about the frightful appearance of the unfortunate driver. 'And you realised that we must be a married couple? How clever of you! How did you discover that?'

'Well, ma'am, you had your wedding ring on, and there were just the two of you, and you were clasped in your husband's arms—' she broke off to sniff sentimentally '—as though you would never be parted, Clay said.'

'Indeed—' Amanda shot a repressive look at the man on the bed who hastily converted a broad grin into a spasm of pain. 'And there was nothing in our belongings?' She tried to recall what she had in her reticule and what she had left with Kate in Norwich. She had changed her reticule for one better suited for travelling and could not recall whether she had transferred her card case.

'No, ma'am, it was a real puzzle. Not that Clay or I would have looked, of course, but Dr Pauling said he had better so we could send a message to your family, but there was nothing. Even the gentleman's card case was empty.'

A puzzle indeed, for what gentleman would be abroad without his card case? It seemed as much a mystery to the stranger, judging by his expression. 'And our baggage?' he asked abruptly.

'Just the two valises, sir.' She gestured to the brown leather bags in the corner of the room. They were very alike, possibly even the product of the same London luggage maker, and it was not hard to see why they had contributed to the impression of a couple travelling together.

Well, at least neither of them had been identified, she reflected thankfully. The news that the widowed Mrs Clare of Upper Glaven House had been found clasped in the arms of a strange man on a stagecoach would be round the county like wildfire! The sooner she was away from here the better.

'Thank you very much, Mrs Clay. Please can you bring me some hot water directly? When I have finished, if you could arrange for one of the men to bring water for my husband and help him to dress and shave, that would be most helpful. I will breakfast in the parlour.'

'Yes, ma'am, of course. Your gown is all brushed out and hanging here behind the screen. Could I be so bold as to ask your name, ma'am?'

'Brown...'

'...Smith,' said the voice from the bed a second later.

'Brownsmith,' said Amanda repressively. 'Mr and Mrs Augustus Brownsmith of London, on our way to visit friends in Holt.'

Mrs Clay bustled out to fulfil her errands, leaving Amanda glaring at the stranger. 'What are you laughing about?' she demanded.

'You are a very forceful young woman, are you not? And I must congratulate you on your quick thinking. But do I really deserve *Augustus*? It was only a very little kiss, if that was your revenge.'

'You...' Amanda knew she was blushing, something which frequently happened despite her best efforts. She had not thought about that swift kiss; the overall shock of the situation had wiped it from her mind. Now it came back with horrid clarity. 'You should be ashamed of yourself! It was quite uncalled for!'

'Under the circumstances, a lot more than a kiss was called for,' he said reminiscently. 'I think I showed admirable restraint.'

'Hah!' Amanda was about to say a good deal more, but the arrival of the landlady with a jug of hot water and a clean towel sent her into retreat behind the screen.

This was a somewhat crude arrangement of cotton panels stretched over a wooden frame and Amanda peered nervously through the gap at one hinge. But the man on the bed, far from taking any interest in what she was doing, had lain back against the pillows with his eyes shut. Angry with him as she was, she could not help but notice with concern the frown of pain as he tried to shift his arm into a more comfortable position. It was not fair to ask him to travel, but they could hardly stay where they were with discovery and scandal a constant danger.

She slipped hastily out of the nightgown, which she presumed belonged to the landlady, had a hasty wash and scrambled into her undergarments and gown, which fortunately she could fasten herself. Then, feeling decently clad at last, she re-examined herself in the mirror.

The face that looked back at her was certainly not that which either her friends or critics would have recognised at first glance. Her mass of dark blonde hair was given to tumbling out of nets, pins or ribbons and falling down her back, but even so, it was always shiny and brushed. Now she winced as she tugged the comb through the tangles, removing several twigs as she did so.

Her admirers maintained that no one could match Mrs Clare's large brown eyes for depth of expression or laughing humour. Her critics, chiefly the matrons of the area who were wary of her attraction for their sons, or her possible rivalry to their daughters, remarked that it was a pity that dear Amanda's nose should be so very straight and her mouth just a touch too wide. All agreed that her chin was determined, which showed either charming independence and courage, or wilfulness and an unfeminine mind, depending on one's point of view.

Amanda herself, although she had her moments of wishing for primrose blonde hair, blue eyes, a tip-tilted nose and a heart-shaped face, was generally neither vain of her looks, nor overly concerned about their failings. After all, her colouring allowed her to wear most shades now she was out of mourning again, her tall figure and long legs showed off gowns to perfection, and incidentally contributed to her excellent seat on a horse.

However, even the most unconcerned young lady of three and twenty could not ignore a reddened cheek and a rapidly purpling eye. But there was no disguising it, for she carried no rice powder in her valise: she would just have to hope that the parlour was truly private.

The stranger's eyes were open again when she emerged, and his expression as he watched her was appreciative. Amanda braced herself for more teasing flattery, but when he spoke it was to observe, 'The sooner we are away from here the better. Doubtless they can hire me a gig. Have you far to go?'

'Once I reach Holt I am close to home.' Amanda folded the borrowed nightgown.

'Will you trust me with your true name and direction, Mrs Brownsmith?' the man asked, the glint of amusement back in his eyes.

'Mrs Charles Clare, of Kelling House—Amanda

Clare,' she replied, fighting the temptation to smile back. 'And your name, sir?'

'Now there, Mrs Clare, you have the advantage of me. I have not the slightest idea.'

Chapter Two

Amanda stared at him aghast. 'You must know what your name is!'

'I assure you I do not. The blow to my head is responsible, I suppose—we must be thankful that, unlike the unfortunate guard, I am not wandering in my wits.'

'And you have realised this ever since you woke up?' she demanded.

'More or less.' The tall man grimaced. 'It came as an unpleasant shock to find you did not greet my presence in the bed with either delight or the faintest trace of recognition. Whilst it is the duty of any gentleman to remember the name of the lady with whom he has spent the night, I am sure it is even more incumbent upon him to remember his own…'

'Do stop rambling—you hardly seem to be taking this very seriously.' Amanda sat on the end of the bed and regarded him with critical eyes. She had no intention of rising to the bait on the subject of their night together. 'What are you going to do about it?'

'Wait until I have shaved, dressed and had my breakfast.' He rubbed a hand over his chin, grimacing at the rasp of stubble against his palm. 'I will think better then.'

Amanda's instinctive retort, that the sooner he began thinking and took their predicament seriously the better, was left unspoken as a tap at the door heralded the arrival of Mrs Clay with more hot water, a bashful-looking potboy at her heels.

'Your breakfast is all set out in the parlour, ma'am, and here's Jem to help Mr Brownsmith.'

Amanda took herself off downstairs, following the tantalising smell of bacon and eggs. Mrs Clay proved to keep a good house, for the neat little parlour shone in the morning sun, there was a fire crackling in the grate and the food was excellent. Although her bruised face made chewing painful, Amanda still managed to do justice to the bacon and eggs and several cups of tea and was just deciding between gooseberry jam or marmalade for her toast when the stranger appeared in the doorway.

He was clean shaven and with his hair brushed, it was only the bruise on his face and the sling supporting his right arm that distinguished him from any other well-dressed gentleman relaxing in the country. Amanda, regarding him critically, saw that yesterday's impression of expensive tailoring was quite correct, and that, furthermore, he was an extremely good-looking man.

She had just arrived at this conclusion as he took a step forward from the threshold where he had halted and she saw he was limping slightly.

'You have hurt your leg!'

'My ankle is slightly twisted, that is all. May I join you?'

'Please do.' Amanda waved him towards the other

chair 'Just pull the bell for Mrs Clay: I can certainly recommend her breakfast.'

'From which I can assume you have suffered no worse hurt from yesterday's adventure than the bruise to you face?' he asked.

'No, none at all, thanks, I believe, to you,' Amanda responded warmly. 'And if you mean that I have a good appetite, you are quite correct: I have so little sensibility that I rarely find myself unable to eat. That was an *excellent* breakfast, Mrs Clay,' she added as the landlady came in. 'I am sure Mr Brownsmith would enjoy exactly the same, if you please. And I would like some more tea and toast.'

The silence that followed the landlady's departure seemed to last a long time. Eventually Amanda observed, 'And have you done any thinking about your predicament, sir?'

'Some about mine, and rather a lot about yours, Mrs Clare.' He seemed considerably more serious than she had seen him before and the twinkle had gone out of his eyes, despite the lightness of his tone. 'Your husband is hardly going to greet magnanimously the news that his wife has spent the night—however innocently—in another man's bed. Assured of my name and station in life, he might have been prepared to take my word for my motives and actions. What he is going to make of someone unable to provide him with so much as a calling card, I hate to think. He has not even the recourse of any affronted gentleman of knocking me down and will have to wait until I have recovered the full use of my arm before issuing a challenge.'

For one reprehensible moment Amanda toyed with the idea of creating a fire-breathing husband complete with horsewhip, before honesty and the sense of what she owed this man got the better of her.

'My husband would always have taken my word, sir, whatever the circumstances. I can assure you, all he would wish to do now would be to thank you for saving me from worse injury than I received.'

He raised an eyebrow. 'You speak in the past tense, Mrs Clare.'

'I am a widow, sir, and have been these past two years.'

'My regrets and sympathy, ma'am. To whom then should I present my explanations and apologies?'

'To no one, sir. I am my own mistress, with neither father nor brothers to thank you for your actions. My husband's cousin and heir, Mr Humphrey Clare, is my nearest male relative, and this need not concern him.' Her tone was crisper than she intended and the man's eyebrows rose, although he made no comment. Humphrey Clare would be delighted to catch out his cousin's widow in some scandalous indiscretion and she had absolutely no intention of giving him the opportunity.

'My situation is easily remedied,' she continued, 'provided I take a little care and have no further ill luck. Once I am in Holt I can make my way home easily enough. But what of yours? I very much regret having to ask you to travel this morning, but it would create a very odd impression if I were to leave without you.'

The stranger remained silent while Mrs Clay brought in his breakfast and Amanda's toast, then, as the door closed behind her, said, 'I have been looking at my boots and my coat.'

'Of course!' Amanda caught his drift at once. 'They are both by very fine makers, are they not? Presumably you plan to visit either your boot maker or tailor where doubtless you will be immediately greeted by name.'

'Exactly.' He seemed amused that her knowledge of men's fashion was so good. 'Then either the mention of my name will immediately bring me to full recollection, or I will at least be able to retreat to a lending library and look myself up!'

'And if they greet you at Weston's or Lobb's with cries of ''Good morning, your lordship!'', what will you do then?' Amanda enquired, buttering her toast. 'Ask them which lordship you are?'

'Hmm, I had not considered that. I wonder if I do have a title? It would be simpler if they call me ''Your Grace'', it would narrow the field. You are right, this is excellent ham.'

'I do wish you would be serious,' Amanda chided, although she was beginning to enjoy herself and could only be thankful she was not in the company of someone thrown into gloom or bad temper by their predicament. 'There may be fewer dukes than other classes of aristocracy, but I can assure you that you are not one of them. I believe I have seen all of those young enough to be you.' She pushed the mustard pot within his reach and added, 'Do you feel as though you have a title? Does being called plain ''sir'' sound odd?'

'How can I tell?' he asked bitterly. 'I am still recovering from being dubbed Mr Augustus Brownsmith.'

Amanda ignored this reproof. 'Of course, you could simply take lodgings in Holt and con the London papers in case your family places an advertisement for you. After all,' she added, glancing at him from under her lashes, 'your poor wife may be frantic with worry, even now.'

'*My wife!*'

'It is not so very improbable. You are old enough to be married. In fact, you may well be the father of a large and hopeful family.'

'I do not feel in the slightest degree married,' he said firmly. 'Surely I could tell that? Would I not feel some anxiety if that were the case?'

'You might be a very bad husband,' Amanda observed, then hastily added as his brows drew together, 'Do you truly not feel any anxiety about your present predicament?'

'Only for you. Otherwise I have to admit to finding it stimulating. I seem to recall being bored.'

'That is interesting,' Amanda observed. 'When you got on the stagecoach you did look as though you were enjoying yourself, almost as though you were on a spree, escaping from something onerous. I must admit to wondering why you should be travelling by stage.'

'That puzzles me too,' he admitted, pushing back his plate and accepting the toast she proffered. 'Something tells me the stage it is not my usual mode of transport. Well, I have no intention of continuing by one! I think our best scheme would be to hire a gig from this inn to take us to Holt. I will then hire a post chaise and go on to London. Once there I will put up at a hotel…'

'Grillon's?'

'No, the Clarendon, the food is better.'

They stared at each other hopefully. 'Does the fact that you know that mean your memory is coming back?' Amanda asked.

'I doubt it—I cannot even think what the Clarendon looks like. Still, there is every chance someone will recognise me and greet me by name.'

'If you do not cut half your acquaintance first!'

'You are a cheerful soul this morning, are you not?'

he teased. 'Still, let us see what my resources are: there is our shot here to be paid, the doctor's bill, the hire of a gig…'

He dug a purse from his pocket, tossed it on the table and reached into an inner pocket. 'I should have a roll of soft in here. Nothing, that is odd, I could swear these are honest people… Still, let us see what the coins add up to.'

But the purse, tipped out on the table, yielded one guinea coin, two shillings, a sixpence and a number of coppers.

Amanda, who knew exactly how little her own purse held, was able to contribute a further ten shillings and a handful of coppers.

They stared at each other aghast, then Amanda said, 'I suppose some passing person may have robbed us before Clay found us, but that is improbable if we had to be pulled from the wreckage. It would seem that the reason you were travelling by stage was because you could not afford to do anything else.' His face was so expressionless that she hurried on, 'But we have enough here to cover our immediate needs. Once we get to Holt I will lend you what you need to get to London.'

'Certainly not!' He got to his feet and limped across to the fireplace. 'Accept money from a lady, when I have not the slightest idea whether or not I can repay it? Under no circumstances!'

He struck the mantelshelf with his clenched fist, the gold signet ring catching the light and Amanda cried, 'Your ring! Perhaps it has your crest on it.'

He came back to the table, holding out his hand and twisting the ring it so she could see the bold single letter engraved on it.

'J,' she said flatly. 'That could be anything: your Christian name, your surname…'

'An ancestor's Christian name,' he finished for her.

'Never mind.' With a good breakfast inside her, her headache clearing and the sun shining, Amanda was in the mood to be optimistic. 'At least I can call you something now! Come along, Mr Jay, I have a plan.'

She stood up and he came round to pull out her chair. As she turned he caught her hand in his and raised it to his lips in a brief, quixotic, salute. 'Just plain Jay, I think, Mrs Clare. You have both spirit and courage, have you not?'

'Nonsense.' Amanda laughed to cover the little *frisson* of pleasure both the caress and the compliment gave her. 'My friends will tell you that I am abominably managing and love nothing more than a mystery. Let us settle our debts with what we have and be on our way. I would have wanted to leave something for the families of the driver and guard, but I will have to send something once I get home.'

The landlord provided a gig and the brown cob to pull it, which proved plain but serviceable. There was a brief tussle for the reins before Jay surrendered and allowed an obviously competent Amanda to drive.

'Good bye, Mrs Clay, Mr Clay! Thank you so much!' she called, waving as the cob trotted out of the stable-yard and out of sight of the inn. 'Thank goodness we are away from there! The Clays are most excellent people, but the strain of remembering who I was supposed to be was giving me a headache.' Amanda regarded her silent passenger from the corner of her eye. He seemed remarkably serious: she hoped he was not going be plunged in gloom by his situation.

However, all he said when he did at last speak was to observe, 'You drive very well, Mrs Clare.'

'Why, anyone could with this solid old fellow.' She laughed. 'A single pair of reins, a quiet horse and a deserted road is no challenge.'

'You are used to more challenging driving then?'

'My husband taught me to drive his team—four beautiful Welsh bays. But since I have been on my own I only drive a pair in my phaeton, which, I regret to say, is a plain low-perch one. It does not do for a widow in a country district to seem to be too dashing, you know. People will talk so.'

'I can imagine that the sight of you driving a team in a sporting vehicle would indeed raise eyebrows! But tell me why—' He broke off and added apologetically, 'Forgive me, Mrs Clare, I should not pry into your affairs.'

'You wonder what a lady who can afford a carriage and pair is doing travelling on the common stage?' she asked.

'I confess, that had crossed my mind,' he admitted. 'Intolerably inquisitive of me.'

Amanda laughed, not noticing the appreciative gleam in his eye at her frank amusement and the way her smile lit up her face. 'Not at all! I am the most inquisitive person myself. The awful truth—and I would not confide this to just anyone, let me tell you—is that I spent all the money I took with me shopping in Norwich and could not afford to hire a chaise to bring me and my maid home again. Shocking, is it not?'

'Surely you could apply to your banker or man of business for additional funds?'

'Well, I *could* have done,' Amanda agreed, looping the rein neatly as they trotted round a bend. 'But Mr

Greenwich at the bank is such a Friday-faced person;
whatever I do he disapproves of. I can hear him now.
"Very unconventional, Mrs Clare, if I may say so." Or,
"Are you sure that is quite prudent, Mrs Clare? So
much money in two days, Mrs Clare?" He makes me
long to run out and do something really shocking, just
to see his face, but I struggle against the impulse, for
he means well.'

Jay observed, with a shake in his voice, 'I can quite
understand that he would be the last person to confess
to that you had outrun the bailiffs and spent your all on
new gowns.'

'New gowns, a *killing* new hat, and the most wonderful taffeta for the drawing-room curtains. It was that
material which did it, for it could hardly be called a
bargain, but I do consider it a false economy to skimp
on drapery, do you not agree?'

Jay considered this. 'I cannot recall ever having had
to make a decision on drapery, but I am sure you are
right.'

'Hmm...that may mean you *are* married and your
wife makes all those decisions, or simply that you have
a very good housekeeper.' She reined in the cob suddenly, then turned him into a narrow green lane running
off the road. 'Listen, something is coming. We are getting near Holt and I do not want to be recognised.'

They waited while a chaise bowled past, apparently
without seeing them, then Amanda concentrated on
turning the cob in the tight space. 'I do worry about
your wife, you know,' she said absently.

'That was neatly done,' he complimented her as they
rejoined the road. 'Why do you worry about her—if she
exists?'

'If she does, the poor woman must be in an agony of worry.'

'Oh, is that what you meant?' Jay enquired innocently. 'I am disappointed.' Amanda flushed slightly but made no rejoinder, so he continued. 'If I am a bad husband, as you suggested, she may be inured to my absence, or even glad of it. Or she may be expecting me to be away some time on my travels. But, you know, I really cannot believe myself to be married.'

'No female face presents itself in your memory?'

'Several,' he observed outrageously. 'But none of them seem likely candidates for respectable domesticity.' They passed a milestone and he added more seriously, 'We are nearly in Holt and you cannot risk being seen with me. Set me down soon, if you please.'

'And how do you propose getting back to London?' Amanda enquired, touching the whip to the cob who responded with a brisk trot.

'That is for me to worry about.'

'Nonsense.' She made no effort to rein in. 'You do not have enough money.'

'This is all very well, Mrs Clare, but I can see the tower of what I assume is Holt church and I really cannot allow you to risk being seen with me so close to the town. Please let me down—I can walk from here.'

'To what end, might I ask?' Amanda retorted. 'With a few coins in your pocket, how do you intend to get back to London? And if you fall ill on the journey, what then? You do not appear to be suffering from concussion, but we cannot be certain there will no delayed effects from the blow to your head.'

'That is my concern,' Jay replied with an amused smile at her vehemence. 'I cannot trouble you any further, nor risk your reputation. You have already done more than enough for a complete stranger.'

'Oh, poppycock!' Amanda turned neatly into a gateway that opened into a piece of rough pasture. Behind the tree tops of a spinney, a roof of red clay pantiles and several smoking chimneys were just visible. She turned the cob to face back towards the road and handed the reins to Jay, sticking the whip into its holder on the side of the gig. 'Now, I have a plan that will allow you to recover your strength and, let us hope, your memory also, in comfortable surroundings and without owing anyone a penny-piece.'

'Indeed?' He took the reins one-handed and regarded her quizzically. 'And just how are you going to achieve this? And what is more, why on earth should you?'

Amanda hopped down from the gig, catching up the skirts of her gown before they caught in the long grass. 'One should make every effort to help one's friends, Mr Jay.'

He said, 'Am I a friend? You hardly know me, and I behaved outrageously this morning, as well you know.'

She smiled up at him, a mischievous twinkle in her brown eyes. 'You saved me from severe injury or worse when the coach overturned, and as for this morning, I understand that many men cannot be held responsible for what they do before they have had their breakfast.

'Now, listen carefully, the roof you can see behind the trees is the Half Moon, which is owned by William Bream. He was our head groom, but he chose not to stay when my husband's cousin inherited and so bought this inn. It was in a terrible condition, and the worst kind of ale house, frequented by all the riff and raff of the neighbourhood. He has transformed it over the last few months and many respectable local people use it now. With three bedchambers and a small livery yard Will is attracting some of the passing carriage trade as well.'

'And you will recommend me for a potboy or an ostler?'

'Certainly not, I doubt you could escape notice for very long in either guise. No, Will is an excellent man, but he has always struggled with his figures and only the other day he was telling me he would have to employ a clerk from the town for several hours each week just to bring order to his book-keeping. My plan is for you to organise Will's accounts in return for your bed and board. In a few days either your memory will have returned or we will have thought of some plan to establish your identity.'

Jay steadied the cob, which was growing restive and trying to snatch a mouthful of grass. 'You, Mrs Clare, are a very managing young lady.'

'I know,' she said cheerfully. 'Mr Humphrey Clare—my husband's heir—says it is my besetting sin. Well, one of them,' she added frankly. 'Will you do it, though?'

'I will, and you have my thanks for it. Tell me, does Mr Humphrey Clare always feel so free to criticise you?'

'Yes, for he is now head of the family, and I am afraid I am a sad trial to him for he does not know what to do with me. If I would only show some feminine weakness and weep on his manly bosom, he would feel much better about it. But never mind Humphrey,' she added as Jay gave a snort of amusement. 'Allow me ten minutes to find Will and explain all to him, then drive into the inn yard. I will go in through the back door and wait inside in case anyone I know should pass.'

Amanda ran across the field, ducked between the two rails of the fence and began to thread her way through the spinney. Once she thought she was out of sight, she paused and looked back. The man she called Jay was sitting staring thoughtfully between the cob's pricked ears, his face impossible to read at that distance.

She stood for a moment, finally allowing the memory of waking up to come back to her, the warm, safe feeling of his body next to hers in the feather bed, the exciting pressure of his lips in that fleeting kiss. 'And that is more than enough of that, Amanda Clare!' she scolded herself out loud, turning to hurry on her way. 'He is probably married with several lovely children and a charming wife, or he is a rake who kisses three different women a day. Whoever he is, he will certainly be on his way and out of your life just as soon as his memory returns.'

Chapter Three

Will Bream was in the stableyard when Amanda emerged through the spinney gate. He came to meet her with a broad smile on his face, which faded as he took in her black eye and grazed cheek.

'Mrs Clare, ma'am! Have you had a fall? Come inside, do, and I'll send for Dr Hoskins this minute.'

Amanda allowed herself to be ushered into the inn but resisted the landlord's efforts to call a groom to fetch the doctor and a maid to bring lavender water. 'No, Will, I am quite all right, I had an accident on the stage yesterday and although it is sore, I do not need the doctor. Now listen, please, for there is not much time. In a few minutes a gentleman is going to drive into the yard and this is what I want you to do…'

At the end of her hasty recital Will, who had been listening with his mouth half-open, began, 'Now, Mrs Clare, this won't do and you know it! Taking up with some stranger when you don't know who he may be and then expecting me to employ a gentleman-born to do my clerking…'

'He saved me from being seriously hurt,' Amanda retorted hotly. 'And I am not asking you to employ him, merely to give him board and lodging in a charitable fashion in return for which he will cast your accounts into order.' He still looked mutinous, so she added coaxingly, 'And if I cannot rely on you to tell me whether he is a fit person for me to be acquainted with, I do not know who I could ask, for you know you are an excellent judge of character.'

'It's no good wheedling me with fine words, ma'am! What your poor husband would say I do not know.'

'He would thank you for taking such good care of me and for helping me fulfil my obligations to a gentleman who was hurt looking after me! Now, here he comes, Will, go out to him, do, before he encounters one of the grooms. Bring him in here.'

Will strode out to the gig, which had stopped under the newly painted inn sign of the half-moon partly hidden behind scudding clouds. Amanda watched his stocky figure, recognising the belligerent set of his shoulders, although his manner was polite enough. If he thought she had encountered a n'er-do-well, Jay would be on his way, never mind what she might say.

But it seemed he passed muster, for Will turned and shouted for the groom, then lifted the valises from the back of the gig himself. Jay climbed down with some care and Amanda saw his mouth tighten into a thin line as his injured ankle took his weight. He limped into the inn and met her in the shadowy hallway with a grin. 'Your faithful landlord is bristling like a bull terrier in case you have brought home an undesirable,' he remarked.

'I trust Will's judgement,' Amanda said primly as she led the way into the parlour. 'Naturally, being a mere woman, I could be sadly deceived in your character and must rely upon a male opinion.'

'You should not pay so much attention to your Cousin Humphrey!' was all that Jay could retort before the landlord joined them.

'The best bedchamber is free, sir, and this parlour is private, you will not be disturbed here. Are these all your bags? I will have them taken up.'

'Thank you. I would be obliged for the loan of some linen,' Jay said, ruefully regarding the state of his cuffs. 'No, not that bag, it belongs to Mrs Clare.'

'Will you lend me your gig, Will, and see that the one in the yard gets back to the inn at Saxthorpe?' Amanda asked. 'I would as soon not send it back from my own home. It was hired by Mr and Mrs Brownsmith, remember.'

'You leave it to me, Mrs Clare. And I'll drive you back home myself in a moment, just as soon as Mr Jay here is settled. I'm not having you gallivanting about the countryside by yourself with your poor face in that state. And not even a veil on your bonnet! What will people think?'

He marched out, shouting for the housekeeper and Amanda turned to peer into the rather dusty mirror hanging by the fireside. 'Oh my goodness, my eye is grown even blacker and more swollen! I look a complete fright!'

Jay's face appeared in the reflection over her shoulder. 'You are a very unusual young lady, Amanda. I sure there are none other of my acquaintance who would not be swooning away or having a tantrum or both despite the fact that the eye will soon subside and the graze is unlikely to mark your very pretty complexion. You are being both sensible and brave.'

'Nonsense.' She laughed, turning away from those penetrating green eyes to hide her pleasure. 'Beside the fact that you cannot recall any of your acquaintance to make a comparison, you forget I am not a young lady, I am an independent widow with no inclination to vapours.'

'Of course, you told me you had no sensibility, did you not?' Although she had turned from the mirror he had not stepped back and she found herself standing very close to him. The faint, warm male scent she remembered from the bed that morning filled her nostrils and she found it difficult to either step away, or make some light remark. She wished he would call her by her Christian name again, she liked the sound of it on his lips.

'You will promise me something?' he asked.

'What?' She kept her gaze fixed firmly on his top waistcoat button.

'Despite your lack of sensibility, your inability to have the vapours and your complete independence— you will go home, let your maid look after you, send for your doctor and rest.'

'I—'

'As you told me just now, you are a mere woman and must rely upon a male opinion.'

Will appeared in the doorway, his brows drawing together as he took in how close they were standing. 'All ready to go, Mrs Clare ma'am. I'll have one of the men take the gig back later. Let's be getting you home. What'll Miss Porter be thinking?'

'Nothing, except whether she should have transplanted the snowdrops under the beech hedge when they finished flowering and not have left them until now, if I know Jane.' She smiled at Jay. 'Miss Porter is my lady companion, but the garden is her abiding passion and unless she was expecting me to have returned with

some new treasure for it, my absence is unlikely to have
come to her notice.'

'An unusual companion,' Jay remarked drily.

'Indeed, and the perfect one to suit my temper! She
gives the appearance of my observing every convention
and yet causes me the least trouble in the world.'
Amanda began to draw on her gloves and look for her
reticule. 'You must not think her uncaring, for she is a
dear friend. She is quite willing to accompany me, or
help with entertaining if I ask, but if left in peace, she
simply vanishes into the garden and terrorises the gar-
deners in the most pleasant way possible.' She retrieved
her reticule and smiled at him. 'I will be off now. Do
rest; I will come and see you tomorrow and find out
how you get on.'

Jay took her proffered hand in both his. 'And you,
too, take care. But do not come here, it would not do
for you to be seen. I will give myself the pleasure of
calling upon you in a day or so, if you will permit.'

Will helped her up into the carriage and watched her
wave goodbye with a disapproving expression on his
face. 'And just why did the gig have to be hired for Mr
and Mrs Brownsmith?' he enquired ominously, turning
into the High Street.

'Well, I could hardly leave Mr Jay there with no
memory of who he was, and with barely a shilling to
his name, and so we had to pretend to be married,'
Amanda explained, reflecting that Will could be somewhat stricter than her governess ever was once he put
his mind to it. She could tell he suspected he was getting only half the story, but there were limits to what
even the most indulged family retainer might ask and
he subsided into silence.

Fortunately Amanda saw no close acquaintance on

the streets and, thanks to Will's brisk driving, they were
out of the little market town before her damaged face
was remarked upon. The road rose and fell as they
crossed the course of the River Glaven, wending its way
to the sea a mile or so to the north. The wooded slopes
gave way to arable fields with trim hedges and every
now and again allowed a glimpse of the roofs and chimneys of Glaven Hall, Amanda's married home, now occupied by Mr Humphrey Clare and his mother.

Will turned the gig into a well-metalled driveway and
soon the façade of Upper Glaven House came into view.
Amanda's home for the past two years was a neat house
of the local red brick with flint panels. Two windows
on each side of the front door were balanced by a wing
on either side, set slightly back from the façade, and
with its restrained pediment the house sat with an air of
unpretentious elegance amid its sweeping lawns and
wide borders, now burgeoning into flower with the
warmth of late spring.

The door burst open as they approached and Kate,
Amanda's maid, ran out, down the steps and arrived
breathless and red-eyed at the side of the gig.

'Oh, ma'am, I've been so worried,' she began, then
gasped at the sight of her mistress's face. 'You are hurt,
ma'am! What has happened?'

'I am quite all right, Kate, there is no need to fuss.
Good morning, Jane,' she added as Miss Porter emerged
from the side of the house, her inevitable garden trug
in the crook of her arm. 'As you can see, I had a slight
accident on the way so was forced to stay the night at
an inn on the road, but it looks far worse than it is.'

'Goose grease,' was Miss Porter's response and she
turned back towards the house. Amanda could hear her

murmuring, 'And if there is any of my witch-hazel infusion left that will help the bruising.'

'Now, Kate, take my valise so as not to delay Mr Bream, he has enough to do without running me about the countryside! Thank you, Will,' she added quietly as she stood beside the gig. 'Please add the expenses of returning the other vehicle to Saxthorpe to my account, and if there is anything over and above Mr Jay's keep, be so kind as to add that too. There is no need to mention it to him.'

The innkeeper shot her a hard look. 'You take care now, Mrs Clare, and I don't just mean your face. Good day to you.'

Amanda followed Kate up to her room and submitted to having her bonnet strings untied and her pelisse removed. It was obvious that she was not going to escape without an explanation to satisfy both the maid and Miss Porter, who had produced a large pot of goose grease and a bottle of her own infallible witch-hazel remedy.

'The unfortunate stagecoach driver suffered a seizure and the coach ended up in the ditch,' she explained, wincing as Jane dabbed her cheek. 'We were all very knocked about,' she added, managing to give the impression that there were several passengers, 'and had to spend the night in an inn.'

Miss Porter gave a little gasp of horror. 'Then it is fortunate indeed that you have not suffered a worse injury! Was anyone else hurt?'

'The driver, I am sorry to say, seems to have died from his seizure, the groom was knocked unconscious and one gentleman suffered more serious, but not life-threatening, injuries.' That was all she was going to say about yesterday's mishap, now she must hope that such a spectacular accident did not reach the local newspaper or cause gossip in Holt.

'It was foolish of me to travel by stage,' she said. 'I do hope neither of you will say anything to anyone about it, I would be so embarrassed if it were to get out.' Embarrassment would be the least of her feelings if it were to become known that Mrs Clare had been staying at a country inn with a gentleman under an assumed name! 'Now, Kate, I would like a hot bath, a light luncheon and then I think I will rest this afternoon.'

Amanda's intention had been to refresh herself and then lie down to think seriously about what could be done to restore Jay's memory, or, if that could not be done, how she could persuade that stubborn gentleman to accept a loan to get to London to pursue his true identity there.

What happened, once she had emerged from a pleasant bath, eaten a slice of cold chicken with bread and butter, drunk a reviving cup of tea, submitted to being smeared once more with grease and dabbed, painfully, with witch hazel and was finally alone and in peace in her bed, was that she fell into a deep slumber.

Amanda woke when the setting sun streamed in through the west-facing, uncurtained, window of her chamber. Rubbing her eyes, she rang the bell for Kate and picked up the set of note tablets that she kept beside her bed in the hope that she might have woken at some point and jotted down a good idea.

She very often did, although sometimes the notes proved unintelligible in the morning. But the tablets revealed only the thoughts of the few days before her trip to Norwich: *Turnips and sheep—write to Mr Coke re pasture; elm trees, how long to reach felling size?; new gown—quilted hem?; point lace or Brussels? Speak to Cousin H. abt. Long End cottages.* And mysteriously, *Dried peas.* There was nothing to help with the problem of Jay.

And a problem it was, not least because one part of her did not want the riddle of his identity solved too soon, because then he would leave. Amanda was not given to self-deception, experience had proved it gave only a false sense of security. She knew she was attracted to Jay, to his expressive green eyes, to the long, lean body that moved with such grace, despite his injuries, to the humour in his voice and the courage with which he dealt with the loss of his identity.

She was just telling herself firmly to stop indulging in daydreams when Kate peeped round the door. 'Are you feeling better, ma'am? Will you be getting up for dinner? Mrs Howlett is roasting a nice joint of lamb, and she says to say there is a buttered crab and some almond tartlets if you could fancy a little of those.'

'That sounds excellent, Kate. Now, if you will just fetch my dark green gown, I will get up.'

The maid hastened about her work, but Amanda, more perceptive now she was rested, noticed that her eyes were still red, her face looked pinched and she showed slightly less then her usual energy.

When Amanda had made her decision not to apply for further funds from her banker in Norwich, she had intended purchasing tickets on the stage for both Kate and herself. But Kate had asked if she could not travel with the packages on the carrier's cart, which made its slow way from the county town up to Holt every week, laden with the orders dispatched by the housewives and yeomen of the market town for those goods that their local shops could not provide.

Kate was very friendly with the daughters of Thomas Green the carrier, and, Amanda suspected, increasingly with young Tom, his elder son and heir to the business. But they were a respectable family, and Kate could do worse than to take up with a well-set up young fellow who worked hard and had a good business to follow. She had agreed willingly enough, telling Kate she could stay and visit with the Greens if the offer was made and Mrs Green was at home. Perhaps there had been a falling-out with Tom.

'And what was your journey back like, Kate?' she asked as the girl stood holding the hair pins while Amanda twisted up her curls into a style suitable for evening wear. 'Did you stay with the Greens?'

'Yes, ma'am,' she said.

Glancing at her reflection in the mirror, Amanda saw Kate was blushing. 'Are they all well?' she persisted. 'Tom, and his sisters?'

'Yes, ma'am.'

As Kate could normally talk the hind leg off a donkey and needed very little encouragement to do so, this was worrying reticence indeed. Could she have fallen out with the young carrier? Perhaps he had found another girl. Amanda resolved to visit Mrs Green before many more days were past. The Greens were her tenants on a smallholding that supplemented the carrying business, and would not find a casual call from their landlady unusual.

'I didn't tell them you were coming back on the stage from Norwich, ma'am,' Kate added suddenly. 'I just said you had let me have a holiday. I didn't think you would want people knowing.'

'Thank you, Kate, that was discreet of you.'

'Well, you did say that if I was to be a proper lady's maid, I should learn never to gossip.' Kate looked so inexplicably depressed by this statement that it was as much as Amanda could do not to demand an explanation there and then.

But dinner needed ordering and she should join Miss Porter in the drawing room, so she contented herself with saying, 'Run along and tell Mrs Howlett that I would like dinner at half past six.'

Miss Porter was sitting by the fireside, perusing a letter when Amanda entered. Her companion, a tall, plain woman in her mid-thirties, had presented herself in answer to Amanda's advertisement for a lady companion just when the young widow was beginning to despair of finding anyone congenial to lend her countenance. She had already rejected two ladies of dubious gentility, another who had not stopped talking from the moment she had entered the room and several of undoubted good birth but with hardly an idea in their head.

Jane, who made no bones about her straitened circumstances, her desire to make her own way in the world and not be dependent on her relatives and her willingness to leave her employer to her own devices just as much as that lady wished to be left, was a breath of fresh air. Even Cousin Humphrey, who, at the instigation of his mother, had had his attorney cast a very sharp eye over Miss Porter's references, antecedents and family, had to confess he could find nothing to criticise.

'Are you feeling rested, my dear Amanda?' she enquired, setting aside her letter and getting to her feet. At all times she appeared cool and reserved, but Amanda knew her manner hid a warm and caring nature.

'Thank you, Jane, I am much better for the rest. Now, do not disturb yourself: tell me how you have been getting on while I have been away.'

The news was little enough: an altercation with the butcher over his account, an accident to the best teapot, some improvements in the new herbaceous border and a visit from Cousin Humphrey.

'Oh dear, I am sorry you had to entertain him alone, Jane. Was he very tiresome?'

'He just wanted to pry about why you had gone to Norwich,' Miss Porter said coolly. 'You may trust me that he got only the most vapid replies. I then asked him if he would give me his opinion as to the state of my compost heaps and he took himself away in great haste.'

Amanda snorted with amusement, then remembered her anxiety about Kate. 'When did Kate arrive home? I thought she was not looking her normal self.'

'Mid-morning today,' Jane replied. 'She said she had stayed the night with Mrs Green. She does look peaky—possibly they all sat up too late last night.'

'I think there may be more to it than that, but I will worry about it tomorrow. Now, let me tell you all about my shopping expedition—I have been quite delightfully extravagant.'

Chapter Four

Kate proved extremely difficult to speak to the next morning. She flitted in and out of Amanda's room performing her duties, but the minute Amanda put down her hair brush and turned to ask the girl to sit and talk she found she had vanished again.

Finally, after breakfast, Amanda tracked her down in the kitchen and bore her off to the back parlour. 'Now then, Kate, something is wrong, I can tell. Do you want to tell me about it?'

She was expecting some tale of a falling-out with Cook or perhaps a lover's tiff with Tom Green, certainly nothing very serious, and was startled when the maid buried her face in her apron and burst into noisy tears. The more Amanda tried to calm her, the worse the sobs became, so that all that was audible from the muffling white cotton was the occasional disjointed word, interspersed with weeping.

'I never should've…without a character…parish… wish I was dead…'

The volume was quite enough to disturb the rest of the household. Howlett the butler put his head around the door, his eyebrows raised in fastidious disapproval at the noise, and was waved away by Amanda. He had no sooner shut the door silently behind him than Miss Porter could be seen, peering anxiously through the window, obviously distracted from her gardening, for her bonnet was askew and there was a smudge of earth on the end of her nose. She too was waved away and Amanda, thrusting a clean handkerchief into Kate's hands, ran to the kitchen herself to fetch a glass of water: she had no intention of involving Cook or any of the maids in whatever was distressing Kate so much.

At last the sobs subsided into miserable hiccups and loud sniffs. Kate emerged from the sodden folds of her apron, her nose red, her eyes inflamed and the snail tracks of tears staining her cheeks. She gulped the water and eyed Amanda nervously.

'My dear Kate, whatever is this all about? How can I help?' Amanda asked gently.

'No one can help, ma'am. Wish I was dead,' Kate muttered again, drawing in her breath for a fresh onslaught.

Amanda decided sympathy would only make her worse. 'Now stop saying that, it is a wicked thing to say, even if you do not mean it! Have you fallen out with young Tom?' Kate drew in a deep, wavering breath, and Amanda said hastily, 'No! Do not try to speak until you have command of yourself, you will make yourself ill. Here, drink some more water.'

Finally, after much sniffing and twisting the handkerchief into knots, Kate blurted out, 'I'm pregnant! And now I'm ruined and you'll throw me out and I'll have to go on the parish, and I'll never be a lady's maid and go to London!'

'Oh, Kate!' Amanda gathered her in her arms and patted the heaving shoulders. 'Do not take on so, of course I will not throw you out! But in any case, Tom will marry you, and just think how happy you will be with your own baby and your own home...' Her voice trailed away. 'You have told him, haven't you?'

'No,' Kate said. 'I wasn't sure, you see, until we went to Norwich and then I went to see a midwife—one who doesn't know me—and she said I was a foolish girl and of course I was pregnant, and I'd better get the father to marry me before it started to show and I made a scandal.'

'You did not tell him last night?' Amanda pulled up a stool beside the girl and held her hands.

'No, because when I got there he was flirting with that Joan from the mill, and I thought, perhaps I'm mistaken in him, and he has lots of girls and he doesn't want to marry me. I won't marry him if he's unwilling,' she burst out with sudden vehemence. 'I don't care what anyone says!'

'Quite right,' Amanda agreed heartily. 'If he does not willingly offer for you, then we will have to think again, but, Kate, I am sure he will. And as for Joan Bridges, why, that girl flirts with every young man, and you can't expect them to behave like clergymen!' Kate began to look more cheerful, and she added, 'And you and Tom can have that little lodge at the south gate—it needs a bit of work, but it will soon be snug, and there's a garden, and a pigsty and room for hens. Why, you will soon be the complete housewife.'

'Thank you, ma'am,' the maid rejoined gratefully, but then added, with a little sniff, 'But I did so want to be a good lady's maid and go to London and work in a big house one day.'

Amanda got to her feet and said, not unkindly, 'Well, Kate, you have made your bed and now you must lie on it.' As have we all, she thought, her face suddenly expressionless. 'Now, go and wash your face, change your apron and you may run down and see Tom now. The sooner you tell him, the sooner we can make arrangements.'

The girl hurried out, already untying the ruined apron and Amanda stood where she was, the bleak look still in her eyes. What she would have given to have had Charles's child… She was jolted out of her reverie by a tap on the window: Jane Porter was peering in again. With a sharp shove Amanda raised the long sash window enough for her companion to bend and step over the low sill into the room.

'My dear! What was that all about? You could hear the girl as far away as the vegetable garden!'

Amanda checked that the door was closed, then said quietly, 'You will not speak of this to the staff, please, Jane, but Kate is with child.'

'Tom Green?'

'Yes, thank goodness, for they are a good, honest, family and he is a hard-working lad. No doubt he would rather have had a few years yet before having the responsibility of a wife and child, but he is no innocent, and he will not be surprised at the consequences of his actions!'

Jane pulled off the old gloves she used in the garden and tossed them on the table. 'Well, he will have to marry her, like it or not.'

'No! I will not have her forced into marriage with a man who does not love her, to someone who is only doing his duty. If he is not whole-hearted, I will just have to find her a respectable place somewhere and she must become a widow for the sake of appearances.'

Jane shot her a dubious look, but did not comment.

She had found Mrs Clare held strong opinions on marriage, and although she was not someone given to vulgar speculation about her acquaintance, she did sometimes wonder about the nature of her employer's own, short-lived, union.

'We will know soon enough if there is a problem,' she said calmly. 'Now, how do you feel, my dear? I am sure you should not be having these problems to wrestle with so soon after your accident.'

'Oh, I am well enough,' Amanda said, raising one hand to her grazed and bruised face. 'If only this would not stiffen up so as it heals—it is most uncomfortable and I must look a complete fright.'

'It is very fortunate that you did not suffer worse injury,' Jane commented. 'And the other passengers, with the exception of the one gentleman you mentioned—they were all unharmed, I think you said?'

Amanda felt awkward. By nature almost transparently honest, she disliked the subterfuge necessary on this occasion. Surely with Jane she could reduce the half-truths to the minimum? 'There was only the one other passenger,' she said, attempting to pass it off lightly.

'You were alone in the stage with a strange man?' Jane queried. 'That must have been most uncomfortable.'

'Why, no, he was a perfect gentleman, kept himself strictly to himself before the accident, and I do believe he saved me from worse injury by er…catching me when the coach left the road.'

'*Catching you!* My goodness, how very embarrassing for you.' Jane paused, then added, apparently inconsequentially, 'And is he a well-favoured gentleman?'

'What has that got to do with it?' Amanda demanded

hotly, then saw the twinkle in her companion's eyes and realised that her very vehemence had betrayed her. 'Yes, Jane,' she admitted with a smile, 'Mr Jay is a very well-favoured gentleman. Not, of course, that I expect to see him again.'

'Of course not,' agreed Miss Porter solemnly.

By the next day, with no word from Jay, Amanda found herself growing restless, whatever she might say to Jane. No news presumably meant that his memory was still a blank, but she was tormented by the desire to go into Holt and find out whether anything, however small, had come back to him.

That would be most unwise, of course, and any lady with a well-regulated mind would have the self-discipline to put him out of her thoughts entirely. No doubt she would eventually receive a note from him telling her that all was well again, or she would hear that he would had secured the resources to make his way back to London.

But Amanda knew well that whilst *she* might consider her mind was perfectly well regulated, Mr Humphrey Clare, his mama and many of the ladies who constituted society in the locality regarded her as headstrong, unbiddable and positively eccentric in the way she managed her life and the landholdings with which she had been so generously endowed by her husband.

Her instinct was to help people, to involve herself in the lives of her friends and those who were her dependents. It was only the fact that she owed Jay much and that he needed her help which made her so anxious, of course; there could be no other reason for wanting to see whether those green eyes still had that mocking twinkle.

At this point Amanda threw aside the quill with which she was casting her household accounts and looked irritably at the ledger in front of her. She had been working on this task since breakfast—a good hour and a half—and very little seemed to have been achieved except a column of figures, which at a second glance did not add up correctly, and a pile of bills from the tradespeople of Holt, still waiting her attention.

Normally this tiresome weekly task took her half an hour: perhaps the knock on her head had caused some ill effects after all. Her concentration was certainly not what it was, she decided, getting to her feet.

Kate, returning yesterday from her encounter with young Tom, had been in a glow of happiness, all her tears gone and full of wedding dreams. There was a great deal to do as a consequence—set the repairs to the lodge in train, speak to Tom to see what additional employment she might be able to put his way, and, not least, find a replacement lady's maid. But it all seemed difficult this morning.

Fresh air and exercise was what she needed, and if that did not clear her mind she would send for Dr Hoskins tomorrow. Amanda took an old bonnet from the chest in the hall where she kept it for when the urge to go for a walk took her, and looked around for Jane in case she wanted to accompany her. But there was no sign of her companion, and, when asked, the butler informed her that he rather fancied Miss Porter had taken the trap and the grey cob and gone into Wiveton immediately after breakfast with some cuttings for the Rector's garden.

Amanda stepped out into the garden, tying her bonnet

strings and trying to decide which way to go. The riverside path would be pretty, with the chance of seeing a kingfisher, but would probably be muddy. A stroll through the lanes risked too many meetings with neighbours, who would be shocked and curious at the sight of her bruised face, and the walk on to the Heath was too tiring given that the ache in her bruised limbs was still not yet responding to hot baths and Kate's vigorous rubbing with embrocation.

In fact, the garden looked very tempting, and even if she was not taking exercise, a stroll along the pathways would be pleasant in the sunshine. Despite the gardener's grumbles about 'wimmin' ordering him about in 'his' garden, he did do what Jane told him and the results of his manual labour and her knowledge and good taste was charming. The late-spring plantings were well advanced and the bees were droning and bumbling. The sunshine had encouraged the birds and several were in full song in the holly trees that edged the lane boundary of the garden.

Amanda finished her wanderings at the little summerhouse. It was screened from the wide gravel path that led round the side of the house from the stable yard by a small shrubbery of laurels. The ladies often took their reading or sewing there on a warm day and Amanda was just wondering whether, if she were to go back into the house for a book to read, she would be able to concentrate on it, when she heard the sound of hooves from behind the high brick wall of the yard and the sound of the groom running out to greet the arrival.

Who could that be? It might be Jane returning from Holt; it might equally be Cousin Humphrey. Amanda stayed where she was, just in case, peeping from between the branches. Booted feet crunched the gravel underfoot and Jay came round the side of the house.

Suddenly the day was perfect. Amanda felt her heart give a little skip of happiness, which she did not stop to analyse, and she turned and ran though the shrubbery to intercept him before he reached the front door.

'Jay!'

He turned and smiled at the sight of her, then came towards her with no sign of hesitation in his long stride. He had a riding crop tucked into his boot and his right hand was thrust into the breast of his jacket. As he took off his hat she saw his face more clearly and realised that, like her own, the bruising was changing colour, but the angry red soreness was disappearing.

'Good morning, Mrs Clare. How are you now?'

'Much better, I thank you, sir, except I still feel some effects from the jolting and I am afraid it will be some days yet before I feel brave enough to show my face in Holt. And yourself?' He had stopped a few steps away and was smiling at her in a way that made her feel pleasantly warm and not a little flustered.

'I too am feeling much better. My ankle is quite well again, but this wretched arm has no strength in it yet. My good landlord and employer gave me the most sluggish beast in his stables this morning, quite rightly judging I could not control anything with the slightest spirit.'

'Would you care to come inside and take a glass of wine?' Amanda wondered where Kate had got to— probably mooning over thoughts of Tom instead of mending hems. But with Jane out, she would have to be found to sit in one corner of the yellow salon and provide the required chaperonage.

'Thank you, no, but I would like to look around your

charming garden, if I may.' He offered Amanda his good arm and she allowed herself to be steered back along the path she had just taken.

'It is nice, is it not?' she agreed. 'But I can take no credit for it, my companion Miss Porter is the ruling spirit here. She cajoles miracles out of our curmudgeon-ly gardener, and is quite an expert horticulturist.' She hesitated as he paused to admire a forsythia's yellow blooms, then asked, 'Is your memory still failing you? Have any recollections come back to you?'

'No, nothing,' he replied. 'Yet I begin to detect some clues. I believe I must own land, for riding here I found myself judging the state of the farms as I passed. Many seem in very good heart and well kempt, and where there was a problem, I caught myself pondering the best solution for dealing with it—draining that flooded field half a mile up the road, for example.'

'That proves you are a good landlord,' Amanda con-ceded, 'but it does not help us, for most gentlemen will own some land—'

She broke off at the sound of another arrival in the stableyard. This time there was the distinct noise of wheels: perhaps Jane had returned.

But the person who came into view though the gaps in the laurels was not Miss Porter in the neat blue habit she wore when driving but a tall, rather portly young man with a dissatisfied expression.

'You will want to go to your—' Jay began but was cut off by Amanda's hand pressed firmly over his mouth.

'Hush!' she hissed.

He obediently stood still and made no attempt to speak, but under her palm she could feel his mouth curve into a smile. The sensation was disturbing and she whipped her hand away, conscious that she was blushing. Out of the corner of her eye she could see that Jay was still smiling slightly, although his gaze followed the other man until he vanished round the front of the house.

'Who is that?' There was the sound of the front door knocker and, after a moment, Howlett's voice informing the visitor that neither of the ladies was at home.

'Mr Clare—Cousin Humphrey,' she whispered back and they heard the butler assuring him that the ladies were not simply Not At Home, but were Away From Home, and unfortunately Howlett could not say when they might return. 'Oh, shh! Here he comes again.'

The two figures in the shrubbery remained still while Mr Clare strode past once more, this time looking decidedly put out. Amanda was just breathing a sigh of relief when a clear voice from the direction of the stableyard said, 'Why, Mr Clare! Good morning. Have you been calling on Mrs Clare?'

Amanda stood on tiptoe and whispered in Jay's ear, 'That is Miss Porter, my companion. Oh my goodness, he is coming back with her!'

'I am glad to see you, Miss Porter,' Cousin Humphrey was saying as they drew level with Amanda and Jay's hiding place. 'Last time we met, you promised me some snowdrops for the flowerbed outside my mama's parlour window, if you recall, and I believe you said they should be lifted while ''in the green''. Do I have the expression correct?'

'Quite correct, Mr Clare. If they are moved while the leaves are still fresh, they will grow again with no trouble. It is, however, rather late, but they should take well enough if you tell your gardener to water them in. Will you not wait here and choose a clump while I fetch a trowel and something to put them in?'

Humphrey Clare could be glimpsed through the laurels peering at the dying snowdrop foliage that carpeted the ground beneath the shrubs. He seemed to find the clumps deeper in of more merit, for after several moments' scrutiny he walked briskly down the path until he found the opening into the shrubbery and began to follow it back.

With silent, cat-like steps Jay began to back away, pulling Amanda gently with him into the shelter of the summerhouse. It was a quaint little structure, built around the trunk of a huge old oak that must have predated the house by hundreds of years. A bench circled the trunk and rustic poles supported the eaves of a sloping thatched roof, which sheltered the bench all the way around. The whole was surrounded by a loop of the path and three tables stood at intervals under the shelter so the ladies could follow the sun around, whatever time of day they sat there.

Jay, avoiding the betraying gravel, moved softly over the grass until the great bulk of the trunk was between them and Humphrey. But he did not release her arm and Amanda found herself standing so close that she could feel the warmth of his body. She risked a glance up at him, but his eyes were looking straight ahead as though he could see Humphrey Clare's movements through the tree. She realised he was listening intently to the sound of booted feet crunching the gravel.

There was a pause. 'He has seen the summerhouse,' Jay whispered in her ear, so quietly that she felt, rather than heard, the words. 'Now, which way…?' She felt his muscles tense, his body balanced to move in either direction. The gravel crunched again and Jay began to edge around the trunk, still holding her to him.

The noise stopped again, and then resumed and paused. It is like Grandmother's Footsteps, Amanda thought wildly as they moved to maintain their distance. But this was no children's game, and, if Humphrey in his guise as Grandmother found them, they would be more than just 'out' of the game.

Jay cautiously took another step, glanced down just in time to prevent himself stepping on a dead branch and swayed to get his balance on one leg.

He caught her eye and grinned and Amanda suddenly found herself in the grip of helpless giggles. Desperately she stuffed her fist into her mouth to stifle the sound. How much longer could they maintain this ridiculous charade? They were almost round the trunk again, on the side nearest the house, when Miss Porter's voice called, 'Mr Clare?'

'Here, ma'am,' he called back. Amanda could hear Jane approaching from the house, and Humphrey walking round the tree to meet her. Suddenly Jay caught Amanda up in his good arm and with two long strides, heedless of broken boughs, swept her round to the far side of the summerhouse. The sound of Jane's approach masked any sound they made and Amanda found herself clinging to him, her face buried in his shirt front, shaking with laughter.

'Hush!' he hissed in her ear. Amanda looked up into his face, saw the answering laughter in it and shook her head despairingly. She simply could not suppress the giggles. It was hopeless—they would be discovered.

Chapter Five

The next thing she knew, Jay had bent his head and silenced her by the most effective method he could have thought of. He kissed her full on the mouth, turning the gasp of amusement into one of shock, then into a little moan of startled pleasure. His lips were warm and gentle but very insistent. She should have been scandalised; instead, she found herself kissing him back with shy responsiveness.

The entire household could have been meeting on the other side of the oak tree for all Amanda was aware as her arms reached up to his shoulders, but Jay, however much she was occupying his attention, had kept his wits about him. Suddenly he was gone. Amanda found herself sitting abruptly down on the rustic bench against the tree trunk, her knees shaking and one hand pressed to her parted lips.

For a moment she was disoriented, then indignant, then, with the sound of heavy footsteps approaching, alarmed. There was a glimpse of dark blue cloth, a rustle of laurel leaves and Jay had vanished entirely, just as Cousin Humphrey, Jane Porter at his heels, came into view. He was studying the ground at his feet and for a moment did not see her, but Jane, with one startled glance at her employer, began to pat her own bonnet in an exaggerated manner.

'Oh, look, Mr Clare,' she exclaimed brightly, causing him to turn while Amanda frantically straightened her own crooked hat and stuffed back several wayward locks of hair. 'That is a fine large clump, is it not? Would Mrs Clare also care for some aconites, do you think?'

Humphrey Clare agreed, holding open the hessian bag Miss Porter had brought while she carefully forked up a clump each of both plants with a hand trowel.

'There,' she said, straightening up and brushing the soil off her gloved hands, 'Now all you need to do is to have your gardener put them in at once before they dry out... Oh, Mrs Clare!' She gave an artistic start of surprise and Humphrey turned.

'My dear Cousin Amanda!' He sounded faintly affronted to find her here and his eyebrows rose at what she supposed must be her dishevelled appearance. Goodness knows what a sight she must present with her old bonnet all anyhow, her face flushed and the half-healed graze on her bruised cheek.

'Cousin Humphrey, good morning. A beautiful day, is it not? I see Miss Porter is finding you some snowdrops: you must be flattered you know, for the Rector declares there is no better strain in the district, and he is a good judge.'

Humphrey, however, was no longer interested in horticulture. 'Cousin, your face! Whatever has occurred?' As always he sounded as though he was more concerned with any potential for local gossip than with anxiety about her well-being.

'A fall,' Amanda replied coolly. 'It looks worse than

it is because of the bruising, but I do not anticipate any lasting damage.' Her mind was racing; should she tell him some thing of the true facts in case news of the stagecoach accident reached him and he put two and two together, or should she say no more? Instinct told her that the less she gave him to chew over the better.

'A fall?' Without asking, Humphrey seated himself beside her and peered at her face. Amanda edged backwards as unobtrusively as she could. At the best of times she disliked the company her husband's cousin and heir; now, fresh from Jay's embrace, his fleshy high-coloured face and staring eyes made her feel positively queasy. 'How did that occur?'

Humphrey Clare was in the invidious position of finding his late cousin's widow extremely attractive and at the same time of disapproving thoroughly of her independence, her intelligence and her spirit. He knew his mother shared his disapproval, but would fail to understand the attraction Amanda had for him, and he rarely did anything that displeased his mama. He also deeply resented the fact that Amanda's late husband had left her every acre of unentailed land—in consequence, she was a considerable landowner—and of acres that he jealously considered were rightfully his. The result was to make him even more judgemental of Amanda's actions and to leave him in a turmoil of suppressed desire whenever he was with her.

Now he leaned forward to peer at her damaged face, but could only look at her bright eyes and the red lips that seemed to him to be disturbingly swollen. The thought that she might have been pleasurably excited by his sudden arrival was so powerfully erotic that he hastily crossed his legs and leaned back, attempting to look nonchalant.

Amanda, who understood his ambivalent emotions towards her rather more clearly than he would have believed, saw nothing particularly odd in his manner. She found his pompous behaviour as head of the family ludicrous and resented deeply his assumption that he could question her actions, but she was far too well bred to show any of this on her face.

'As I said,' she responded, 'I had a fall. It was an accident.' She managed to assume a pious expression and added, 'Naturally, I am taking care not to go out where I might be seen until it is healed. I would not want to cause any comment—people will indulge in such ill-bred speculation and ask such impertinent questions.'

Miss Porter hastily stifled a snort of amusement, but Mr Clare did not appear to connect the comment with his own behaviour. 'Indeed,' he agreed gravely, 'I have often had occasion to remark so to Mama. Doubtless it is the restricted life of the countryside: in town, where society is so much more select, a greater restraint obtains.'

Humphrey liked to give the impression that he moved in the highest circles in London and that only his devotion to the estate kept him in the country. Amanda, who had experienced enough of the Season to have observed Society closely, rather doubted both his social standing and his vision of London life. She was saved from making any observation however by the sound of hooves on gravel, which faded away as the horse left the stableyard.

'Now, who could that be?' Humphrey enquired, with what Amanda regarded as an altogether too proprietorial manner.

'Um...' It would be Jay, of course. He must have

made his way silently out of the shrubbery, skirted the house and approached the yard from the opposite direction and was now riding away. To say she did not know would be a direct lie, and for the life of her she could not think of a convincing answer.

Miss Porter came to her rescue. 'It was the hack from the Half Moon. I noticed it when I came back. Doubtless one of Will Bream's people with a message.'

Amanda shot Jane a look of pure gratitude, but Humphrey had found another ground for disapproval. 'What has that man Bream to do here? If he is too puffed up with his more-than-generous legacy from your late husband to continue his previous employment at the Hall, he should mind his own business. It does you no credit, my dear Mrs Clare, to have dealings with a common alehouse keeper.'

Behind Humphrey's back Jane shook her head warningly and Amanda swallowed most of the retort she had been about to make, saying merely, 'He supplies the ale for the servants' hall here.' She got to her feet, relieved to find that her treacherous legs would support her once more. 'Would you care to take luncheon with us, Cousin?'

Humphrey, who caused both ladies much resigned irritation by always timing his visits to coincide with one meal or another, accepted with an alacrity that would have been flattering if Amanda did not know that Mrs Clare senior was finding keeping a good cook at Glaven Hall well nigh impossible.

'Has Mrs Clare been fortunate enough to find a new cook?' she enquired as they sat down at length in the small dining room. A hasty retreat to her room, a splash of water on her face and the vigorous application of a hairbrush had restored her appearance somewhat, but she could only be grateful that Humphrey had been districted enough by her bruised face not to notice quite how dishevelled she had been.

'No,' he sighed, accepting a platter of cold meat and forking a more than generous portion on to his plate. 'Poor Mama has had to suffer a string of lazy, incompetent, unsatisfactory cooks since the Howletts saw fit to move here with you. But what should one expect in the country? It is not good for her health to be so troubled by these problems.'

Amanda knew perfectly well that it was nothing to do with the location and all to do with the endless nagging and interference that Mrs Clare senior considered to be essential in managing servants. Mrs Howlett's opinions on the subject had been entertaining, but in the interests of domestic discipline Amanda had had to repress her weekly bulletins from Glaven Hall where some of the old servants still continued, being unable to find alternative employment locally and unwilling to leave the neighbourhood.

'Perhaps you should take a wife, Cousin Humphrey,' she said sweetly. 'A younger lady to take the cares of domestic duties from your mother's shoulders.'

For a long moment Mr Clare made no response, apparently engrossed in the well-cooked beef, fine homemade relishes, excellent bread and freshly churned butter before him. Then he looked up, his gaze travelling round the well-kept, charming room until it rested on Amanda opposite him. 'Yes,' he said slowly, as though entertaining a completely fresh idea. 'Yes, perhaps I should.'

Amanda stared back, appalled at the results of what she had meant as a secret joke. Now, it appeared, she had made Humphrey realise that, in addition to the desire she knew he kept trying to suppress, she was an excellent housekeeper and would ensure the domestic comfort of any husband.

Jane had recognised this too and, as soon as they had managed to see him on his way at the end of the meal, she shut the parlour door firmly and exclaimed, 'My dear Amanda! What have you done?'

'Acquired a suitor, it seems, unless a little reflection reminds him just how very unsatisfactory I am in every other way than my housekeeping!'

'You will tell me if I overstep the mark,' Miss Porter said, taking the chair opposite Amanda's and reaching for her sewing, 'but we have discussed Mr Clare's apparent admiration of your…er…looks, before now. Can it be that you have modified your opinion of him?'

'Certainly not!' Amanda exclaimed, stabbing herself painfully in the thumb with her needle and getting a drop of blood on the hem of the nightdress she was hemming. 'Now look what I have done!'

'Then it was not the sight of Mr Clare that made you flush so when we found you in the garden?'

'No, it was not, as you well know, Jane. The only flush Cousin Humphrey brings to my cheeks is one of annoyance at the impertinence of his manner and questions. But I must thank you for your quick wits about the horse in the yard—I was quite lost for an explanation.'

'I assume the messenger was your mysterious fellow traveller, Mr Jay, is it not? Whatever had he said to make you blush so? And why is he using the Half Moon's hack?'

'He is staying at the inn,' Amanda answered, her head bent, apparently concentrating on binding her thumb with her handkerchief so as not to get any more blood on her sewing.

'At the Half Moon? A gentleman? Surely the Feathers would be more his style?'

'Um…' Amanda was not hesitating to tell the whole story because she did not trust Jane or her discretion but because she suddenly felt very shy indeed at the thought of talking about Jay. She bit her lip, then took a deep breath and said, 'He is staying there because he has no money. I suggested to Will Bream that he could earn his keep by bringing order into Will's accounts.'

'You did say he is a gentleman?' Jane queried, receiving a silent nod in return. 'Then why has he no money?'

'He does not know why—he lost his memory when he was struck on the head in the accident.' She met Jane's startled look and added, 'I could hardly abandon him after he saved me from much worse injury. I believe he could have prevented the blow to his head if he had had his hands free when the coach toppled into the ditch.'

'So…' Jane said thoughtfully. 'We have a brave, well-favoured and resourceful gentleman, who has no money, no memory but who causes you to blush and become flustered and who trysts with you in the shrubbery.' She waited for Amanda's rather rueful agreement, then added, 'But you know nothing about him! He could be married, he could be escaping from a scandal, from gaming debts… Has he been kissing you?'

'Yes,' Amanda said baldly, deciding she might as well be hanged for a sheep as a lamb. 'And I spent the night with him at the inn.'

'*What?*' Jane swallowed. 'You really should not say such things, Amanda—for one dreadful moment I thought you meant you spent the night in the same room as him.'

'I did, in the same bed.'

'But…but what is to be done?'

'Why, nothing, Jane dear.' Amanda did her best to look unconcerned and sophisticated. 'We were both unconscious. The landlady, a well-meaning soul, thought we must be man and wife. Naturally, when I awoke and discovered what had occurred I gave her a false name and we brushed through it well enough. But you can see, we had to leave the inn together or it would have had a very odd appearance.'

Jane was silent for a moment. 'Did he…did he take advantage of the situation in any way?'

'No! Not at all! Well,' Amanda, incurably honest, added, 'not once we had woken up. And it was only a kiss,' she hastened to explain at the sight of her companion's expression.

'Only a kiss—and he kissed you in the shrubbery?' She hardly waited for Amanda's nod. 'What can he be thinking of, to put you in such a position if he does not know whether he is married or betrothed, or in any way eligible?'

'Eligible for what?' Amanda demanded, flustered at this perfectly justifiable line of questioning. 'This is merely a flirtation, if that! And anyway, he says he does not feel married.'

'Oh, really?' Jane enquired darkly. 'Well, we will see about that!'

'Jane! What are you intending to do?' Amanda's sewing slid from her knees to the floor, quite unheeded.

'I hope I know my duty as your companion,' Miss Porter said firmly. 'I may be a spinster, but I am older than you and, grateful as I am for my position here, I cannot let it blind me to an unpleasant responsibility. I must talk to this man.'

'You cannot! Oh, how embarrassing! Please, Jane, do not think of it.' Amanda leaned forward and seized Miss Porter's hands in both of hers. 'Please!'

'Either I speak to him or I see no alternative but to seek the Rector's guidance. Or,' she added, a look of painful determination on her thin face, 'Mr Clare's.'

Amanda could see that her companion, hitherto entirely malleable to her wishes and tolerant of her oddest starts, had made up her mind. 'Very well, Jane,' she capitulated meekly. 'When will you go to the Half Moon?'

'Tomorrow at ten,' Miss Porter replied, apparently too anxious about the situation to be suspicious of Amanda's surrender. 'I must think carefully about how to approach this: I have never had to recollect a gentleman to his duty before. I shall go out into the garden, if you will excuse me.'

Amanda sat back in her chair, her brain spinning. She must prevent Jane from lecturing Jay at all costs. It would be dreadfully embarrassing and, even worse, could lead him to believe that she was attracted to him to such a degree that her companion found it necessary to intervene.

Hastily she got up and opened her writing desk. Her first three attempts at a note were torn up, at a great waste of hot pressed paper, before she managed a simple request that Jay call on her at a quarter to ten, *exactly*. On re-reading, she thought it seemed more like an agitated demand, but it would have to do. She added, *Do not tell Will where you have gone, only that you will be back about eleven o'clock, and do not, under any circumstances, take the main road here—ask him to show you the way across the fields.*

Goodness knows what he would make of that, but if Will Bream told Jane she only had an hour to wait she would not turn the gig around and come straight home. Now all Amanda had to do was to think what she was going to say to Jay when he did arrive. My companion thinks you are flirting with me? My companion thinks I am in moral danger from you? Miss Porter says you are no doubt married? Jane thinks we should not meet again, and I cannot bear that?

Well, the last was undoubtedly the truth, unpalatable though it was. Not, of course, that this was anything more than her anxiety to solve the problem of Jay's identity! And, she added, the fact that I find him very attractive, that I enjoy being kissed by him and that it is wonderful to be flirted with again.

She wandered out into the hall where the late afternoon sunlight was slanting through the windows and through into the yellow salon. She stood looking up at the portrait of Charles Clare, which hung over the mantle facing the door. The artist had caught the essence of the man, the decent, direct expression as he stared out across the rolling acres he had loved so much, the humour in the eyes and in the turn of the lips, the line that responsibility had set between his brows.

'When I'm gone,' he had said one afternoon, very shortly before he died, waving aside her spontaneous protest. 'When I am gone, you find yourself someone to love you, someone who will give you happiness again.' She had tried to speak, but his thin hand had silenced her with a gesture so weak it had frozen her heart. 'I have left you well provided for. Every acre that is not entailed—and only this house and the Home Farm are—I have left to you. There is no condition on this, no restriction. When you wish to remarry, I know I can trust your judgement, Amanda. Be happy again, that is all I wish for—promise me that.'

She had mourned him deeply, honestly, for a year; then, gradually, the sunlight had come back into her life, the demands of the land she had inherited and all its people ceased to be a burden and became a purpose that brought satisfaction and an ambition to learn more, do better, create something. She thought of Charles often, never forgot to raise her eyes to the portrait when she entered the room, but now it was a gentle grief, a regret, and she knew she was ready to do as he asked and to move on.

But she never found anyone who was more than a friend and as the months passed she began to think she was fated to be a widow all her life. She could have gone up to London, she knew. A wealthy, young, attractive widow would have no trouble finding beaux aplenty, but something in her revolted at the thought of setting out deliberately to find a husband.

And now it seemed she *had* met someone for whom she could feel the tug of something more than friendship. And he was most likely married, or engaged, and her duty was quite plain: to stop this before she began to feel anything more for him and before he stopped flirting and began to entertain the same sort of feelings.

Amanda bit her lip painfully, then tugged at the bell-pull until Howlett appeared. 'Please see this is delivered to the Half Moon this afternoon.' She handed him the letter and added, 'Is Mr Pococke still in the stableyard?'

Her estate manager had been there a while ago with a builder, deciding on repairs to the coach-house roof: a lengthy discussion with him about the merits of plant-

ing turnips—as the famous Mr Coke of Holkham, just
along the coast, advised—would take her mind off her
personal affairs if nothing would!

It proved so effective—for Mr Pococke was less convinced by the radical agriculturist's theories than his
employer was and was prepared to put up a spirited
argument—that Amanda was surprised to be handed a
letter by Howlett just as she entered the hall for dinner
that evening.

'Came by way of the stable lad up at the Half Moon,'
the butler remarked. His face was as expressionless as
usual, yet something in his tone alerted Amanda to the
fact that her household staff were aware that something
was afoot.

'Indeed, I wonder what it might be,' she replied
coolly, slipping it into her reticule. 'Please serve in
twenty minutes, Howlett.'

The letter, directed in a totally unfamiliar hand,
seemed to burn through the reticule as dinner proceeded
through its courses. Normally the two ladies had more
than enough to talk about, whether or not they had company, and Amanda would have enjoyed recounting her
battle over the turnips with Mr Pococke. Tonight, however, Jane was too distressed by the thought of the painful duty that lay ahead of her tomorrow and the fact
that for the first time in their happy relationship she was
disagreeing with her employer—and over such a matter!—to do more than talk in the most stilted manner.

Neither was sorry when the tea tray was removed and
they could make their way to their chambers. As soon
as she was alone Amanda slit the seal on the letter. As

she had guessed from the black, arrogant hand, it was from Jay.

'It will be my pleasure to do as you ask' was all the note said and across the bottom of the sheet was scrawled the single letter *J*.

Chapter Six

Jane set off the next morning in the gig at half past nine, dressed as though for church. She had made a little speech after breakfast, much to Amanda's embarrassment, although she could not help but be touched by her companion's desire to protect her, at whatever cost to her own equilibrium.

'My dear Mrs Clare, I would not do anything to cause you distress, as I hope you know,' she had begun, her voice strained. 'But I cannot allow you to walk heedlessly—in your innocence—into a situation of the utmost peril to your reputation and your peace of mind. This man must be warned off, and it is my duty to do so.' She had hesitated, the tip of her nose pink with barely repressed emotion. 'And if you feel I have overstepped the mark, I quite understand if you wish to terminate my employment.'

'Oh, Jane!' Amanda hurried around the table to put her arms around her friend. 'As if I would do such a thing when I know you are only doing what you feel to be right!'

Her conscience pricked her at the thought of deceiving Jane, and she knew it showed exactly the sort of moral weakness that her companion was so anxious to save her from. Amanda waved Jane goodbye as she drove off with her face set in the solemn lines of someone carrying out an unpleasant duty, but the minute the gig was out of sight she called Kate and dispatched her on an errand to Cook at Glaven Hall.

'I have promised her the receipt for pickled walnuts and I keep forgetting to give it to her,' she said with perfect honesty. 'Mr Clare is very partial to them it seems. Here it is—and Kate, if you wish to call and see Mrs Green on your way back, that will be quite all right.'

The maid hurried off, only too happy to be sent on such a pleasant errand on a sunny morning and Amanda set herself to freshening the flower arrangement on the console table in the hall.

Her stratagem worked: she heard the sound of gravel crunching under booted feet and had whisked the door open before Jay had had a chance to raise his hand to the knocker.

'Good morning,' he said doffing his hat as he entered and looking around for the butler to hand it to.

'Good morning. Here let me take those,' Amanda responded, relieving him of his hat, gloves and whip. But instead of placing them on the chest in the hall which usually received callers' hats, she carried them with her into the yellow salon.

She turned, waiting for Jay to follow her and saw from his amused glance at her scattered flowers on the hall table that he knew she had deliberately let him in without the servants knowing.

'You are a notable strategist Amanda,' he remarked, smiling. He closed the door behind him as she put down his things. 'And no chaperon? Now what are you about? Your letter was very mysterious.'

'I needed to speak to you alone,' she admitted. She looked him firmly in the eye, then let her gaze drop, confused. She had known it was going to be difficult, but now, with him standing before her, watching her closely between narrowed green eyes it seemed impossible.

'It sounded urgent,' he said helpfully. 'Has any rumour of our accident reached the area?'

'Oh, no, nothing like that.'

'And you are quite well, not suffering any ill effects? Your face is healing well.'

'Oh, yes, quite well, thank you.' This was ridiculous. She walked to one of the wing chairs beside the fireplace and sat down, gesturing him to take the other.

Jay came towards her, and as he did so, saw the portrait hanging over the fire. 'That is a very fine piece of work,' he remarked, stopping to study it more closely, his head tipped back to take it in. 'I imagine it is very like—the artist has caught a considerable personality there, behind a quiet exterior.'

'Yes, indeed,' Amanda agreed warmly. Those who did not know Charles well had often mistaken his quiet, calm exterior for blandness or a lack of character. It pleased her that Jay should see through that at once.

'Your father? It has a place of honour.'

'My father? No, indeed not, that is my late husband.'

'Your husband!' He turned to stare at her, all the amusement gone from his face. 'But this man must be twice your age, at least.'

'Charles was thirty-three years my senior when we married,' she said quietly.

'And you were how old?' Jay demanded.

Shaken by his vehemence, Amanda stammered, 'Ni-nineteen.'

'Nineteen! And who was responsible for selling you into that bargain?'

'No one! I was not *sold*—how could you use such a term!' She was becoming angry now, but not as angry as Jay, whose voice and dark expression made her shrink back momentarily.

'Are you telling me you loved him?' He took an angry step away from her, then spun round to face her again.

'No…not at first…but I sincerely admired and liked him. He was a gentleman who could not help but command respect.'

'What possessed you to enter into such a marriage?' Jay was not compromising either tone or expression, despite her own pale face and shaking voice.

'I was in a position where… My situation was such… Mama…'

'So your mother forced you into it?' His tone was biting and his expression so bleak that she hardly recognised him.

Suddenly Amanda found her shock and alarm swept away by her own anger. 'No one forced me. I made a rational decision that led to a very happy, if short, marriage. It is none of your business and I will not be interrogated, shouted at and hectored!' She was on her feet now, confronting him across the width of the hearth, her hands clenched into fists at her side, tears of fury and distress starting to roll down her cheeks.

Jay was staring back at her and for a moment she could not tell whether he was about to take her by the shoulders and shake her or walk out of the room. But as she stood there she saw his eyes lose their focus; he raised one hand to shield them and with the other groped for the back of the chair to support himself.

'Jay!' She was at his side in an instant, steadying him, not knowing whether to leave him and call someone to go for the doctor or to try and get him to sit down.

But the weakness was over almost as soon as it had struck him. He lowered the hand from his eyes and looked at her, his pupils wide and dark. 'Amanda? What happened? You are crying.'

'You were shouting at me,' she said as prosaically as she could, rubbing her eyes with her free hand while trying to press him down into the chair with the other. But he was stronger than she and resisted, pulling her round to face him properly.

'*Shouting at you?*' He closed his eyes for a moment and when he opened them again his gaze was the lucid green she was used to. 'What on earth... Amanda, my darling, I am so sorry!'

Her lip trembled as reaction set in and with a muffled oath Jay pulled her tight into his arms, wrapping her in an embrace against his chest. Whatever had prompted that extraordinary outburst she did not know, but she felt safe again, only so shaky...so very shaky.

'I'm sorry,' she said, her voice muffled against his coat, 'but I think I am going to cry.' And she did. She could not remember the last time she had had this luxury, letting all her emotions out in the arms of someone who simply held her gently but firmly and did not tell her to control herself, or behave as befitted a lady. Nor did he seem embarrassed. And somewhere, behind the storm of tears, was the echo of his voice saying *my darling...*

Eventually she stopped with a little hiccup and simply stood, her face against the now damp broadcloth of Jay's coat, feeling strangely at peace.

She felt his grip slacken and he moved, turning her until he could press her down gently into the chair. He produced a large handkerchief from his pocket and handed it to her. 'Quite clean,' he said prosaically. 'The Half Moon has an excellent laundry maid.'

'I know, she used to work at the Hall,' Amanda said, blowing her nose vigorously into the white linen. 'I am sorry, I must look a fright, my nose always goes red when I cry.'

'*You* are sorry!' His vehemence made her jump. 'My word, Amanda—what happened, what did I say?'

'You do not remember?' She looked at him anxiously.

'Yes…no. I can remember being angry, but it was not with you, it was something in my past all mixed up with whatever it was that started this.' Jay rubbed his forehead and say down abruptly in the opposite chair. 'Can you bear to tell me about it—exactly what happened?'

'Yes, very well.' Amanda sat up straight, the handkerchief forgotten in her hands. 'Do you recall why you were here this morning?'

'Yes, you sent me a note last night.' Something of his old humour showed in his face as he added, 'A more mysterious mixture of precise instructions and vague intentions I have never read.'

'Jane—Miss Porter, my companion—is even now at the Half Moon, waiting to bring you to a sense of your duty. She feels she must warn you not to visit me again in case you compromise my reputation.' The words were out before she could feel any of the discomfort she had expected. Fortunately, Jay appeared to grasp the problem without further explanation.

'So, she considers me to be a shady cove, does she?'

'She fears it—if a shady cove is what I think. I had to tell her about your memory, you see, and what happened after the accident. She thinks you are doubtless either a rake or married, or both, and, whichever it is, I should not be seeing you.'

His mouth was twisted into a rueful smile. 'And I suppose if I tell her I do not feel in the slightest bit married, and that if I am a rake, which I feel is more likely, I promise to be on my best behaviour, she is unlikely to be convinced?'

'Exactly. And however unmarried you feel, you may well be wrong, or you may be betrothed. And in either case you ought not to be…to be…'

'Kissing you?'

Or calling me your darling, she thought, but said only, 'Yes.'

'Hmm.' He regarded her thoughtfully from under lowered brows. 'We can discuss that in a moment. But what did you expect to achieve by sending me the message? You can hardly hope to keep the pair of us shuttling back and forth across country every time she sets out to lecture me on my duty.'

'I was embarrassed—I thought I should explain in case you thought I had sent her.'

'Because you could not give me my marching orders yourself?'

'Yes. Not that I should not do so,' she added, then gave herself a little shake and continued more firmly, 'Anyway, you arrived, and I let you in without the servants knowing you were here, and you were going to sit down so that we could talk, when you saw the portrait over the mantle.'

Jay tipped his head back to look at it and his face darkened. 'It is coming back—but an old memory, not what has just happened.' He closed his eyes in an effort of concentration. 'There was a lady, a beautiful young lady with blonde hair. Very straight hair. And blue eyes, and the most lovely, gentle smile you have ever seen.' His voice seemed to be coming from a long way away and Amanda sat still as a mouse, terrified of breaking the spell. 'And she was going to marry an old man, an old, debauched man. And there was nothing I could do to stop it, and I was so angry…' His eyes snapped open. 'That is all I can recall and, what there is, is all distorted.'

'Then discovering I had married someone so much older than myself disturbed that memory, and all the anger came back,' she suggested eagerly. 'We just need to find some other clues that will trigger memories and sooner or later something you say will identify you.'

'You would risk another outburst like the one I appear to have subjected you to?' he asked incredulously.

'Yes, of course, if it helps. Now I know what to expect, I will not be frightened.'

'Did I frighten you?' Jay demanded, leaning forward and taking her hand.

'Yes, but only for a moment, then I was angry. And then…upset, because of Charles. But you are unlikely to hit on anything like that again.' She ought to tell him to let go of her hand, but the warm pressure of his fingers was so right, it was an effort to move her hand.

'You see, you suggested that I had been sold into marriage in some way, and that was far from the truth. Yet, if I am honest, my conscience did trouble me, for

I did not fall in love with Charles.' She bit her lip. 'But he knew why I married him and understood the circumstances, and I vowed I would make him a good wife, and I did.' Her voice softened and she almost forgot where she was, looking back. 'I began by truly valuing him and liking him, and I came to love him. And I do believe he was happy with me. He never reproached me for not giving him an heir.'

'How did you come to marry him?' Jay prompted.

'Mama was widowed when I was twelve. I have no brothers or sisters. I did not understand at first, but I think she must have been a very poor manager, and our trustees were not sympathetic. By the time I was seventeen it was obvious that there was no money for a come-out; in fact, we were hard put to maintain a respectable appearance. But by then I was old enough to take a hand, and whatever poor Mama's problems in handling money, I have not inherited them! I shocked the trustees by nagging them until they took more of an interest, and I introduced what economies I could and started to save.'

Jay released her hand and sat back, an expression of intense interest on his face. Amanda, still lost in the story, continued. 'I am, if nothing else, practical, and it seemed to me that our only hope was for me to make a respectable marriage. I could have supported myself by becoming a companion or a governess, but that would not have kept Mama as well. But to make a marriage I needed a Season, and it took me until I was just nineteen to save enough for the bare minimum of suitable clothes. Then I managed to persuade a distant cousin to sponsor me—her daughters were still too young, so I was no trouble to someone who loved parties—and there I was, launched on my first and only Season.'

'I wonder if I met you.'

'I think I would have remembered, but do not forget, this was a very muted come-out! No vouchers for Almack's, no fashionable parties.'

'But you were a success.' It was a statement, not a question.

'Goodness, no!' Amanda laughed. 'I was just a provincial nobody. And I soon realised that being practical about money did not mean that one was necessarily practical about life. Somehow I had imagined that there would be someone, and our eyes would meet, and that would be that. He would not worry about my lack of money for he would not be on the catch for a rich wife, and I would be sufficiently well born to satisfy his family.' She laughed again at the memory of the naïvely romantic girl she had been.

'It is not like that, of course, as you would know if you could remember London society and the Season. Prince Charming did not come along, I received two offers from men I thoroughly disliked, one from a gentleman who did not have marriage in mind but quite another arrangement, and I was beginning to despair, when along came Charles.'

'But you did not love him.' Jay's face, shadowed by the wings of the chair, was unreadable.

'No, but he loved me. He had been a childless widower for many years and told me he had had no thought of marrying again until he met me. I was honest with him about my circumstances, and my feelings, but he just brushed that aside. I did try to dissuade him, but in the end he convinced me that we could both be happy. And we were,' she ended simply.

'And your mama?'

'She died a year after we were married.'

Jay made no reply, but something in the quality of his silence made her blurt out, 'I would still have married him if I had known. Do not assume I was making some sort of sacrifice for her.'

'No, I can see that you did not. You made an honest bargain by all accounts, and it seems, from what I hear around about, that you repay his memory by being at least as good a landlord as he was.'

'Am I the subject of much gossip, then?' Amanda could not decide whether she was put out that she was talked about, or flattered that her reputation as a landowner appeared to be so good. 'I know I am much disapproved of by the older ladies for taking such an interest in farming and the tenants' housing.'

'Not gossip,' Jay corrected with a smile. 'Just interest.' He hesitated and Amanda saw his mouth twist wryly. 'I had the impression of a lady who had been much in the world, someone who was awake to all suits.'

'Well, and so I am—now,' she responded firmly. 'You should see me haggling at market when I take my corn to be sold, or my fleeces, and the quite brassy way I write to Mr Coke at Holkham for his advice on farming matters without going through my estate manager as a respectable lady should!'

Jay raised one eyebrow. 'I do not deny that you are a remarkable landlord, a highly practical manager and have scant regard for the conventions. But—'

'I knew there was going to be a *but*,' she interrupted ruefully. 'I ask you here to save you from a lecture and now you are going to lecture me!'

'I would not dream of it. No, what I am trying to say

is that your companion is quite right to want to warn me off. I had not realised I was dealing with someone so sheltered from the ways of the world—one quiet Season, then whisked off to the country by a doting older husband.'

'Are you trying to tell me that you thought I was the sort of dashing young widow—and yes, I did see enough of society in my one Season to know they exist—with whom you could enjoy a pleasant flirtation?' Amanda demanded.

Jay stood up and walked away to look out of the window. 'To start with, yes.'

'Indeed! And then?'

'I stopped thinking about flirtation.' He did not appear to be going to add anything to this.

'You *are* a rake, sir!' she said warmly to his unresponsive back.

'Very likely. I did warn you.'

'Well, I feel extremely sorry for your poor wife if you are apt to career around the countryside with hardly a penny piece in your pocket, looking for dashing widows to flirt with!'

That did make him turn. Jay strolled back to lean against the wing armchair, looking down at her. 'I hardly think setting out with my pockets to let would be a very satisfactory strategy if I wanted to attract a flirt! No, there is some other explanation behind the odd start that found me in that stagecoach.' He sat down again abruptly and looked across at her, his face serious. 'Before that extraordinary brainstorm just now, I could have sworn I was unattached and heart-free when I set out on this adventure.'

Amanda wished she could be as certain, but one thing from his flash of memory earlier did lend some credence to his feeling. 'Perhaps you have never recovered from losing the blonde young lady you were speaking of and never formed another attachment?' she suggested.

'Wearing the willow for years for my lost love?' he quizzed. 'I wonder just how long ago that was? I am left with the most extraordinary impression of power-lessness, which argues that I was very young. But this is beside the point: I now have no confidence at all in that certainty. If my mind can hide what was obviously such a powerful memory, there is no saying who I am or what my circumstances. Whether I am married with six children, or, as I believed, a single man not averse to the company of ladies, either way I am an unsuitable person to be associating with you. Especially when you consider the manner of our meeting.'

Amanda struggled to keep her feelings from showing on her face. Jay was rapidly becoming more than a chance-met stranger in need of help, more than a friend. Without her realising it, he had become essential to her happiness. What she knew was the right thing to be doing was becoming harder by the minute now that he was agreeing with her.

'What exactly are you saying?' she enquired, trying to sound unconcerned with his answer.

'That we see no more of each other,' Jay stated baldly. 'I am, of course, for ever in your debt for res-cuing me, but I have allowed myself to become too attached to your company and too heedless of the risk to you.'

Amanda wondered if she could manage to see him to the door without bursting into tears. She did not dare think about what he had just said about her company but summoned up every ounce of self-discipline, fixed a social smile on her stiff lips and said calmly, 'You are no doubt correct, sir. But you know that curiosity is my besetting sin—you will write and tell me how you get on, will you not?'

'Of course.' He was gathering up his hat and whip, drawing on his gloves, readying himself to walk out of her life. From the deep, shared intimacy of their conversation only a moment ago they now seemed like strangers, formally bidding each other good day. Jane would be proud of her, for she had succeeded in everything her companion had desired. Jay was going out of her life.

Chapter Seven

Jay was standing to one side of the door, one hand on the handle ready to open it for her, when it swung inwards abruptly, causing him to step back.

'Well, Amanda, that was a morning wasted!' Miss Porter marched into the room and began untying her bonnet strings. 'I waited and waited at the Half Moon, with Will Bream assuring me that Mr Jay would be back directly, but there was no sign of the wretched man. Possibly he has recovered his memory and gone about whatever mysterious business brought him to the area, for I cannot disguise from you my grave doubts about his respectability, whatever you may say.'

She tossed her bonnet on to the chair and began to unbutton her pelisse, oblivious to Amanda's expression of mixed horror and amusement. Behind her back Jay also appeared to be struggling to keep his countenance. The strain of preparing herself for a delicate and embarrassing interview, heightened by the long wait, had obviously overcome Miss Porter's normally reserved nature and she was now thoroughly annoyed.

In a voice which shook, Amanda suggested, 'A shady cove, you mean, Jane?'

'Really! My dear Amanda, where did you hear such an expression?'

'From the *wretched man* in question.' Jay stepped forward, his hand held out as Jane spun round to confront him, her complexion turning from red to white in confusion. 'I do beg your pardon, ma'am, for inconveniencing you.'

'Inconveniencing me—' Jane began as Amanda hurried forward.

'Jane, may I introduce you to Mr Jay. Mr Jay, Miss Porter, my companion.'

The effect of the formal introduction was enough to restore Miss Porter to something approaching her normal reserved calm. She shook hands stiffly and observed, 'Good morning, sir. There is no need to apologise, you had no way of knowing I was seeking an interview with you.'

Amanda had the grace to blush, but Jay merely bowed and observed, 'However, I now know something of your intentions and I hope I may put your mind at rest by telling you that Mrs Clare and I have just been discussing the matter and agreeing that it would indeed be prudent if I avoided her company.'

'Oh!' Miss Porter was obviously taken aback by this immediate capitulation, but recovered swiftly. 'You had this discussion without a chaperon in the room?'

Amanda and Jay spoke together. 'On a matter of such delicacy, ma'am...' and 'Let me ring for tea, you must be fatigued, Jane. Mr Jay, will you not join us?'

To her obvious surprise, Miss Porter found herself seated by the hearth with Jay helpfully placing a small side table within her reach and Amanda making brisk social chit-chat.

'Mr Jay has been admiring the garden, Jane, and I

have told him it is entirely your creation. Ah, Howlett, tea, if you please.'

'Yes, ma'am.' The butler shot a glance at Jay. 'I beg your pardon, sir, I did not hear your arrival.' He bowed and went out, his expression as bland as usual, yet Amanda was left with the distinct impression that he knew more than he betrayed. The servants' hall were obviously well informed about their mistress's new acquaintance. She only hoped that they had no idea of the circumstances of their first meeting.

She turned back to find that Jane had been seduced—no other word seemed appropriate—into telling Jay all about her revival of the garden. He was leaning forward, all attention and encouraging nods as she recounted the problems of rampant brambles, neglected shrubberies and the constant battle with the cantankerous gardener.

Amanda made no attempt to interrupt. She suspected that Jane could not suspect a man who showed such an interest in mulch and black spot in roses of having evil designs upon her friend, and however much her head told her that she and Jay were right to keep their distance, she found it mattered very much that Jane should like him.

'You are very knowledgeable about horticulture, Mr Jay,' Jane observed after Howlett had deposited the tea tray and left.

'I fear I know nothing about it at all,' he replied, accepting a cup from Amanda. 'Thank you, Mrs Clare.'

'You seem so interested.'

'I can certainly admire the product of taste and hard work, Miss Porter, but I fear I can find no information in my brain beyond the merest commonplaces on the subject.'

'Oh, dear.' Jane sighed and offered him the plate of

biscuits. 'Will you not try one, sir? They are still warm from the range and Mrs Howlett is a fine cook. You must build up your strength,' she added.

'Bodily I am greatly recovered, ma'am, as I trust Mrs Clare is. But much as I have to agree with you on the excellence of the biscuits, I am afraid any amount of feeding is not going to assist my memory.'

'Well, what are we going to do about that?' Jane demanded.

Amanda's lips curved into a little smile. Even through the fog of unhappiness that seemed to be gathering around her heart, her irrepressible sense of humour could not but respond to the sight of Jane, fired up to help the very man she considered so dangerous.

'There is nothing you can do, Miss Porter. We have all agreed—have we not?—that my continued association with Mrs Clare may expose her to the possibility of associating with someone whom she is better off not knowing, and, at worst, the risk of the truth of the coach accident becoming known.'

'Hmm.' It was obvious to Amanda that, having met Jay and realised she was not confronting the lecherous, yet insinuating, adventurer she had been expecting, Jane was no longer so anxious to send him about his business. 'It would appear to me,' she said thoughtfully, 'that our best defence against the true story coming out is to restore your memory, sir, and to establish you where you ought to be, in your true character.'

'Restored to your family,' Amanda added firmly. She found that conjuring up a mental picture of a young wife with children clustered around her did nothing to help her aching heart, but did much to stiffen her resolution to do the right thing.

'Another blow to the head might help,' Jane pronounced, oblivious to the look of mock alarm on Jay's face. 'If I were a betting woman—which of course I am not—I would—'

She broke off as Jay said sharply, 'What did you just say? I beg your pardon, ma'am, but if you could just repeat that last sentence.'

Puzzled, Jane obliging repeated, 'If I were a betting woman—'

'That is it!' Jay turned triumphantly to Amanda, his face alight. 'A bet! That was why I was on the stage with my pockets to let.'

'But who made this bet with you? And where?' she demanded. 'If we can but find one of those two facts, surely the whole puzzle will unravel.'

'That is the devil of it,' he admitted, apparently not noticing Miss Porter's cluck of disapproval of his language. 'I suspect I had had a fair bit to drink at the time. All I can remember is a small group of men around a table and one of them saying, ''You wouldn't be so very superior about my shortcomings if you had to manage without your guineas, your servants and your calling cards for a week or two.'' I assume I had made some remark that had touched a raw nerve with him.'

'And he and his friends made a wager with you that you could live without any of the benefits of your station in life for a fortnight!' said Amanda delightedly. 'Surely we can gather some useful information from that?'

'We already knew that I could afford a good tailor and bootmaker and that I can support at least the appearance of a gentleman. All that this tells us is that I have been known to drink too much in male company and have made at least one foolish wager.'

'Oh,' said both ladies together in a joint sigh of disappointment.

'We must not be downhearted,' Miss Porter stated after a moment's reflection. 'We have agreed, have we not, that it would be imprudent for you and Mrs Clare to meet in circumstances that might present the slightest appearance of intimacy. But now that I am involved, I see no reason why we cannot continue to assist you, if only at a distance.'

Amanda did not know what to say. Jane had obviously forgotten any suspicions she might have had that Amanda's feelings were involved in any way beyond an eagerness to help someone in difficulties. She wanted to stay in touch with Jay so much, yet knew that it was wrong to do so. For a long minute she kept her gaze fixed on her hands, closed tightly on each other in her lap, then raised her eyes to find that Jay was watching her with an expression she could not fathom.

'Jane, I really do not—' she began, and the door opened.

'Mr Clare, ma'am,' Howlett announced. 'Shall I bring fresh tea?'

'Yes, please do,' Amanda said, fixing a smile on her lips. Why on earth had she not told Howlett she was not at home to visitors? Then she realised that Humphrey would have seen Jay's horse and it would have made him curious if he had been denied admission when another morning caller was already there.

'Please come in, Cousin. Mr Jay, allow me to present Mr Clare. Cousin Humphrey, Mr Jay, who is a visitor to these parts.'

The gentlemen shook hands and took their seats. She saw Humphrey's eyes narrow in calculation, for she had instinctively presented him to Jay and not the other way around, implying that Jay was of the higher status. Humphrey, who was particularly sensitive about his position in society, and would dearly have loved a title, however minor, was doubtless running through a mental list of county families in search of Jays.

'One of the Hampshire Jays?' he enquired, so obviously fishing that Amanda winced.

Jay leaned forward and, with an air of confiding in a gentleman likely to instantly comprehend, announced, 'I am travelling incognito, sir.'

'Indeed?' Cousin Humphrey looked surprised, as well he might at this revelation, but almost at once a smug glow came over him. Amanda recognised the signs. Humphrey liked to believe that he was awake upon every suit, and would have sooner have been seen on the dance floor in riding breeches as admit that he had not the slightest idea what Jay was talking about.

'As a man of substance, a notable local landowner,' Jay continued smoothly, keeping eye contact with a mesmerised Humphrey, 'you will understand how delicate these matters can be.'

'Of course, of course,' Mr Clare huffed. Amanda met Jane's horrified eye. What was Jay leading up to?

'The slightest rumour, and the price soars, as I am sure you are well aware,' Jay continued, his voice dropping slightly so Humphrey had to lean towards him as though sharing a secret.

'And you are acquainted with my cousin...'

'Mrs Clare is spoken of locally with great respect as a landlord well versed in the latest agricultural theories. I presumed to call and have been most kindly received. You too are spoken of widely in connection with land management.'

He was outrageous! Not a single word was an untruth, but the implication was that Jay had called upon her to discuss Mr Coke's theories and that local opinion had told him that Humphrey was an equally advanced landlord.

'So you are interested in acquiring agricultural land,' Humphrey ventured, light finally beginning to dawn, 'and such a considerable amount that you are viewing the area incognito so as not to force up the price!'

Jay simply leaned back in his chair, steepled his fingers and smiled a slight, saturnine smile. 'I can see, Mr Clare, that everything I have heard about your intellectual powers are nothing less than the truth.'

Amanda closed her eyes, quite unable to risk meeting Jane's. Just how much flattery would Humphrey accept without becoming suspicious? Apparently an unlimited amount, although thankfully Jay appeared to feel he had said enough.

'You may count upon my discretion, sir,' Humphrey announced, with the air of a High Court judge delivering a judgement.

'And now I must take my leave and not encroach upon Mrs Clare's kindness any longer.' Jay stood and turned to Amanda as Jane pulled the bell cord for the butler. 'Your thoughtfulness means a great deal, ma'am. Be assured I will communicate what success I have.'

'I wish you an early success, Mr Jay. Good day, sir.' She stood and held out her hand.

As he took it in his he met her gaze; something there seemed to arrest his attention, for he murmured, 'What is it?'

His back was turned to Jane and Cousin Humphrey, effectively shielding them as she replied, low-voiced, 'I wish you had left before Jane came back.'

She did not expect him to understand her—indeed,

she hardly understood herself—but his voice had a sudden edge as he said, 'So do I.' Then he had released her hand and was turning to the others. 'Good day, Miss Porter, Mr Clare.'

Howlett shut the door behind him and the exchange of words as the butler ushered him out of the house were distantly audible through the panels.

Amanda returned to her seat by the hearth wondering, with a strange feeling of detachment, whether she was about to faint.

Cousin Humphrey did not appear to notice anything amiss. 'Mysterious fellow, that,' he remarked, reaching for yet another ratafia biscuit. 'Obviously a gentleman. Spotted the incognito at once, of course—you noticed the way he admitted it the moment I began to probe, I am sure.'

Amanda watched him as he munched his way through the sweetmeat. It seemed everything was magnified and sharp, as though seen through the hand lens her father had let her play with once when she was a child.

And like the creatures under that lens, Jane and Cousin Humphrey and all the things in the room, although perfectly in focus, were remote and unreal: Humphrey with his rather too-shiny striped waistcoat was a fat beetle; Miss Porter, fastidiously dabbing her lips with a napkin, a crane fly, all angular limbs and muted colouring.

Amanda concentrated on them desperately, as though Cousin Humphrey's every word was a life-line to stop her from bursting into tears and exposing her feelings and her vulnerability.

Inside her chest everything seemed to hurt—as her heart beat, as she breathed, as she swallowed minute sips of tea. She understood now why she had told Jay she wished he had left immediately.

They had reached a moment of decision and were doing the sensible, right thing, however painful she found it and she had felt a merciful sense of numbness. That would wear off, of course, but she could bear that, keep it to herself and learn to live with it in private until the inevitable letter came telling her that he was restored to his true identify, to his real life—to his real family.

But now she had seen him with others for the first time without his attention focused on her alone, and it was as though she was catching a glimpse of that real self for the first time. Why did that make it so much more difficult?

'Yes, mysterious,' Humphrey was continuing, frowning. 'But sound, I felt, very sound.'

'Sound?' Miss Porter queried, raising an eyebrow at Amanda.

'Yes, obviously a progressive man, and recognised another when he met one. Advanced ideas of course, but no harm in that, none at all.'

Both Miss Porter's eyebrows rose, as much in surprise in Amanda's lack of response than at Humphrey's opinion. He was a disastrously conservative landowner at a time when life was changing rapidly for both landlord and agricultural worker and he had consistently deplored Amanda's interest in the reforms of Mr Coke of Holkham.

Seeing Jane's face, Amanda pulled herself together. She was not in the slightest surprised that Mr Clare was adopting this attitude: he had obviously been impressed by Jay, flattered by his words and was hastily aligning his *spoken* opinions to mirror the other man's. 'You feel his ideas have some merit?'

'Well, of course, with a male intellect applied to these questions there is much worth considering.' Humphrey was never happier than when his opinion was sought, and Amanda had never known a lack of knowledge of a subject inhibit him in giving an opinion. 'I know you have dabbled in this to some extent, my dear cousin, but you would do well to leave such matters to men of understanding such as Mr Jay and myself. A lady cannot be expected to understand the subtleties.'

Yesterday Amanda would have enquired sweetly as to his last year's corn yield or the weight of his wool clip, then artlessly let him know what her lands produced. Now she let his patronising comments slide by unanswered.

Miss Porter hastily enquired, 'So you do suppose Mr Jay's business to be the acquisition of agricultural land, Mr Clare, as you said?'

Humphrey regarded her solemnly. 'Of course—why, his confidence in me was such that you heard him admit as much. But there is more to it than that. I am convinced he is in search of a major estate. Why else such discretion? Why else the need to linger in these parts? There are one or two families hereabouts whose affairs are, shall we say, shaky.'

Miss Porter, apparently sensed the need to carry the burden of the conversation herself and spare Amanda, whom she could tell was not herself. 'But there have been no advertisements of sale, Mr Clare.'

He regarded her with a patronising smile. 'Of course not, Miss Porter. Mr Jay is testing out the land, gathering the opinion of informed persons such as myself and then will doubtless make a discreet call upon his chosen landowner and conclude a shrewd bargain with someone only too happy not to appear to be making a forced sale.'

Humphrey was happily constructing bricks out of the few straws that Jay had so carefully strewn in his path. Amanda let her mind wander and suddenly realised why watching Jay with Humphrey and Jane had been so revealing and so painful.

Jay had been someone quite out of the ordinary, almost a fantasy. But for Jane and Humphrey, he was a chance-met gentleman about whom they were forming an opinion as they might about any new acquaintance. Jane obviously found him intelligent, charming and sympathetic, for Amanda knew her reserved nature too well to mistake the signs of approval in her open manner towards him.

Humphrey, while approving him as a gentleman and a knowledgeable landowner, was unmistakeably somewhat jealous of him. To Amanda, Jay had been simply Jay—a man who had insidiously become important to her happiness.

Now through Humphrey's eyes she saw a tall, handsome man, one with assurance and breeding. Even without their shared secret and intimacy, this made him a dangerously attractive man—and one from whom she had just parted forever.

And a good thing too, she told herself firmly. *Or you'll find you have fallen in love with him—and then where will you be?* And a small voice seemed to whisper in response, *Too late, Amanda, too late…*

Chapter Eight

Quite how long Amanda sat there lost in these disturbing thoughts she had no idea, but a small cough from Jane recalled her to the fact that they had a guest, however unwelcome. Cousin Humphrey had apparently asked her a question and was waiting for an answer.

'Yes, of course,' she said at random, forcing a smile.

'Excellent, excellent,' Mr Clare responded heartily, getting to his feet in a small shower of biscuit crumbs. 'It is fortunate that it is fixed for Monday evening. Your face is healing very well, but I would not want dear Mama alarmed by the sight of such an unladylike disfigurement.'

It was an effort to keep the polite smile fixed as she tugged the bell-pull, but as soon as Humphrey had been ushered out Amanda exploded, 'Insufferable man!' She took an angry turn around the room and came to a halt in front of her companion. 'And what have I agreed to for Monday night, Jane?'

'I did think you were not quite attending to the conversation, dear,' Jane replied mildly. 'We have been invited to dinner at Glaven Hall.'

'Oh, no, I *am* sorry, Jane dear. It is bad enough to

endure an evening there without inflicting it upon you as well. I wonder why he included you on this occasion, you usually manage to escape.'

'I am afraid Mr Clare does not always have the, shall we say, imagination, to realise that by ignoring a paid companion he may be giving offence.' Jane's tone was dispassionate. 'However, now he is courting you, he obviously feels it is proper to include your companion as chaperon.'

'Do you truly think he is courting me, Jane?' Amanda plumped herself down in the chair again with rather more force than elegance. 'I did wonder when I saw that look in his eyes the other day. I fear my good housekeeping outweighs my other faults.'

'And your land.'

'How lowering to be admired by such a man and for such reasons.' Amanda cupped her chin in her hand and gazed dismally out into the garden where a light drizzle was beginning to fall. 'Just look at that weather! Would it be very unworthy to hope he catches a cold riding home?'

'Yes, most unworthy,' Jane agreed. 'However, I do not think Mr Jay admires you for either reason.'

'Please, Jane, do not speak of him so. We are all agreed, are we not, that it is better if he and I do not meet.'

'Well, as you know, I did think that would be best,' Miss Porter said thoughtfully. 'But that was before I met him. I flatter myself on being a good judge of character, and I cannot believe he is anything but a gentleman of breeding who wishes you only good.'

'That is as may be,' Amanda retorted, trying to convince herself as much as Jane. 'But he says himself he is probably a rake, and, although he is convinced he is not married, who knows what attachment he is bound by.'

Miss Porter inclined her head in silent agreement, but after a moment's thought remarked, 'It is interesting to meet a rake. I suppose he would naturally be a man of handsome appearance and charm, but I had expected to find such a man sadly dissipated in appearance.'

'Really, Jane! What an improper observation! He will probably *become* dissipated in appearance; after all, he is comparatively young.' They looked at each other for a moment, then Amanda was suddenly struck by a thought. 'What *do* you think he would say if he could hear us?' And with one accord they dissolved into giggles.

Amanda eventually emerged from her handkerchief, mopped her eyes and remarked, 'I feel better for that. It was doubtless what Mrs Clare senior would describe as an unseemly fit of hysterics, but I refuse to be downhearted about the situation. I am sure we will find some way to restore Mr Jay to his true identity.'

Looking at her over-bright eyes and determined smile, Miss Porter thought, *All very well, but is it going to restore your heart, my dear?*

The next morning, Saturday, dawned bright and fresh with the air washed clear by the previous day's drizzle. Amanda lay in bed, firmly talking herself into the frame of mind usually associated with New Year's resolutions. She reached over for the tablets she kept beside the bed, turned to a fresh page and sucked the end of her pencil. *Number 1: No daydreaming.* Not, of course, that she would close her mind to thinking about ways of helping Jay, but these thoughts would be purely practical and directed towards helping a distant friend. *Number 2:*

Kate re. Wedding. Banns? Cottage. She must talk to
Kate about arranging a wedding day as soon as possible
before there was any sign of the baby, and early enough
that curious neighbours would not start adding up dates
when it did arrive. A special licence would hasten matters, but that in itself would cause speculation. She
would see what the young couple thought.

Amanda chewed the end of the pencil some more
then added *Number 3: New lady's maid. Local? Norwich agency? London.* London was a very tempting
thought. It was a long time since she had stayed in town
and it was common knowledge that a flurry of shopping
and dances was exactly the remedy for an aching heart.
But she could not go not knowing what was happening
to Jay, and once he was recovered he would almost
certainly be going there himself and she shrank from
appearing to follow him. No, London would have to
wait. She would make enquiries about suitable local
girls and resort to the Norwich domestic agencies if
necessary.

That left one more item for her list. *Number 4: What
to do about H?* What to do about Humphrey indeed!
To fall out with him would be most unseemly and
would create local gossip and comment of a most undesirable sort. Much as she disliked him, he *was* the
head of the family now and she owed him and his
mother the respect owing to that position.

Would he believe her if she simply declined him politely when—if—he proposed? She suspected he would
not take 'no' for an answer without very good reason.
She had no other plausible suitors, for she had been in
deep mourning for a year, half-mourning for a further
six months and was only now beginning to take her
place in the somewhat restricted local society. She sus-

pected that once she began to attend more local assemblies and dinner parties again she would find some eligible suitors appearing from the ranks of the local landowners, for word of the young widow with her generous portion and good lands would soon spread.

Amanda might be unconcerned about her looks, but she was aware she was accounted handsome by even the most exacting critics, so there was nothing to stand in the way of her receiving the flattering proposals that had been so lacking when she had first come out.

But she could hardly throw herself into a social whirl simply to surround herself with enough suitors to keep Humphrey at a distance, especially when she had no intention of accepting any of these imaginary men. A pair of lazily amused green eyes came to mind at this point and Amanda tossed aside pencil and tablets and scrambled out of bed, tugging the bell-pull as she did so.

Kate appeared with the water ewer and observed her mistress as she walked across the room. 'You are moving so much more easily, ma'am. Are your bruises better now?'

'Do you know, I think they are, Kate. I feel hardly a twinge, and my face is almost better.' She pulled off her lacy nightcap and shook out her hair. 'Kate, I want to talk to you about your wedding plans. I think the banns had better be called as soon as possible—unless you were thinking of a special licence.'

Kate nodded vigorously as she poured steaming water. 'I was talking to Tom last night and he suggested a licence too, but I think it'll make folk talk, so we are going to see Vicar tomorrow so he can start the banns on Sunday, then we can be married in four Sundays' time.'

She chattered happily while Amanda washed and sat in her robe, brushing out her hair, then asked, 'What will you be wearing today, ma'am?'

The sunlight sparkled off the cut-glass bottles on the dressing table and Amanda decided she could not bear to be inside any longer. 'My riding habit, Kate. It must be well over a week since I was last riding—it will shake out the cobwebs.'

She pulled a face at the sight of her habit as Kate lifted it out of the clothes' press. 'Oh dear, I wish I had thought to bespeak a new one while I was in Norwich. That one really is the most depressing colour.' She had bought it when she had come out of full mourning and had begun to ride about again, but the kindest description she could think of for the colour was greyish mouse.

Kate helped her into the long skirt and tight jacket and she bundled her hair into a net. 'It will have to do for now, I can hardly make another trip to Norwich so soon just for a riding habit, and none of the local tailors is up to a really fashionable lady's habit. Perhaps I will wait until I next go to London.'

'Oh!' Kate's lip quivered at the thought of missing the long-dreamed-of trip to town, but she sniffed resolutely and picked up Amanda's hat, gloves and whip to take downstairs, ready for when she wanted to go out.

Over breakfast Amanda politely asked Jane if she wished to ride too, but, as she expected, Miss Porter declined. She was an excellent whip and an energetic walker, but always declared she felt off balance in the saddle. 'Where will you go, dear?'

'Down to the coast and across the marshes to the seashore,' Amanda decided. 'I have missed the sea this past week.' The butler came in with fresh toast. 'Howlett, please send round to the stable and ask them to saddle up Jupiter. I will be riding after breakfast.'

'Well, take care—and do take a groom,' Jane urged, more in hope than expectation. One of the things that caused eyebrows to rise locally, at least among the matrons who did not quite approve of Mrs Clare, was her habit of riding out alone.

'Nothing wrong with that,' their husbands would counter. 'Mrs Clare is a good landlord, and a good landlord rides their lands.'

'She should take a groom with her,' their wives would argue. 'After all, she is a female.' At this the men's eyes would tend to take on a thoughtful look and their spouses would wisely change the subject.

Amanda laughed without answering her companion and reached for the cherry preserve.

Her bruises were rather more painful than she had thought when she began to trot out of the yard and she realised that at some point during the accident she must have sat down hard on her behind. However, her grey mare Jupiter had a beautifully even pace, and once the first stiffness had worn off Amanda was soon relaxing. This had been a good idea, for her mount was fresh enough to give her both exercise and something to concentrate on and within a few minutes the nagging unhappiness about Jay, if not forgotten, was less overwhelming.

Jupiter trotted down the lane between high hedges and stretches of finely made cobble- and brick walls that marked the edges of some of her neighbours' parklands. Now and again she saw someone she recognised and waved, but did not stop until she met the Rector, off on some errand of mercy in his pony trap.

He pulled up and doffed his hat, obliging her to stop also. Jupiter sidled and snorted but Amanda held her with a firm hand and exchanged polite conversation about the weather and how improved the ring of bells was now the entire peel had been tuned and re-hung. 'And I believe I will be seeing you on Monday evening at Glaven Hall,' Mr Maddison added. 'I am sure it will be a most interesting gathering.'

Describing an evening at Glaven Hall with Mrs Clare senior presiding over the dinner table as 'interesting' was, Amanda felt, carrying charity too far, even for the Rector, but she smiled and agreed she was looking forward to it. At least the addition of the Maddisons to the party promised a more stimulating evening than she had feared, for Humphrey had probably invited several other couples while he was about it.

'Until Sunday service then, Rector.' She smiled as he shook the reins and the fat pony ambled on its way. They were almost at the village green in Wiveton; within a few minutes, she was trotting over the humped-back bridge spanning the Glaven and heading into the little port of Cley. Although all but the smallest craft now had deserted its wharf for Blakeney, it was still busy and Amanda enjoyed the change of scene as she wove her way slowly amongst fishermen, housewives out for the morning's provisions and small groups of labourers hanging around in the hope of a day's work.

Then she was clear of the village and was at last able to give Jupiter her head. The ruler-straight line of the grass bank stretched before them from the coast road to the great shingle ridge hiding the sea. Waders and ducks rose screeching and flapping from the marsh as the horse passed by, then settled in wheeling clouds behind them. All too soon Jupiter was plunging to a walk as her hooves met the deep, loose shingle of the ridge. Snorting, she laboured up the side, sliding as she did so and forcing Amanda to hold tight to the pommel to keep her seat. Then they were at the top and the sea stretched cold and grey before them.

'All the way to the North Pole', Charles had said when he first brought her here, and even on a warm day like today she imagined that she caught the sharp scent of snow on the wind. Ridiculous, of course, but the thought was romantic and she always enjoyed the sweeping views to the west where the shingle rose gradually into low cliffs and to the east where the great spit of Blakeney Point curved out from its root, where she stood, to its tip guarding the anchorage.

Amanda scanned the sea for seals, for one could often see their black heads looking like human swimmers bobbing in the shallows. Sometimes there was even the excitement of sighting the great fins of basking sharks, but today there was only the passing white gannets and flocks of gulls to enliven the waves.

Sitting still for a while reminded her of her bruises and she decided to walk a little to stretch her legs. Jupiter made her usual fuss about having to scramble down the shingle bank again, but was happy enough to be tied to a post near a patch of short grass and left to graze while Amanda swung the long skirt of her habit over her arm and set off at a fairly brisk pace along the path on the landward side of the bank.

The bulk of Blakeney church with its little lantern tower to guide the sailors slowly grew larger to her left as the marsh between the coast road and the spit grew wetter and wider and began to be broken up by muddy channels. The tide was out, but as she walked Amanda saw that it was turning and the water was rippling and running back to cover the mud.

At last, rather out of breath, she scrambled up the bank to the top again. In the distance she could see Jupiter, head down, cropping grass. Near the horizon she could make out sails and just along the beach in the shallows a black head was bobbing—a seal at last. Amanda had walked rather further than she had planned and was beginning to think a rest would be a good idea. Almost opposite the seal the sea had thrown up a tumble of something—an old net, perhaps—and she decided to walk that far, then sit down and have a rest. If she sat quietly, the seal might come quite close in.

The shingle made walking difficult and, head bent, she trudged on, the wind snatching at her hat until at last she sank down, just under the top of the ridge, and pulled off hat and veil. The seal had gone, but with the little protection of the ridge the sun was winning over the wind and she sat hugging her knees, gazing with unfocused eyes over the waves.

Now she had stopped moving, Jay filled her thoughts again. What was he going to do if his memory did not return soon? If only he would accept a loan from her, but she knew he never would. He had recalled playing cards: perhaps he was such a good player he could win enough to finance a trip to London. But he would still need a stake.

At this point the seal bobbed up again, then vanished almost at once. Vaguely wondering why it was so shy, Amanda relapsed into her thoughts again. Time passed and still she sat there, the wind stirring her hair, her mind anxiously running round schemes, none of which, on closer examination, proved practicable in the slightest.

There was the seal again…no! Not a seal, a swimmer, a man rising from the sea and beginning to walk out of it, the water sluicing down his shoulders and chest, down to his waist, down…

Amanda buried her face in her hands and sat hunched where she was, praying that her drab riding habit would afford her some invisibility. She risked a quick glimpse from between her fingers: he had reached the point where the seabed rose sharply to the shore and with a scrambling stride was almost clear of the water.

With an awful inevitability she recognised that the swimmer was Jay, and also, as she reburied her flaming face in her palms, that he was quite naked.

She heard his feet crunching through the stones, then they stopped and she realised that what she had vaguely assumed was a pile of old nets must be his discarded clothing. At least he was getting dressed! Amanda pressed her fingertips to her eyelids until she saw stars, but nothing could banish the image of that tall frame, the broad shoulders and muscular torso tapering into the narrow waist, the long legs darkened with wet hairs, the dark chest hair narrowing downwards…

She felt hot and cold and realised her breath was coming short. If the shingle had opened up and swallowed her she would have been glad of it, but all she could do was sit there, her ears straining until they caught the crunch of footsteps again. They gradually faded away and she realised that he was not going to approach her.

Hardly able to breathe, Amada raised her head and looked around her. Jay was walking as briskly as possible on the shifting surface, away from her and towards

where she had left Jupiter. Had he seen her? It seemed
too much to hope that he had not. Had he recognised
her? That too seemed only too likely. He must have
been treading water out there for many minutes, hoping
she would walk on, or back, and let him get out of the
water. Finally the cold must have driven him out.

Amanda crouched there, shivering with reaction,
watching Jay's receding figure. After what seemed like
an hour, but was probably only ten minutes, he cut up
off the beach to climb the ridge and dropped from sight.
He would make better time on the grassy strip on the
landward side and would soon reach the marsh bank.
Which meant she must walk back along the beach or
he would see her as he walked inland.

With a heavy sigh Amanda got to her feet and picked
her way down the beach, hoping for at least a ribbon
of hard sand to make her going easier, but the rising
tide had covered it and she trudged on, perversely grateful for the effort of walking. She focussed on each foot-
step, forcing herself to think of nothing else until at last
she reached the log, bleached by the sea and tossed high
and dry by the winter storms, which acted as a marker
for the point where she had to turn her back on the sea.

Jupiter was waiting patiently, one hoof cocked, head
drooping, but she whickered at the sight of her mistress
and butted her gently with her soft muzzle when the
usual caress and titbit was not forthcoming. Amanda led
her over to the stile which made a convenient mounting
block and turned her head inland. The long path on the
top of the embankment was empty.

Amanda let her breath out in a long sigh and tried to
think rationally about what had just occurred. 'Pull
yourself together!' she admonished herself. 'What a fuss
about nothing. You have been a married woman after

all. It was embarrassing of course, but nothing to get into a state about.' Jupiter twitched her ears, enjoying the sound of Amanda's voice. 'I am not going to see him again, which is a blessing.'

Jupiter walked on, but there was nothing further from her mistress who appeared rather depressed with the effect of her thoughts, for her hands dropped to the mare's withers and the reins slackened. Jupiter ambled along and at the coast road, when there was no direction from her rider, turned west instead of heading back into the village. Sometimes Amanda went that way—it was longer, but there was the opportunity of a good gallop over the heath as a reward for the steeper climb up.

Amanda sat, hands unmoving, eyes focussed on something entirely other than the passing countryside, until Jupiter stopped at a gate. 'What!' She started as if woken from sleep and realised that the mare had found her own way almost to the heath. 'Oh, Jupiter, I am sorry! Are you very bored? Never mind, we will go through here and have a good gallop, it will do us both good.'

Drawing up at the gate off the heath five minutes later, Amanda reflected that the gallop might have done Jupiter some good, but it had had the most extraordinary effect on her. She had fallen into a rather hazy daydream of the morning when she had woken in the inn bed beside Jay and her mind, shying away from the all-too-naked reality of what had just occurred, had been soothed by the memory of his warmth, his deep, slow breathing and of the safety she had felt, drowsing beside him.

The gallop had aroused an entirely different feeling of urgency and restlessness. She felt hot and cold all at once, wanted to gallop again, feel the wind in her hair, the power of the horse carrying her along, muscles surging beneath the saddle. 'What is the matter with me?' she whispered as she trotted sedately back along the lane, ducking her head to avoid the blossom which was beginning to cover the hedges, bending the boughs low. Perhaps she was sickening for a fever. It would account for her ridiculous over-reaction to the encounter on the beach, her absence of mind, the strange feeling that still possessed her.

Jane was in the stableyard as she rode in and her expression as she greeted her confirmed Amanda's diagnosis. 'My dear, are you quite well? You are so flushed. I do hope you have not overdone things.'

Amanda slipped down gratefully from Jupiter's back and handed the reins to the groom. 'I think I must be developing a cold, Jane, I feel so very odd.'

Jane put her hand under one arm. 'Amanda, you are positively trembling. Come up to bed at once and I will make you a saline draught. Reaction to the shock of your accident, that will be it, mark my words. That sort of thing will lay even the healthiest person open to a cold. Let us hope it is nothing more serious.'

Chapter Nine

Tucked up in bed by Jane, a hot brick at her feet, a saline draught forced down, Amanda found herself curiously willing to play the invalid. She had never felt quite like this before: even when Charles had died she had not wanted to hide away. There had been people to see and to comfort, just as she had needed comfort. There had been tasks to carry out and she had done all of that without shirking anything, even coping calmly with the unwelcome arrival of Cousin Humphrey and his mother, indecently soon after the funeral, to take up residence.

Perhaps she really was going to be ill, and not hiding as her conscience kept telling her, whenever she allowed herself to listen to its promptings. *You do not want to think about him*, it nagged her. *You are in love with him and now you desire him.*

'I am not! I cannot be!' she said out loud so vehemently that Jane, who had popped her head around the door to enquire if she would like a little chicken broth for luncheon, was alarmed.

'Oh dear, you are delirious,' she gasped, hurrying

into the room and placing one cool hand on Amanda's hot brow. 'I shall send for Dr Hoskins.'

'No, please, do not do that.' Amanda caught her hand and forced herself to smile reassuringly. 'It is nothing more than a delayed reaction to all the excitement with the accident, and Jay's predicament and so on. And I am worried about Kate, and finding a replacement for her.' All of which was quite true and nothing at all to do with the state she was in. 'I am sure that a day resting will do me a power of good, Jane. I will have a little broth and spend the afternoon with one of the books I brought back from Norwich. After that, and a good night's sleep, I will be right as rain in the morning, Jane, just wait and see.'

The first part of her remedy worked perfectly. The broth was reviving, Miss Austen's *Pride and Prejudice*, which she had unaccountably missed when it was published, was engrossing and made her laugh out loud, and she was able to address the supper that an anxious Kate brought up with relish.

'You see, Kate, I will be perfectly all right in the morning and able to go to church. I would not want to miss hearing your banns read.'

But the good night's sleep which Amanda had predicted proved to be far from reality. She certainly slept, but it was a sleep full of dreams so vivid and explicit that she finally awoke as the clock chimed five with the bedclothes in a tangle around her limbs and her breath coming fast as though she had been running.

Even with returning consciousness the dreams did not fade, leaving Amanda staring wide-eyed into the dawn light, remembering images of her body clasped in Jay's arms, their limbs equally naked, his mouth hot and possessive on hers, kissing her with an intensity that neither of his previous kisses had achieved. Her breathing was still ragged, her body felt almost unbearably tense and she was filled with a deep, aching longing.

Amanda scrambled out of bed, poured cold water from the ewer into the basin and splashed her face, towelling it roughly until she felt fully awake and the trembling in her limbs stopped. Shaken, she got back into bed, plumped up the pillows and sat watching the brightening dawn.

Was this desire, then? She had been brought up to understand that ladies did not experience this sensation, that the physical act was, if one was fortunate, not too unpleasant, and was the price one paid for a happy marriage, children and the comfort of an affectionate husband.

Charles had treated her from the first as though she was infinitely fragile and as though he expected her to be deeply shocked by the whole physical side of marriage. She had never seen her husband naked, for he always spared her blushes by drawing the curtains and extinguishing the lamps before coming to bed. His love making had been gentle, and over sooner than she had expected. At first it had been every bit as painful and embarrassing as she had feared, but as she grew to trust him it became simply something that had to be gone through in order to achieve the companionable presence of a satisfied and kindly husband in her bed.

She enjoyed sleeping by his side, listening to him breathing, feeling safe and loved. She had enjoyed their early morning conversations, both of them in their nightgowns, sitting up against the pillows, sipping their chocolate and planning the day.

His kisses were pleasant, but she had felt none of the

more exciting sensations that occasionally she heard whispers of from her faster acquaintances. And she had no one to ask whether this really was all there was to the marriage bed.

The sight of Jay's raw physicality had shaken her to the core and had brought into focus all the feelings that being with him had stirred in her, made the remembered touch of his lips something infinitely dangerous and exciting, full of longing and desire.

I told you so, jeered that inner voice she had so vehemently denied the day before. *And he has gone and you will never see him again.*

Her treacherous imagination took her back to the bed in the Lamb and Flag. What would have happened if she had not opened her eyes, but had let herself fall into his embrace, let that brief kiss linger, allowed his arms to hold her, his legs to tangle with hers, his body to roll her into the deep feather mattress and his weight to cover her?

He would have made love to her, that was what would have happened, and she would have discovered what it is like when a man treats a woman not as a child bride, not as a fragile piece of porcelain, but as a flesh-and-blood creature capable of as much passion and pleasure as he was. And now she would never experience that.

The sound of the household waking up and going about its business finally roused her from her thoughts. Today was Sunday and somehow or another she was going to get up, put on her Sunday clothes and her Sunday face and struggle to school her thoughts into calmness and reverence.

Once she and Jane were walking at the head of the little procession of servants wending their way to church, prayer books in gloved hands, best hats and bonnets firmly on heads, she began to feel more in control. It was amazing what the discipline of routine and the need to behave properly in front of the servants could do for a breaking heart.

Jane was inclined to fuss over her at first, but Amanda's apparent serenity, her lack of a fever and her determination to attend Matins soon set Miss Porter's mind at rest. Several friends and neighbours greeted them as they met and mingled at the north porch. The servants, whispers hushed, made their way to their pews in the rear of the church, the bell ringers shuffled in from the tower arch and Amanda and Jane made their way down the aisle to where their high box-pew sat just across from that belonging to Glaven Hall.

Amanda knew very well the comforts hidden behind the high panelled door. Charles had had the velvet cushions replaced, she had embroidered the kneelers herself over several long winter months and there were even velvet curtains on brass rods to draw to keep the draughts from penetrating where the oak panelling met the grey stone of the pillars.

Her own pew now was less imposing, as befitted one of the lesser households in the valley. The verger was opening the door for her with a bow when Cousin Humphrey stood up in his pew, making Jane jump. 'Will you not join me, Cousin?' he enquired. The verger hurried to open that door in turn, almost tripping over his long verge as he did so. Amanda had no wish to join her cousin, but she had even less desire make an exhibition of herself arguing about it in front of a full congregation.

'Thank you, Cousin, thank you, Mr Berry, come,

Jane,' and she stepped into the box, blithely ignoring the look of chagrin on Humphrey's face. He had had no intention of inviting the companion, now he had to shuffle along the bench to make room as the two ladies bowed to Mrs Clare senior and took their places.

If Amanda had wanted to find a counter-irritant to her thoughts, she could not have done better than to sit with Mr Clare. Her attempts at quiet reflection were broken into by him officiously finding her place for the next reading or hymn; he dropped his hat, enquired in a loud whisper if she felt at all cold as he had a rug under the seat for such an eventuality and instead of being able to listen closely to Mr Maddison's sermon, she was mortified by him nodding vigorously and exclaiming 'Quite right, sir!' all too audibly at intervals.

His mother merely sat bolt upright, fixing Amanda, whenever she caught her eye, with a fishy stare that appeared to blame her for Humphrey's excesses. Finally the Rector began to read the banns. When he reached the announcement for Kate and Tom Green, Mrs Clare's expression became even chillier and her mouth set into a thin line of disapproval. Amanda knew she was imagining the worst and wondered just how, short of an untruth, she was going to protect Kate's good name when the village tabbies began to gossip.

As the service ended she was careful to stand well clear of the pew door to make it very obvious that she expected Humphrey to give his mother his arm and allow her to take precedence as he was showing alarming signs of ushering Amanda out first.

Her good manners did not save her from a vigorous interrogation as soon as she had shaken hands with the Rector and was outside the church, waiting for her little household to reassemble.

'This is very sudden, the marriage of that maid of yours, is it not?' Mrs Clare demanded. 'A scrambling way of doing things, I declare, one could almost imagine she has need for haste.'

'Surely not,' Amanda replied calmly. 'If that had been the case, why, they could have married by licence. Jane, where can the boot boy have gone to, can you see him anywhere?'

'A licence!' Mrs Clare was aghast, the black beads in her bonnet flashing with her vehemence. 'Aping her betters!'

'No doubt, ma'am,' Amanda responded, apparently giving it little importance. 'Where has that boy got to! I have no intention of leaving without him and having him arrive back at goodness knows what hour, covered with mud. Not upon a Sunday, in any case.' She saw Jane hurrying the miscreant back from a hiding place amongst the tombstones and turned her attention back to Mrs Clare. 'It is a very long-standing attachment, ma'am, so I am not at all surprised, although sorry to be losing such a good servant, of course. May I walk with you to your carriage?'

Mollified, if still inclined to speculate, Mrs Clare allowed herself to be guided firmly down the churchyard path. Amanda was relaxing when her next sharp question made her jump.

'What do you know of this man Jay that Humphrey has taken up with? A Captain Sharp, is he?'

'I know very little of his circumstances,' Amanda replied truthfully, trusting that the warmth of the sun would explain any colour in her cheeks.

'You have had him in the house, for that is where Humphrey came upon him.'

'Oh, yes, but one is duty bound to entertain and assist

visiting gentlepeople. Although who am I to remind such a notable hostess as yourself of the fact? Mr Jay was brought to my attention as a gentleman enquiring about agricultural matters and I was happy to give him what information I have. Naturally, he found his meeting with Mr Clare of inestimable interest.'

The combination of Amanda's disinterested tone and her flattering remark about Humphrey did much to lull Mrs Clare's suspicions. 'I am sure he did,' she retorted sharply, but with a pleased glint in her eye. 'I am glad of your opinion of the man—not that your experience is wide, but I have no reason to believe you do not recognise a gentleman when you see one.'

'Thank you, ma'am, praise indeed,' Amanda murmured. 'Here is your carriage, I will bid you good morning.' They exchanged bows and Amanda walked briskly away, cutting the corner to avoid meeting Humphrey as he bustled after his mama.

Jane occupied the walk back to the house with a discussion of the best way to discipline the boot boy—'An incorrigible child!'—appreciation of the Rector's sermon—'Always so much matter for contemplation afterwards in Mr Maddison's addresses, do you not think, dear?'—and very mild praise for the floral arrangement at the altar—'Such a lack of imagination when one thinks what a wealth of bloom is available just now.'

It was not until the ladies were ensconced in the parlour with a half-embroidered kneeler apiece for the Lady Chapel on their laps that she spoke of what had obviously been filling her mind. 'I was so taken aback by Mr Clare's actions this morning! He has never done such a thing before.'

'I know.' Amanda sighed, reaching for her embroidery scissors. 'I felt so conspicuous. Why, he could hardly have made his intentions clearer if he had posted a notice in the porch!'

'How did his mama react?' Miss Porter enquired. 'I could not see her face without bending forward, and naturally I could not do that.'

'She was not pleased, although she was distracted by the news about Kate's marriage. If she does make her feelings plain to Cousin Humphrey, do you think that will be enough to discourage him?'

Miss Porter set a few stitches thoughtfully. 'If it were just a passing fancy, it might, but reflect, dear, we have decided that not only does he covet your lands and appreciate your skills as a housewife, we had long recognised that he was attracted to you...that is he found you attractive—' She broke off blushing.

'I suppose it is too much to hope that his relationship to Charles puts him within the prohibited degrees of marriage for me?' Amanda exclaimed, suddenly hopeful. 'They are listed in the prayer book.' She picked up the book from the table beside her and riffled through the pages. 'Here we are...parents, brothers, uncles... No, if he had been Charles's uncle, then it would be forbidden, but there is nothing at all about cousins.'

'You will just have to tell him the truth, that is all,' said Miss Porter firmly. 'His mind is not elastic, and it may take several repetitions before he gives up, but surely that is the only way.'

'Tell him that I do not think we should suit, you mean?' Amanda asked, resuming her stitching.

'Of course, if that is the only reason,' her companion answered calmly, apparently not noticing the hectic blush which rose in Amanda's cheeks. 'Do you think this dull gold is better for the lettering here, or should I use the brighter yellow?'

The night brought no better rest for Amanda. The feverish dreams persisted and by the morning she felt so tired and out of sorts that her normal sense of humour had quite deserted her. Despite the fact that Jay had remained true to his word and had not contacted her since Friday, she found herself blaming him for the nature of her dreams, just as though he had been indulging in the most persistent attentions to her.

How dare he intrude into the calm, happy, orderly world she had built for herself? How could he flirt with her so carelessly, charm her with that lazy smile, those deep green eyes? Why could he not be a gentleman and endure a little cold while she took the air on the beach?

The entire household felt the change in Amanda as she swept down to breakfast. Not that she exhibited the slightest ill temper to anyone, for she would have been ashamed to do so, but the string of orders she delivered left no one in any doubt as to her mood.

'Kate, it is about time that all the clothes presses were emptied and aired and fresh wormwood hung up for the moth. And when you have done that, please reline all the drawers. Mrs Howlett will give you fresh lavender to refill the lavender bags. Jane dear, shall we turn out the linen cupboards as we have been promising Mrs Howlett we would do this month past? A complete new inventory is needed, she tells me.' She paused for breath and surveyed her staff, apprehensively assembled in the hall.

'Howlett, I cannot think why, but all the windows look smeary in this sunshine. Please set the footmen to work on the inside and the grooms can get out the ladders and do the outsides. And do you not feel it is about time the cellar was reviewed and we decided what new order to send off to Grimble and Hodgkiss in Norwich? I do not want to risk having inadequate wines when we have company.'

She spotted the boot boy trying to vanish under the stairs. 'And you, Jeremy, can blacklead every grate in the house until Mrs Howlett is satisfied.'

Leaving them breathless behind her, Amanda picked up the sheets of paper that contained the linen inventory and swept upstairs. 'Come along, Jane, let us start with the cupboard on the top landing.'

By mid-afternoon the staff were hot, bothered and dusty, but the windows sparkled, the grates gleamed and a substantial order was sealed, waiting to be dispatched to the wine merchant.

Jane, who after one intent look at her employer's expression had shaken out sheets, tugged at hems and condemned worn pillow cases for dusters without complaint all day, finally sat back on her heels and announced. 'I think that is the very last sheet in the house, leaving aside what is on the beds, of course.'

Amanda wrote the last correction on the inventory and conned it critically. 'I do not know what the servants do to their sheets! I could swear that we ordered twelve new pairs last year at this time and there is hardly an undarned one in the house. But beside that, and an order for some new pillow cases, I do not think things are too bad.'

She put down her pen, untied her apron and tossed it on to the table, noticing her companion's weary stance for the first time. 'Oh, Jane, I am sorry! Are you very tired? I should have noticed, and we hardly stopped to eat.'

'It is quite all right, my dear.' Miss Porter got to her feet and folded her apron. 'It is no bad thing to do such a task all at once, and I am sure we will suffer no harm for having had a light luncheon. After all, we are dining out this evening.'

'Oh my goodness, I had quite forgotten.' Amanda brushed her hair off her forehead and regarded the smudge on the end of Miss Porter's nose. 'A hot bath for both of us, I think. What shall we wear?'

'You said that Mr and Mrs Maddison have been invited, which probably means that several other couples have as well. Mrs Clare would regard that as an economy to return all her outstanding invitations at one time. Therefore we had better look our best, do you not think so? It will hardly be a family dinner.'

'Yes,' Amanda agreed. The anger with Jay was still running hot in her veins and the thought of dressing up, of putting on her jewels, of making an impression, was very tempting. Perhaps some single gentlemen had been invited. In that case, she would flirt—very discreetly, of course. That would show him, she thought, although how he would be expected to know about it, she had no idea. 'Yes,' she repeated. 'Let us dress up, Jane, I am sure Mrs Clare would appreciate it.'

Chapter Ten

Amanda stepped down from the carriage outside Glaven Hall in the full knowledge that she was looking magnificent. She was not vain about her looks, nor was she given to dressing to make an impression, although Charles had liked it when she had appeared on his arm in striking gowns and wearing the jewels he had bought her.

But she did enjoy beautiful clothes. In recent times the opportunities to dress her hair, take the diamonds out of their box and show off her latest gown had been few and far apart, so she intended to make the most of this one.

The gown she had decided on for this evening was one of her purchases in Norwich, an over-dress of the palest sea-green gauze draped elegantly over the under-tunic of a deeper shade of the same colour in a fluid silk with a deeply beaded hem. The neckline was almost plain, with just a thin line of the same beading, but it skimmed low to show off her bosom and shoulders, which were lightly veiled in a gauze scarf that the vendeuse had assured her was, 'Just the colour of the sea-foam, madame.'

Diamond-drop earrings trembled against her neck, the matching necklace was simple enough not to distract from her pale skin, yet flashed with the true depth of stones of the first water. She hesitated over her hair, which was piled high with one curl tumbling artlessly down, then fastened the two diamond pins just where the curl twisted free of the coiffure.

A touch of rice powder where a critical eye might discern the faded bruise, a final touch of jasmine water behind the ears and on her lace handkerchief and she was ready.

Jane was full of admiration at the effect, and more than happy to receive compliments in return for her neat but elegant gown of bronze silk with a braided hem. 'We are very fine,' she commented as the carriage turned into the long drive up to the Hall.

'Indeed we are,' Amanda agreed, her eyes sparkling, her smile rather more brittle than her companion was wont to see it. All that was wrong with her, she had decided, was a lack of society. If she mixed more, met more men at dinner parties or on the dance floor, then she would not be so ridiculously affected when one of them paid her some attention. The disturbing impact of a pair of green eyes, or a length of well-muscled leg, would soon be put in proportion.

In this combative mood Amanda swept up the front steps and smiled brilliantly upon her startled host, who suddenly felt as though a biddable and pretty kitten had turned into a veritable tigress. She shook hands with Mrs Clare and allowed herself to be shown into the long drawing room where she had entertained on many occasions herself.

As she and Jane had speculated, it was indeed full with perhaps twenty couples and she was glad she had dressed for the occasion. One or two of the faces were unfamiliar, although she guessed that no one was there from very far afield from the fact that everyone she could see was engaged in very easy conversation. And there were certainly at least half a dozen men in their twenties and thirties, ideal to begin her resolution to put the memory of Mr Jay firmly into proportion.

A small knot of guests who were partly obstructing the doorway broke up to allow her through and she was immediately greeted by Mrs Maddison. 'Good evening, Mrs Clare. What a very enjoyable gathering, to be sure. May I make my nephew Mr James Williams known to you?'

Mr Williams proved to be amiable, admiring and eager to make conversation. 'Allow me to find you a chair, Mrs Clare. Here, perhaps, away from the crush by the door?'

Amanda let him guide her into the room, refused the chair and set herself to make small talk. The young man soon found himself joined by several others: two were the sons of local landowners, another the junior partner of the leading Holt firm of attorneys.

Somehow Amanda became aware that she was becoming the centre of attention. Why, she did not quite know. Several of the ladies were at least as well gowned as she and there were also a number of handsome women in the room against whom she knew herself to be quite eclipsed in looks. Nor was she talking loudly or making any attempt to draw attention to herself. And yet her mood seemed to communicate itself to those around her, spreading a dangerous edge of excitement.

Then the pattern of groups at the far end of the room shifted and reformed and she found herself looking down the expanse of floor to one man who was standing alone in front of the wide marble fireplace. It seemed to Amanda that the voices in the room fell silent, then the swell of conversation filled her ears again as Jay walked towards her, his eyes fixed on her face.

He paused as a footman passed him with a tray of glasses, lifted two of them and walked on. As he reached her he nodded pleasantly to the young men surrounding her, said, 'Gentlemen,' and they seemed to melt away. Amanda found herself standing alone with him, perforce having to accept the champagne flute he was holding out to her.

'Good evening, Mrs Clare. You are in great beauty tonight.' His eyes lingered like a caress over the smooth curves revealed by the low-cut dress and came to rest on her face.

'Good evening, Mr Jay.' She managed to smile as she said it, but her voice was hard.

Jay's eyebrow lifted and the green eyes lost their habitual look of sleepy amusement. 'You are not pleased to see me? Have I done something to offend you?'

'You can ask me that?' she hissed, then turned and smiled at a passing matron. 'Good evening, Mrs Wilmott, yes indeed, the flower arrangements are quite lovely.'

Jay continued to look politely baffled. 'I really do apologise, Mrs Clare, but you have me at a loss.'

'Saturday!' Amanda snapped. 'Need you ask?'

'Ah!' Oh, provoking man! As if he had not known all along what she was talking about! 'You are angry with me for not stopping to greet you? But I thought we had agreed it would be better if we did not meet.'

'*Greet me?*' Amanda's voice rose to an unflattering squeak and she hastily lowered it. 'How could you suggest such a thing when you were…you had no…your clothes…'

'Well, naturally, I mean after I had resumed my clothing—' He broke off to move aside for a couple making their way down the room. 'But as you seemed unwilling to acknowledge me, I did wonder if you had failed to recognise me, so I thought it better to leave.'

'Recognise you!' Amanda gasped at the effrontery of the man. 'Of course I recognised you!'

Jay said nothing, but his expression was so wicked that Amanda wanted to slap him. 'I mean…that is, of course I did not recognise you immediately with no clothes…'

He was obviously struggling now with a strong urge to laugh, but Amanda was saved from blundering any further into the morass by the arrival of Mr Bateson, an elderly farmer who took an avuncular interest in his young neighbour and who had apparently caught the tail end of what she had said.

'Mrs Clare, how very lovely you look this evening my dear. And you have found a gentleman willing to discuss clothes with you, have you? Keep a firm hold of him, not many gentlemen will do more than worry about the *bills* for the clothes, now will they, sir? Ha!' He ambled off in search of the footman with the tray, leaving a fulminating Amanda behind him.

'And where did you get that suit of evening clothes, might I ask? Or have you found someone from whom you *are* prepared to borrow money?' The suit was of good quality, but the jacket stretched taut across Jay's shoulders in a way that even the most extreme dandy might consider too tight.

'They were left by a gentleman who did a midnight flit from his accommodation at the Half Moon without paying his shot. He overlooked one portmanteau and Bream has been keeping hold of it to see if the money turns up. The housekeeper took in the trousers, but could do nothing about the shoulders—it would appear that the owner was a portly man of unimpressive physique.'

'You really have no need to angle for compliments about your figure, sir,' Amanda said icily.

'Amanda.' He took her gently by the elbow and steered her closer to the first of the pairs of long windows overlooking the terrace. Without making a scene she could hardly resist, but her arm was stiffly unresponsive under his fingers. 'Amanda, what exactly are you so angry about? I am sorry I gave you a shock on the beach, but although I am more than willing to lay down my life in defence of your safety or your honour, I am damned if I am going to freeze to death to preserve you from a few blushes!'

'Freeze to death?'

'Have you ever swum in that sea at this time of year?'

'No, of course not, this is hardly Brighton!'

'Well, it is damnably cold, I can tell you. I had gone with Bream down to the harbour in Blakeney while he was about some business and on impulse got one of the fisherman to row me over to the Point. I thought a brisk walk would do me good, but I got more than I bargained with on that shingle. It wasn't long before my ankle was hurting like the devil again. I decided a quick plunge would reduce the swelling. I had swum for about five minutes and decided I had better get out again before my blood turned to ice when you appeared.'

'Well, what do you expect?' Amanda demanded, suppressing her anxiety that he had damaged his ankle. 'It is a public beach, after all.'

'As you yourself said, it is hardly Brighton. I think I can be excused for not expecting young ladies to be wandering down it. I thought I could stay where I was until you turned round or passed by, but no, what must you do but sit down virtually on top of my clothes.'

'I wanted to think,' she said indignantly.

'Well, you certainly gave me furiously to think. I could die of cold—and I assure you I was rapidly losing all feeling in my legs—or I could get out, expecting you to modestly avert your gaze while I did so.'

Amanda blushed. 'I was shocked, and then, of course, alarmed.'

'Alarmed? What by? I can assure you, you have nothing to fear in the way of amorous attentions from a man who has been immersed in freezing water for ten minutes!' He was sounding every bit as angry as she was now, and the effort of having to conduct this argument in whispers while maintaining the appearance of normality was helping neither of them stay calm.

'Sir!'

'Oh, really, Amanda! If you had been an innocent débutante I might have been a gentlemanly fool and let myself sink without trace. But you have been a married woman, for goodness' sake! Please do not try and tell me you have never seen a naked man before.'

'I...' Amanda felt the tide of crimson rise up her throat and suffuse her face. 'How dare you?' She looked frantically around, but there was nowhere to hide her blushes without everyone noticing. 'Oh, go *away*!'

With an abrupt bow Jay turned on his heel and took a hasty stride away from her, then, obviously recollecting where he was, began to stroll slowly across the room. She watched just long enough to see him caught up in a conversation with a group of men around Humphrey before turning her burning face towards the windows.

Had anyone noticed? She struggled to take deep, slow breaths, willing the blood to leave her face. After what seemed an age she felt the heat subside, but did not turn when Mr Williams joined her. She could see his reflection in the glass and pretended to be admiring the darkening garden beyond the terrace.

'A very fine view in daylight, I recall,' he remarked. 'May I fetch you another glass of wine, ma'am? Oh, I see you have not finished that one. Would something else be to your taste?'

She could hardly spend the rest of the evening with her back to the room. Taking a deep breath, Amanda turned and smiled at the young man. 'No, but thank you. I shall finish this. It is indeed a fine view. From the terrace you can see down over the lake, which is not large, but does sit very prettily in the landscape.'

The champagne was crisp on her tongue and she sipped it gratefully. Whether it was the effect of undemanding conversation with a pleasant young man, or the wine that calmed her, she did not know, but by the time dinner was announced Amanda was feeling able to face the rest of the evening. Unless, of course, that involved any further contact with Jay.

Unfortunately, he was placed on the opposite side of the long table to herself, although not directly in front of her. With the first remove of dishes she spoke to her right-hand neighbour, a local landowner whom she suspected Humphrey had invited to meet Jay. There were rumours that he might have to sell land to meet the debts of his sons. However, he seemed in a good mood for someone on the verge of bankruptcy, so Amanda put the rumours down to mere speculation and had a pleasant discussion about the success of a locally bred racehorse, the very fine memorial glass window that had been erected in a nearby church and the shocking rise in poaching nationally.

With the second remove she turned, obedient to etiquette, to converse with her left-hand neighbour. This brought her diagonally in line with Jay, who had similarly turned. Conversation was more difficult with this gentleman, a somewhat studious young man who obviously found making small talk with ladies a strain. The effort not to raise her head and meet Jay's eyes was enormous.

Eventually she gave in and flashed a quick glance across the table, but he was apparently engrossed in what his neighbour, a very pretty relative of Mr Bateson, was telling him. She gave a little trill of laughter and he smiled, then looked up so quickly that Amanda was unable to glance away in time.

Their eyes held, but this time the smile stayed in his, not mocking her, but gentle. Amanda managed a small, answering smile and turned back to the young man, her heart beating oddly.

All the ridiculous anger had gone, drained away as suddenly as it had possessed her. Of course it was not Jay's fault that she had come across him on the beach, and he had been perfectly reasonable to expect her to turn away at once, and, in any case, not to be too shocked. How was he to know what a strangely sheltered marriage she had had? She ought to apologise to him, but that would not be easy without telling him more than she felt able to about very private memories.

She glanced across once or twice more during the course of the meal, but did not catch his eye again. Whether he looked at her she did not know, although she felt his presence as strongly as though he were sitting next to her. Finally Mrs Clare got to her feet, gathered the ladies with a glance and led them from the room. Behind them the sound of scraping chairs as the men resumed their seats was cut off by the closing doors.

Several ladies slipped away at once to the bedrooms set aside as retiring rooms and Amanda followed them. She peered anxiously into a mirror and placed a dab or two of rice powder on her cheeks, but the hectic blushes of the evening did not appear to have inflamed her injured face and there was nothing in her appearance to cause comment.

How was it possible to be so filled with churning emotion and yet show nothing of it on the outside? she wondered. Are we all hypocrites, hiding our innermost thoughts, showing only a social mask to the world?

'You are thoughtful, Mrs Clare,' one of the ladies observed.

Amanda forced a light laugh. 'I was just thinking how easily we hide our innermost thoughts behind our social faces. We are all so accomplished at it, are we not?'

'Indeed, yes.' It was the young lady who had sat next to Jay at dinner, engaged now in teasing out the curls which clustered on either side of her face. 'Take Mr Jay, for example. Why, he chatted to me so very pleasantly all through the second remove at dinner and I am sure his mind was quite elsewhere.' She pouted slightly, for she was not a girl used to taking second place in a man's thoughts. 'He is very good looking, is he not, Mrs Clare?'

'I suppose so, I am not really acquainted with him.'

'Are you not?' the older woman enquired, a slight

smile on her lips. 'You found plenty to talk about before dinner.'

Inwardly Amanda winced. So they had been noticed after all. 'We found we did not agree on everything we discussed,' she said with a careless laugh. 'There is nothing like a disagreement to prolong a conversation, is there?'

Conversation amongst the ladies was general and Amanda found relief in sitting quietly and allowing her seniors to carry the weight of it. Jane made her way over and sat beside her.

'Mrs Clare was remarking upon your gown very favourably to me. I think she is beginning to approve of you.'

'Oh, never say so!' Amanda whispered back. 'Her disapproval and opposition are my chief weapons against Humphrey!'

'Have you seen that Mr Jay is here?' Jane enquired with a sideways glance.

'Indeed I have.' Amanda hesitated, but the need to confess her bad behaviour was too strong. 'I have had a quarrel with him,' she admitted.

'A quarrel? Here? What about?'

'Yes, here. And it was really about nothing at all. It was my fault, I behaved very badly.'

'Well, you must find the opportunity to apologise,' Jane said robustly, inwardly smiling to herself. In her experience—admittedly as an onlooker—it was a sure sign of building attraction when a man and a woman quarrelled over nothing. Just so long as she was right about Jay…

The evening was becoming sultry and Mrs Clare senior suggested that the ladies might like to return to the long reception room and have the doors on to the terrace thrown open. 'I believe there are enough married ladies here to chaperon the débutantes if anyone wishes to take a turn outside,' she announced with surprising benevolence.

The reason for this soon became apparent when the gentlemen joined them. Amanda saw Humphrey exchange a pleased smile and nod with his mama when he saw the open windows and he turned from her to scan the room.

Before Amanda could avoid him he was at her side, one slightly damp palm under her elbow. 'Do come out on to the terrace, Cousin,' he urged.

'Of course, how delightful. But only if the others join us,' Amanda responded with a merry laugh. 'I cannot risk my reputation by being seen alone with you!'

Apparently taking this as flirtation, Humphrey preened himself and was soon urging other couples outside.

It was a lovely night. The moon was almost full, the sky spangled with stars and the air still warm enough to be comfortable. But it was not a night to find oneself being steered inexorably towards the steps to the lawn by a persistent and unwelcome suitor. 'You are lovely, you know.' Humphrey was breathing hotly close to her ear. 'Come down here where we can be alone and let me show you how I feel.'

Amanda gave a squeal and pulled her arm free. 'Oh, a bat! A bat! It will get in my hair!' Unbalanced by her movement, Humphrey grasped the balustrade for support, missed and sat down hard, and painfully, on the top step. Amanda slipped silently away and took refuge in the bushes that fringed the terrace, safely out of sight.

But her escape had not gone unnoticed. A dark figure appeared before her, its sleeve brushing the branch, and a wave of scent from the tumbled blossoms washed over her. 'Amanda?'

'Jay!'

They stood for a moment, neither able to see the other's face in the dark, then both spoke at once.

'Jay, I am so sorry, I was completely unreasonable—'

'Amanda, I should never have teased you. And I made assumptions—'

'Go on,' she urged as he broke off.

'Not here, come down these steps, I think your cousin has retired inside to nurse his dignity.'

Amanda allowed herself to be steered down the shallow flight of steps, across the grass and into the little stone temple, which commanded a charming view of the lake. Now the moonlight bathed its columns in light and tipped the little wavelets on the water with sparks of brightness. The scent of jasmine followed them, lingering on the sleeve of Jay's coat as he raised one hand to rest it against the column behind her head.

'Beautiful,' he said. His voice deepened slightly, and he quoted, 'The moon shines bright; in such a night as this, when the sweet wind did gently kiss the trees and they made no noise, in such a night—' He broke off. 'No, I cannot recall the rest.'

Amanda sighed. 'Is it Shakespeare? "Did gently kiss the trees"… That is lovely.'

Jay did not pursue the elusive quotation. After a moment he said, 'Amanda, I am sorry. I teased you when you were upset, which was unforgivable, and I had no intention of shocking you so.'

'No, it was my fault. I reacted—overreacted—so foolishly. I was…upset that we had parted with so much unresolved. I had no right to lose my temper like that, and, I must admit it, I do not know why I did so.'

There was silence. She was very conscious of his arm so close to her bare shoulder, of his warmth, of the scent of his citrus cologne underlying the jasmine. She had only to lean back a little and her skin would touch his sleeve. What would he do if she did that? She made no move except to turn her head a very little, but it was enough.

His voice was husky as he said, 'I am not made of stone, Amanda.'

She was aware suddenly that she was shivering; a fine vibration seemed to posses her body, centring on a deep, swirling ache inside her. Something caressed her shoulder, then she realised it was her own curl, moving as she shivered, disturbing the jasmine scent on her own body, sending it warm and sweet to his nostrils.

Then he moved.

Chapter Eleven

Startled by the swiftness of Jay's movement, Amanda was momentarily confused, then saw that his long stride had taken him across the full width of the little temple to stand facing her across the marble floor.

'I am not made of stone,' he repeated. 'We agreed it would be better not to be together.'

'Yes,' she agreed, uncaring that her voice shook.

'Do you know what I want to do at this moment?' His voice sounded curiously angry.

She shook her head.

'I want to take you in my arms and kiss you until you beg me never to stop. I want to pull that lovely gown from your shoulders and kiss your naked body in the moonlight and then I want to make love to you, here on this marble floor.'

There was silence as he finished speaking. Amanda found she was gripping the column behind her with both hands. The swirling tension inside her made it difficult to hold on to any sense of reality. 'Yes,' she faltered, unsure whether it was a question, a plea or simple agreement.

Jay moved again sharply to turn his back on her. She

saw the ring on his hand flash in the moonlight, transformed from gold to silver by the light, as he hit his clenched fist against the column next to him. 'And I am going to do none of those things because I do not know who I am and I suspect I have hurt you quite enough already—' He broke off, then added, 'I have been dreaming.'

'What do you dream about?' she asked, knowing she dare not do what her senses were screaming at her to do and cross the distance between them.

'I dream the same dream every night,' he said bleakly. 'I dream that I will never discover who I am.'

'I cannot believe that,' she protested. 'You will find out, I promise we will find out.'

'And if we discover I have the wife and children you are in the habit of warning me about?' Something of the old humour was back in his voice, but there was bitterness behind it.

'Then you will be happy to have rediscovered them,' Amanda promised, trying to make herself believe it. 'You will go home and this will be the dream that will fade away like mist in the morning, or the characters at the end of a play.'

'And you?'

'I will be glad for you. Not every play can have a happy ending,' she added, almost to herself. She could not stay there, it was unbearable for her, utterly unfair on him. 'Wait for five minutes, I will go back to the house. Good night, Jay.'

Somehow Amanda found herself back in the reception room, her absence apparently unmarked. Guests were beginning to make their farewells and she cast around for Jane, who suddenly appeared at her side.

'There you are, dear. My goodness, Amanda, you are as white as a sheet!'

'Humphrey attempted to lure me down to the lawns.'

'Then the sooner we leave the better! What an unfortunate experience.' They found themselves almost at the door. 'Oh, goodnight, Mrs Clare, what a delightful evening. Thank you so much for the invitation.'

By the time they had retrieved their wraps, the coach had been called and they were seated, Jane's head was nodding and she soon dropped off to sleep. Amanda was alone with her thoughts for the short distance between the Hall and her home.

The intensity in Jay's voice as he had made that declaration! She felt the shivering begin again at the memory of it. That had been desire: pure, unalloyed, intense physical desire, and she had felt it too. No wonder it could bring down nations, wreck alliances, ruin lives: she had no idea it could be so all consuming.

But it was not love. He had never spoken that word. And without love she could never give way to desire, and, unless he was free, she could not allow the word to be spoken.

That she loved him she was certain now. But who was this man she loved? Someone with no name, no past, no present. And if his dreams told the truth, he was also a man with no future. The carriage pulled up with a jerk as the sleepy driver misjudged the position of the front door, and Jane woke.

'Are we home? We must go straight to bed! What an eventful evening this has been.'

The next morning brought an unexpected note for Amanda, just as she was sitting at her little writing desk penning a few words of thanks to Mrs Clare for the previous evening.

It was from Humphrey's mother herself. 'Look at this, Jane.' Amanda handed her companion the note. 'It has just arrived.'

'How strange. She says there is a matter of some urgency upon which she wishes to consult with you and urges you to call this morning. I would have thought she would be resting after her exertions last night, not sending out notes to solicit calls.'

'I suppose I had better do as she asks,' Amanda said, still puzzling over the note.

'Can you not put it off until tomorrow? You are looking sadly pale, my dear. Did you not sleep well last night?' Jane enquired solicitously.

'Oh, as well as can be expected after last night's excitements,' Amanda said lightly. And as well as one might expect after receiving a passionate declaration from a man who wishes to make violent love to you in the moonlight, she could have added with some justification. 'I will walk over, the fresh air will do me good.'

'Would you like me to come with you?'

'No, please do not disturb yourself, Jane dear. I can tell you are tired too, and I fail to see why both of us should dance to Mrs Clare's bidding. She probably wants to tell me that the recipe I sent by Kate for pickling walnuts is quite incorrect, and she wonders at it that I have been using such an inferior receipt for so long.'

Jane laughed at this and returned to the long letter she was sending to an elderly relative who would enjoy every detail of a party such as the one last night. Amanda changed her slippers for a pair of boots, swung a pelisse around her shoulders and set out briskly for the Hall.

Using the shortcut across the park it did not take her long, and she was soon knocking on the wide front door through which she had once walked in and out by right. It was a strange sensation, which she found took several minutes to subdue on every occasion when she called.

The butler ushered her through to the library, which surprised her, for she had expected Mrs Clare to be receiving in the morning parlour. All was explained, however, when Humphrey got to his feet from the depths of one of the leather wing-chairs.

'My dear Amanda—' he began.

'I do beg your pardon,' Amanda cut in. 'I must have failed to make myself clear to Peters. I have called to see Mrs Clare, she sent me a note this morning.'

'No, there has been no mistake.' Humphrey was looking inordinately pleased with himself. 'Mama wrote the note, but at my request. I knew you might feel a slight reserve at calling on a gentleman, yet I felt we could be uninterrupted here.'

'Indeed, I do feel such a reserve,' Amanda said firmly. 'I have no chaperon with me.'

'Mama and the housekeeper are both about somewhere,' Humphrey assured her.

'Then let us call one of them.'

'No, no!' Humphrey had moved surprisingly quickly and before she knew what he was about he was beside her, one arm hovering at her back, urging her towards a chair. 'After all, what need of a chaperon do you have in your own cousin's house?'

Common civility prevented her from making the honest answer and Amanda allowed herself to be seated. 'In what way can I assist you, Cousin?' she enquired coolly. 'Miss Porter is not feeling quite well this morning, and I really do not want to leave her too long.'

'Too much champagne, eh?' Humphrey chortled. 'You indulge a paid dependent too much, my dear.'

'Miss Porter is a dear and loyal friend,' Amanda replied repressively. She did wish he would sit down and not lurk about just behind her chair. The high back and enveloping wings restricted her view and made her feel quite trapped.

Suddenly he was beside her, clumsily falling to one knee and catching her right hand in both of his. 'Amanda! My darling!'

'Mr Clare!'

'Call me Humphrey, I beseech you.' His plump cheeks were shiny with emotion. Amanda wriggled back into the chair, but it only made her feel more confined.

'Please, sir, this excessive display of feeling...'

'It comes from my heart, beloved!' What on earth had he been reading? Ignoring her shocked expression and efforts to free her hand, Humphrey ploughed on with what was obviously a prepared speech. 'For many months my admiration for your many fine characteristics has been growing to the point where I cannot hide from you any longer my ardent desire to make you my wife.'

'But, Mr Clare, I know you have often disapproved of my actions and beliefs. How can you think that I would make a conformable wife to you?' Amanda had a sinking feeling that appealing to reason was not going to work, but she had to try.

'Once we are married, I know that these odd starts, these little acts of feminine rebellion, will cease. You need firm guidance, the protection of a virile and energetic husband. You nobly supported my ailing and elderly cousin, now take your reward for faithful duty!'

'Charles was not elderly and I did my best to be a good wife to him because I most truly loved and valued him!' Amanda flashed back. 'My reward, if indeed I deserved one, was in his love and companionship.'

Humphrey gave a little shudder of what appeared to be excitement. 'Oh, your spirit! How I long to subdue that, teach you to love and obey me!'

Amanda felt queasy. Her hand was beginning to hurt in his grip. Against her instincts she tried wheedling. 'Please, Humphrey,' she whispered, 'you are hurting my wrist.'

'Fragile flower!' He released her wrist only to grip her hand and begin to shower kisses upon it. His mouth was wet and the touch of it on her shrinking skin disgusting. Her struggles only seemed to inflame him more and before she knew what was happening he had pressed her back in the chair and was trying to kiss her mouth.

Once, early on in their courtship, Charles had rescued her from the amorous advances of some buck who had caught her alone in a theatre box while the rest of the company was temporarily absent. Having hit the gentleman neatly on the point of the chin, he had shut the door of the box and proceeded to show Amanda exactly how to best apply her knee should she ever find herself in such a fix again.

She had never required the lesson before, but now, with a mental whisper of thanks to Charles, Amanda used her knee as he had told her. The effect was miraculous. Humphrey went red, staggered back clutching his groin and began whooping for breath.

Amanda did not stop to see how much damage she

had done. She was out of the chair, through the door and into the hall in a moment, considerably startling the butler. She paused in front of the cheval glass and adjusted her bonnet. 'Good day, Peters, thank you.' She hesitated on the threshold. 'I do not think Mr Clare wishes to be disturbed for a while. He is thinking something over.'

The butler bowed and shut the door. Amanda suppressed a desire to sit down on the front step and give way to strong hysterics, but instead walked across the gravel sweep, down the sloping lawn and towards the point where the river opened into the lake. She could follow the path to the weir, cross on the footbridge and cut back to Upper Glaven House from there. It would give her a chance to compose herself before recounting the experience to Jane. Just at the moment she doubted if she could articulate a single coherent word.

Two declarations in the space of a few hours. But what a difference in them. One of passion and desire, the other soliciting marriage. But it was the latter that filled her with disgust. Her hand felt damp from Humphrey's grasp and his kisses. Her wrist hurt too, perhaps enough for there to be a bruise tomorrow. She would bathe it in the river where it pooled at the weir.

The tranquil river began to gurgle and eddy as she walked upstream towards the weir. Just before it there was a crescent cut in the bank where the grass sloped to a little beach. She crouched there and rinsed her hand in the cool water, dipped her handkerchief and wrapped it around her wrist. That was not a bruise she wished to explain to anyone.

Amanda walked on, around the bend to the weir, and realised she was not alone. It was a good fishing spot, Charles had told her, and guests at the Hall often took a rod and line there. The man sitting with his back against the bank, legs stretched out, and the rod propped on a rest beside him, did not appear to be a keen angler, however, more someone enjoying a sleep in the sunshine.

He was not asleep. As she stopped he opened his eyes and regarded her steadily. 'Hello, Amanda.'

'Hello, Jay. I did not look to see you here. No, please do not get up.'

He sank back on to the turf. 'Your cousin pressed me to try my luck with his fish. It seemed a relaxing thing to do.'

'Have you caught anything?' She sat down too, perhaps four feet away from him.

'No, I have not even baited the hook.' His eyes scanned her face. 'Amanda, last night…'

'Last night the moon was full and the air was full of dreams. I am sure that whatever happened and whatever was said were simply part of those dreams.'

'Do you believe dreams come true?'

'Some of them. Others do not. We must wait and see, and perhaps not stand in the moonlight exchanging dreams. Sometimes the morning brings too much reality.' Her voice must have shaken, for Jay twisted to look sharply at her.

'What has happened? You are too pale—and your wrist…have you hurt it?'

She had thought that she was coping quite well with the shock of Humphrey's proposal, but the warmth in Jay's voice quite overset her and she gave an abrupt sob, stifling it with her hand.

'Amanda!' He was on his knees beside her, reaching for her, but she held him off with her bandaged hand. 'What has happened? Let me look.'

He unwrapped the wet handkerchief with gentle fingers, peeling it back to reveal the reddening marks of a male grip imprinted around the narrow wrist, overlaying the fragile bones.

'Who did this to you?' His voice was coldly angry.

'Humphrey. Just now, he was proposing.'

'Proposing! By breaking your wrist?' Jay got to his feet. 'Wait here, I will not be long.'

'Where are you going?'

Jay looked down at her. 'To find Humphrey Clare and break his jaw for him. That should prevent him making any further proposals—of any kind.'

'No! Please, Jay, please do not.'

'He has insulted you, he has hurt you. Someone must call him to account for it.'

'Jay, I do not want you to do this. He will not try again, believe me. I cannot afford a scandal and if you and he fight there will be certain to be talk.'

'I have no intention of fighting with him. I have every intention of beating him within an inch of his life.'

'If you go, I will cry,' Amanda stated flatly.

'Do you expect that to stop me?' There was a faint edge of amusement in his voice.

'No,' she admitted honestly. 'But I thought it worth a try. Please, Jay, I promise he has not got away scot free.'

He dropped back to the grass beside her. 'What did you do to him?'

'Charles showed me how to deal with that sort of advance. By using my knee.'

Jay gave a shout of laughter. 'You kneed him in the groin?'

'Yes. It worked very well. He went red and whooped. A bit like a turkey.'

Jay was almost helpless with laughter now. 'I wish I had seen it,' he managed to gasp.

'Would it have hurt a lot?' Amanda was ashamed to find she hoped very much that it would.

'I think you may be certain you could have done nothing more painful to him,' Jay said, dragging a pocket handkerchief out and mopping his eyes with it. 'A man is very vulnerable in the, er…groin area.'

'Good.'

'Can you bear to tell me what happened? It might help.'

Amanda found it did indeed help to recount the entire episode, from the letter from Mrs Clare to the butler's impassive expression as he had let her out.

'The man's a fool,' Jay observed dispassionately. 'Of all the insane ways to propose, pinning you in a chair and slobbering all over you.'

'He did slobber too,' Amanda recalled with a shudder. 'All up my arm.'

Jay gently took her bruised hand in his. 'Now that was very ill advised of him. When kissing a lady's hand, the last thing one wants to do is to kiss it.'

'What do you mean? That does not make sense.'

'Like this.' Jay lifted her hand to his lips and gave it the merest touch with his lips. The sensation was intense, delicate, yet sent shivers up her arm. 'But one does not want to let go at that point: the fingers can achieve so much more than the lips in this situation.'

Mesmerised, Amanda felt his fingertips gently caressing the inside of her wrist, so lightly that the bruises did not hurt, so sensitively that she felt as though every nerve was exposed to his touch. 'And then, of course, there is the thumb.' The ball of his thumb began to move insidiously against the swell at the base of hers. Amanda felt a little moan escape her lips.

'You see, there is absolutely no need to slobber all over a lady at all.' He leaned down the bank and rinsed out her handkerchief, wrung it out and bound it gently around her wrist again. 'There.'

'Thank you,' Amanda said shakily, clasping both hands firmly in her lap. 'You promise you will not do anything to Humphrey?'

'I promise.' He leaned back, his eyes on the stream as it chuckled and swirled its way towards the lake. 'Tell me something.'

'Yes?'

'What is Coke's Clippings?'

Of all the questions Amanda might have expected, this was the last. 'Coke's Clippings? Why on earth do you want to know about that?'

'Someone mentioned it last night and it was suddenly very familiar—and important. I could hardly expose my ignorance by asking anyone there.'

'It is the name given to the gatherings that Mr Coke holds every year at Holkham during the shearing. You know he inherited the estate from a relative when he was a young man? No? Well, he knew nothing about agriculture, but he saw that so much needed to be done, if only he knew how to go about it. So he began asking knowledgeable men to visit him at the shearings, and gradually it grew and grew into one of the great events in the countryside.' Amanda's admiration for her famous neighbour showed in the pride in her voice.

'People come from all over the world—America, Russia even. He holds open house for many guests and feeds all who come. From being a young, ignorant man he has become the expert and people come to sit at his feet and learn. It is a social event as well, with country people, yeomen, tradesmen as well as the aristocrats and landowners all meeting and exchanging ideas. Mr Coke is a very great man.'

'Indeed, he sounds it. Do you attend?'

'Yes, every year. At first I went with Charles and we used to stay at Holkham Hall. Now I go for one day only, but I would not miss it for the world. It is next week: will you come with me?'

Jay looked thoughtful. 'Yes, I will. I have no idea why it should stir the slightest memory for me, but something tells me that the answer to this puzzle of my presence here lies at Holkham.'

Chapter Twelve

'The first day of the gathering is Wednesday next week,' Amanda said, reluctantly standing up and brushing off her skirts. 'Just look at the state of this dress!'

Jay, who had got easily to his feet and was holding out a hand in case she still felt shaky, laughed. 'Hardly surprising! First crushed by Humphrey's not inconsiderable weight and then sat on amongst the damp grass of the river bank. No,' he reassured her as she twisted round to look at the back of her skirts, 'no grass stains. Would you like me to drive you to Holkham on Wednesday?'

'Thank you, but no, I will drive Jane and myself in the phaeton with a groom up behind. It is what I normally do and any change from that might cause comment. But I would be very glad of your escort if you can prevail upon Will Bream to lend you something better than that slug he has been mounting you on. I know he has a very nice young hunter in his stables that he refuses to let me ride.'

Jay grinned at her. 'And why not, might I ask?'

'He says it is too big, too strong and not a lady's

mount. He is hoping to bring it on this year and sell it next hunting season for a good profit.'

'And if I borrow it you hope to wheedle me into letting you ride it at some point in the journey?'

'Certainly not! The thought had not crossed my mind,' Amanda said indignantly. 'I just thought it would suit you very well. It is a thought, though… I am sure my saddle would fit in the phaeton—'

'No! If Will Bream says it is too strong for you, that is the end of the matter. That man's judgement is uncommonly sound.'

Amanda wrinkled her nose. 'He is too protective of me. He was devoted to Charles, you see.'

'From what I can see, you need all the protection you can get,' Jay said grimly.

'Surrounded with rakes as I am?' Amanda teased, skipping neatly onto the plank bridge across the weir. 'We will meet you at the crossroads at eight of the clock on Wednesday morning. Will will show you where.'

'Until Wednesday, then,' Jay raised a hand in farewell. 'Unless you need me. Send at once if Mr Clare gives you the slightest annoyance; you have no idea how I long to have an excuse to break my promise to you and hit him from here to perdition.'

Amanda's sunny mood lasted just as far as the garden gate, then reaction set in. She had enjoyed telling Jay how she had bested Humphrey, had loved being there on the riverbank with him. The memory of his caress still tingled in her palm.

Now the nausea that Humphrey had evoked returned, along with the nagging worry of how she was to maintain some sort of relationship with the Hall when she no longer trusted him to be in the same room with her.

To make a break with the Clares would cause a scandal all around the district.

And Jay's conviction that the Clippings held a clue had sounded so optimistic that she had not thought through what it might mean. On dragging feet she wandered round, through the shrubbery and sat in the summerhouse, one hand cupping her chin.

Jay could be wrong and they would find no help there. Or he would discover who he was and what he was doing in Norfolk—and find that he was married or affianced. Or, having recovered the knowledge of his true identity, he might not be the same person as he appeared now and his feelings for her would be different too.

Whatever those feelings were. He desired her, that was very apparent. But did he love her? Was he simply not saying those words in case he proved not to be free—or because that was not what he felt?

From being full of optimism, Amanda gloomily concluded that the odds against this whole adventure having a happy ending were stacked high against her. She tried telling herself firmly that if Jay was restored to his rightful place, whether or not that included a wife, that must be a happy ending, but this very proper reflection did not provide the comfort it should do.

'Amanda! Mrs Clare!' It was Jane calling. Amanda called back and after a moment Miss Porter peeped around the side of the tree. 'Did you want to be alone, dear? Only I saw you come in the gate and you looked so serious I was quite worried. Is anything amiss at the Hall?'

'Come and sit down, Jane.' Amanda patted the bench beside her. 'I need to tell you what has occurred and it is better out here: I would not have the servants hear for anything.'

Jane listened wide-eyed to the tale of Humphrey's declaration, the tip of her nose growing pinker and pinker as her indignation rose. 'And your wrist!' She unwrapped the handkerchief and tutted in dismay at the sight of the marks on Amanda's arm. 'The brute! Oh, for a man to call him to account!'

'I have just spent some time making Jay promise he would do no such thing,' Amanda admitted. 'I came across him fishing down at the weir, and he could see I was upset. Foolishly I blurted it out.'

'And you managed to stop him taking any action?' Miss Porter sounded sceptical. 'Mark my words, he will have gone up there the moment your back was turned.'

'He promised me,' Amanda assured her. 'I told him what a scandal it would cause. Oh, Jane, what are we to do if Humphrey calls? Or Mrs Clare invites me to the Hall? It would cause such talk if I stop going there or receiving them. And we meet so often—in church every week, in other people's houses…' Her voice trailed off.

Miss Porter looked thoughtful. 'You go nowhere you might meet him alone. Kate or I will always go with you. If he calls, I will sit with you. When we meet them, we will speak with perfect cordiality, but without the slightest note of encouragement.'

'It sounds very unpleasant,' Amanda said drearily. 'I have never liked them, but I do so hate being on cool terms with anyone.'

'It may not be for long,' said Miss Porter, then looked extremely confused.

'Whatever can you mean, Jane?'

'Oh…er…they may go up to town, or visit relatives. Or you may go to town.'

Amanda regarded her quizzically. What on earth was causing poor Jane such embarrassment? Possibly she had been too frank in describing Humphrey's assault. She changed the subject.

'Jay heard someone talking of the Clippings last night and has a strong conviction that if he goes there he may solve this puzzle of who he is and what he is doing adrift in the countryside.'

'How strange. Is he certain?'

'How can he be? But it seems so improbable that it may be true—it is not the sort of thing you imagine. Anyway, I have suggested he escort us on Wednesday and we will see what results.'

The rest of the week passed uneventfully. There was an ominous silence from the Hall and silence also from Jay, although one of Amanda's grooms reported seeing 'that fine new hunter of Will Bream's' being exercised on the heath by the mysterious gentleman from the Half Moon. 'He can't half ride, ma'am,' the man added. 'That's a fierce strong beast, but he don't mess about with that gentleman up.'

By Sunday Amanda was able to remove the broad velvet band she had been wearing around her bruised wrist and the ladies set off for church in a spirit of considerable apprehension.

Miss Porter was filled with a mixture of nervous indignation, a fear of there being a scene on sacred ground on the Sabbath and a fixed resolve to preserve Amanda from the disgusting clutches of Mr Clare at whatever cost to herself.

Amanda, while sharing her concerns about encountering Humphrey in full view of the local congregation, was finding that with every day that passed the cold, tight knot of uncertainty in her stomach got worse and worse. She went over and over in her mind the various outcomes from their visit to the Clippings and the more she thought, the more fearful she became. If only she knew the worst, somehow that would be better than this awful uncertainty.

They arrived before the party from the Hall and reached the safety of their high-walled pew with relief. Amanda sank to her knees and tried to compose her mind but she found all that filled her thoughts was the image of Jay. She was so shocked and horrified at herself that she pushed the hassock aside, and knelt on the cold, hard stone until she could achieve a coherent frame of mind and offer up penitent and reverent prayers. Still shaken, she sat and read some of the more severe Old Testament prophets until the wheezing of the organ bellows and the first notes brought the congregation to their feet.

The Clares had entered and taken their places unseen by her, which was a blessing, but in her present frame of mind she found herself wondering if she should not approach Humphrey afterwards and make some offer of reconciliation.

Further reflection decided her that to risk a scene in the churchyard would defeat the whole purpose of such an approach. Instead she must act as if nothing had happened and receive what friendly overtures might be offered.

It was a subdued Amanda who emerged into the sunshine after service and although her heart sank at the sight of Mrs Clare senior beckoning her towards where she sat in her barouche, she obediently walked over. Of Humphrey there was no sign.

'Good morning, ma'am.'

'Good morning, Amanda. Please be so good as to step into the carriage. Wilkins! Get down from the box and go to their heads, I wish to speak to Mrs Clare.' She waited while Amanda sat opposite, then fixed her with a quelling stare. 'I suppose you think you know what you are about, trifling with my son's affections in this callous manner?'

'Trifling, ma'am? I protest, I have done no such thing. I found myself unable to return Cousin Humphrey's sentiments and told him so. To have led him to believe I felt anything else would indeed have been trifling.'

'And all the encouragement you have been giving him these last months?'

'Encouragement?' Amanda's voice rose and she hastily lowered it. 'I have done no more than act in a neighbourly way and as I hope I should to my late husband's kinsman.'

'So you say now.' Mrs Clare regarded her through narrowed eyes. 'Something has occurred. You have decided you have fatter fish to land and have cast aside my worthy son in the process. Well, at least he has had his eyes opened. I can only trust for the sake of this family's reputation that whatever you are about now will not cause a scandal. Good day, Amanda.'

Amanda was so angry she could not reply, simply bowing abruptly to the older woman and jumping down from the barouche without waiting for the groom to hurry to the door. Would that spiteful creature start spreading gossip about her? Had she realised the attachment she felt towards Jay, or observed them at her party? Would she find herself stigmatised as the sort of fast young widow she had teased Jay about and be cut by those worthy neighbours whose good opinion mattered to her?

All the way up the hill Amanda struggled with her anger. If she could forgive Mrs Clare, would that not go some way to mitigating her wandering thoughts in church? It would at least be good discipline. By the time she reached home and Jane asked her what had transpired, she was able to reply moderately.

'She reproached me for refusing Cousin Humphrey. She feels I have given him unwarranted encouragement. I can understand her anger: she is ambitious for him and my land would be a considerable benefit to him.'

Monday brought a note from Jay. *I have identified our meeting place and will be there at 8. Do* not *bring a saddle—under no circumstances are you riding this horse. J.*

That produced the first gurgle of laughter from Amanda that Jane had heard for almost a week and she nodded to herself with a little smile, which soon vanished when she thought of all the things which could go wrong with the plans she fondly imagined for her friend.

The house was all of a bustle from early on Wednesday morning. The phaeton was loaded with rugs and a picnic hamper in case of a change in the weather or a delay on the road. Indoor shoes were slipped in bags under the seats in case Mr Coke should come across them and invite them into the house to eat, Amanda brought her most frivolous new parasol and Miss Porter her largest umbrella.

At last Ned swung up on to his perch at the back, Miss Porter settled her rug around her knees, Amanda took up the whip in one hand and gathered the reins into her hand, tightly gloved in York tan leather. 'Let go their heads,' she called and the pair, tossing their manes, trotted smartly out of the yard.

'They are very fresh this morning,' Miss Porter commented, holding rather more tightly onto the edge of her seat than usual.

'I have had them inside for three days on double rations of oats,' Amanda admitted as the horses shied skittishly at a milestone.

'Why ever did you do that?' her companion demanded. 'You will be exhausted at the end of the journey if they continue to behave like this.'

'Jay does not believe I can handle a difficult horse. I intend to show him I can manage two. I only wish this were a high-perch phaeton.'

Jane cast up her eyes, but refrained from comment. After a brisk mile during which the pair fought every inch of the way to get the bit between their teeth and Amanda fought just as determinedly to get them to keep to a trot, the crossroads came in sight with a lone rider waiting beside the milepost.

Jay rode forwards, touching his whip to his hat brim. He looked the pair over as Amanda brought them to a halt and remarked, 'Good morning, Miss Porter. Have you been feeding these beasts double oats, Mrs Clare?'

Amanda chose to ignore the question. 'Good morning, Mr Jay. I hope you have not been kept waiting?'

'Indeed, no, you are commendably prompt.' He wheeled the big bay horse and fell in beside the carriage, his eyes on Amanda's hands on the reins. After a few minutes he let his attention relax, but she was very much aware of the scrutiny. It appeared she had passed muster.

In her turn she glanced at his mount. 'That is a well set-up animal of Will's.'

'Yes,' Jay agreed. 'It is up to my weight and more. I may well make him an offer.' He saw the question in Amanda's eyes and added, 'If things work out.'

There was not much she could add, with a groom standing behind and well within earshot. Amanda let the greys lengthen their stride a little and once she was confident they had steadied, cast a surreptitious glance at Jay riding alongside the phaeton.

He seemed in his element astride the big bay. Amanda was conscious of long legs gripping the saddle above boots polished to a high gloss. His riding coat sat well on broad shoulders and the laundry maid at the Half Moon had produced linen that shone in the sunshine. He was riding one-handed, the other, holding the crop, resting lightly on his thigh. The horse moved beautifully, with a long, even gait, but Amanda was not deceived by its apparent docility: its ears flicked continuously and the one eye she could see rolled back and forth as it assessed its chances of getting away from the man who was mastering it with such confidence.

They rode on in silence for a while, passing through the little coastal villages and skirting the coastal marshes that ran between each settlement. At last the road opened out with not so much as a packhorse in sight and Amanda called challengingly, 'Would you care for a race?'

Jay did not hesitate, but drew the bay onto the wide grass verge and said, 'To that bend? Very well, at your mark, Miss Porter!'

'Oh, dear!' Miss Porter gripped the seat with one hand and her hat with the other. 'Very well... Go!'

Amanda sprang the pair, who gathered their hind legs under them and took off at a gallop. There was a whoop of exhilaration from the groom, clinging on for dear life behind, and the sound of hooves on grass as the hunter got into its stride.

Not daring to turn her head and see where Jay was, Amanda gasped, 'Do we have a lead, Jane?'

'Yes... No!'

The bay swept up level with them, then gradually lengthened its stride until it was neck and neck with the pair. Jay glanced round: his teeth white, then he leaned over the horse's neck and urged it forward. But the pair were into their stride now, full of fidgets and over-excited by the presence of the big horse. They responded to Amanda's voice and she found she was laughing out loud with the excitement as they gained ground.

The bend was nearing. Jay was going to win, as she expected, the pair with a full carriage behind them were no match for the hunter, but she had acquitted herself well, she felt. At that moment a farm cart began to back out from a concealed gateway in front of Jay. He shouted, but the carter was apparently oblivious.

Amanda tried to judge the distance. Could she pull up in time?

Even as she thought it, Jay yelled, 'Whip them up!'

Jane gave a little shriek, the groom could be heard uttering a string of blasphemies, but Amanda understood him at once. For the first time she laid the whip across the horses' backs and they hurtled towards the closing gap. Then they were past in a swirl of dust and at the edge of her vision she saw the hunter leap the cart in a powerful arc, Jay poised low over its neck.

Amanda pulled up, the horses coming to a stand in a snorting, head-tossing slide. Jay reined in beside her as behind them the cart rumbled out on to the road.

'You win, Mrs Clare,' he said, one hand gentling the sidling horse. 'That was fine driving.'

Jane glanced from one to the other of them and saw the look that passed between them. She let her breath out in a gasp, then hastily straightened her bonnet. Miss Porter considered herself immune from the tenderer passions, but that shared, intimate glance made her feel both hot and cold all at once.

Amanda simply smiled, shaking her head. 'No, you would have won easily if it were not for that prodigious jump.' She twisted in the seat, 'Are you all right Ned?'

'Bloody h— I mean, yes, thank you, ma'am.' The groom gingerly unclenched his hands from the rail. Jay turned the hunter and walked it back towards the carter who was standing, cart and horse still across the road, regarding them with some astonishment. Amanda saw a coin change hands. 'Cor, ma'am,' the groom continued, 'that Mr Jay can't half ride. The width of that cart in one jump, didn't even bank it! Must have thigh muscles like iron.'

'Er, yes.' Amanda, trying not to think about that, turned back and patted her hair into place.

The rest of the journey proved uneventful, although the closer they got to Holkham, the denser the traffic of carriages and riders became. Amanda broke off several times to wave to acquaintances and was aware of Jay, eyes shaded under the brim of his hat, scanning faces as they passed.

Amanda, knowing the routine of old, joined the

queue of carriages approaching the stables and pad-
docks where the visiting horses would be accommo-
dated for the duration of their owners' visits. Once they
were fairly close to the Hall she reined in and called to
the groom, 'Can you take them now please, Ned?'

Jay swung down out the saddle and handed down first
Miss Porter and then Amanda. The groom hesitated.
'Shall I take your horse in, sir?'

'No, better not, he is more than inclined to take lib-
erties in strange hands, I will walk him up. Where may
I meet you, Mrs Clare?'

Amanda handed her whip up to Ned, then turned to
scan the parkland, which stretched before them from the
Hall down to the lake. 'I want to start at the shearing
pens, if that is agreeable to you. Miss Porter and I will
go into the Hall to sign our names in the book—you
had better not add a forgery! Shall we meet at that grove
of oaks just there?' She pointed to a knot of evergreen
holm oaks halfway between the house and the shearing
pens. 'It would be easy to miss each other if we go
separately into that crowd.'

Jay agreed, and strode off after the phaeton, the
hunter following behind and shying at every passing
creature. Amanda heard Jay's voice. 'Come on, you
fool. Have you never seen a sheep before?'

'Well!' Miss Porter commented as they walked up to
the Hall. 'That was a very exciting race. How very well
Mr Jay rides: one would go so far as to say he looks
magnificent on a horse.'

'Indeed.' For once the image of Jay thus conjured up
did not hold Amanda's attention. 'Jane, do you feel we
are being watched? I have the nastiest prickling between
my shoulder blades.'

'Of course we are being watched! Well, at least you

are because you look so fine, my dear, and we have many acquaintances who will be looking at us, I am sure.' They reached the doors and were ushered in to sign the visitors' book and to seek out the retiring rooms set aside for the ladies.

Jane was just brushing out the dust from her hem when a tall woman came up and greeted her warmly. 'Miss Porter! How glad I am to have come upon you. Mr Coke has been making some improvements to the garden and has invited some interested ladies to walk round with the head gardener. Will you not join us?'

'Lady Grahame.' Miss Porter and Amanda curtsied slightly.

'Good morning, Mrs Clare, I did not see you there. Will you join us?'

'I thank you, Lady Grahame, but I must decline: I am expected at the shearing pens directly. No, Jane,' she added as she saw Miss Porter was about to make her own excuses and insist on escorting her. 'You go with Lady Grahame, it sounds too interesting an invitation to resist. I shall be quite all right—as always, Mr Coke's outdoor staff will be all over the grounds to keep an eye open for undesirables.'

Emerging into the sunshine at the top of the steps, Amanda unfurled her new parasol and scanned the scene before her. The greatest activity at the moment was at the shearing pens, but groups of men were gathered around various wagons, temporary pens set up all over the grass or pieces of agricultural machinery, which were drawn up in lines.

Ladies strolled amongst them and the occasional knot of children, laughing in excitement, tumbled past. Over to one side a piece of turf had been roped off and

Amanda guessed that Mr Coke's Eleven would be challenging a scratch team of farmers that afternoon.

There was no sign of Jay, so she walked down the steps and began to make her way towards the grove of trees. It looked pleasantly shady, but so far the day had not become so hot that anyone was seeking out its cover and it was slightly set aside from the main route down to the pens. Amanda stopped once or twice to shake hands with old friends and to be introduced to new acquaintances. It was comfortable, happy throng and she could find no reason for the sense of unease that gripped her again. She gave herself a determined little shake: of course no one was following her, it was just the apprehension she had been feeling all week about the outcome of this day.

The grove when she reached it was empty: the queue at the stableyard must be worse than usual, she decided, strolling across the grassy area ringed by the trees and the scrubby underbrush, which often concealed deer. Now it was uncannily silent and deserted. As she thought it a pigeon erupted in panic from the boughs above her, making her jump and a twig snapped on the grass behind.

'Jay!' Amanda turned thankfully, then froze, for the man making his way across the clearing towards her was not Jay.

Chapter Thirteen

'Cousin Humphrey! What are you doing here?' So that was why she had been experiencing such an unpleasant sensation of being spied upon ever since she had arrived. More annoyed than alarmed, for, after all, they were surrounded by people, even if they were out of sight, Amanda allowed him to walk up to her. It was better that they had this confrontation here—she had no desire, if she had to speak to him at all, to risk a scene where everyone could see them.

'I have as much right to be here as you,' Humphrey observed in a knowing tone, which set her teeth on edge. 'There is no need for me to enquire what you are doing, is there? And it isn't taking an interest in agriculture. I saw you arrive with that Jay fellow.'

'I thought you admired Mr Jay,' Amanda observed coldly.

'Nothing wrong with him, whatever his real name is, but I know a rake when I see one, and I can guess what you are about with him, madam! And it isn't selling him land,' he added with a coarse chuckle.

'How dare you—' Amanda began, but Humphrey was ploughing on.

'You turn down an honourable proposal from a respectable man to go flaunting yourself about with a London buck...'

'Honourable proposal! It was no such thing. You tricked me into calling, you mauled me, insulted me, insulted Charles's memory...'

'And it isn't an insult to his memory for you to be carrying on with that man when you are hardly out of mourning?' Humphrey's face was red with fury and through her own gathering anger Amanda realised that the wound to his pride of her refusal was made even more painful by his suspicion that she preferred the superior attractions of the mysterious stranger.

'I am not "hardly out of mourning",' she protested, 'and I am not "carrying on".' At this point her own innate honesty made her realise that in the eyes of most members of polite society that was exactly what she was doing, and she blushed scarlet.

Humphrey saw the betraying colour and closed in. 'You see! You cannot deny your shameful conduct. Well, madam, if you can give it to him, you can damn well give it to me too,' and with that he seized her in a bear hug and pushed her back against the nearest tree.

Amanda was momentarily made breathless by both the crudity of his words and the violence of the attack. Then she tried to push him off while simultaneously straining to raise her knee or kick him. But Humphrey had learned from their previous encounter and he was giving her no room to hit back.

With space, and the advantage of surprise, she had defended herself easily; now Amanda found herself crushed by his weight and was utterly powerless. At Glaven Hall she had never feared more than embarrassment and his unpleasant kisses, but now she was becoming seriously frightened that he meant far, far, worse. All fear of attracting attention was long gone: the appearance on the scene of a dozen sturdy yeoman was what she prayed for and she opened her mouth to scream, only to have it closed by Humphrey with his own.

It was the most disgusting experience she had ever had. His mouth was wet and loose and he was trying to force her lips open with his tongue while one hand pushed off her bonnet and the other groped at her clothing. Amanda shut her lips tightly and tried to twist her head away, but to no avail and she was becoming terrifying aware than he was bearing her downwards towards the grass.

Then suddenly he was gone from her. Amanda staggered back and clutched the tree behind her for support. By the time her head had cleared, Humphrey was flat on his back two yards away, his hands to his face and blood trickling from between his fingers.

'Jay! Oh, Jay!' Amanda hurled herself into the arms of her rescuer and clung to him. It felt so good to be held like this. The smell of clean linen, the scent of him, the heat of anger that was rising from his body all made her feel utterly safe. He held her tightly to him, his face buried in her hair until at last she relaxed enough to loosen her grip.

He tipped up her face gently. 'Amanda, darling, what did he do to you? Are you hurt?'

She shook her head, bending it to avoid looking into his eyes, so dark with anger that they looked more black than green. 'No... He grabbed me and pushed me against the tree and he kissed me.'

'I told you I should have dealt with him on the last

occasion. When you feel a little better I will take you up to the house and then I will come back here and—'

'No, Jay.' Amanda clung to his arm, still too shamed by the recollection of Humphrey's words to look up at him. 'He was angry because he said I was flaunting myself with you. He accused us of…of…' The crude words failed her. The sound of a faint snarl was all the response she got, so she faltered, 'If you fight him he will spread it all over the neighbourhood. Oh, Jay, I know I have behaved imprudently, but I could not bear it if I lost my reputation.'

There was a silence, then Jay said, 'I see. What do you want me to do with him?'

'No…nothing. He has been humiliated, surely he will do nothing—oh, Jay, look out!'

Over his shoulder she saw Humphrey, blood-streaked face contorted into rage, stumbling towards them a broken branch in his hand.

Jay swung round, pushing Amanda behind him as he did so and flinging up one hand to catch at the branch. But he was off-balance, hampered by the woman so close behind him and he missed, only succeeding in deflecting it from hitting him in the face. Instead, it caught him a glancing blow on the side of the head, which sent him reeling.

Amanda could not see his face, but Humphrey could and whatever he saw there turned his own frustrated anger into quivering terror. He turned to run, was caught by one shoulder, spun around and hit squarely on the jaw with the full force of Jay's right fist. Amanda would not have believed that a man of his weight could be sent flying through the air if she had not just seen it. Humphrey landed with a thud on the turf, lay motion-

less, then with a whimper began to scrabble feebly away
on hands and knees.

But he was safe from pursuit. Jay staggered, clutched
his head in both hands and sank to his knees. Amanda
knelt beside him, one arm around his shoulders, trying
to search through the thick hair on the side of his head
for a wound.

'Jay! Jay, speak to me! Where are you hurt?'

He shook his head, winced, then sat back on his heels
staring at her. She saw his eyes were open, the pupils
wide and black and his expression unfocused as it had
been when he had lost his temper over Charles's portrait.

Terrified that Humphrey's blow had done real damage, Amanda did not know whether to stay with him or
run for help. Then the unfocussed gaze sharpened and
he said, 'Amanda?'

'Yes, yes. Keep still. Can you sit back against this
tree while I go for some help?'

'Amanda.' It was a statement. His hand closed around
her wrist, preventing her from getting to her feet. He
paused, then said, 'And we are at Holkham? At the
Clippings?'

'Yes, but do not try and think! You need to rest.'

'It is all right. The bast—sorry, the wretch, must have
caught me in the same place as the blow during the
coach accident. Where is he?'

'Trying to hide under a bush,' Amanda said wither-
ingly. 'Never mind him now... Jay, stop it, you should
not be getting up!'

Doggedly he hauled himself to his feet and stood staring at Humphrey who stared back, transfixed, from his
position on the ground. Slowly Jay walked across the

space between them until he reached Humphrey's sprawled figure.

'You have hurt and insulted this lady who should expect nothing but support and protection from you. You deserve that I should call you out for that.' His voice was frigid with anger and contempt. 'You have attacked an unarmed man with his back to you. Again, for that I should call you out. But Mrs Clare is too sensitive of any scandal attaching itself to the name of her husband's family, however richly its present head may deserve it, and I shall therefore let you go.'

The expression of relief on Humphrey Clare's face was pathetic to behold and Amanda looked away from him to Jay, too worried about the effect of the blow to concern herself with the figure quailing on the ground. But Jay's next words riveted her attention as nothing else could.

'Before you crawl away, remember this. If one word of this gets out, if I hear a single whisper of speculation or one slighting word about Mrs Clare, I will seek you out and force a quarrel on you in the most public place I can contrive. And just in case you are in any doubt about who you are dealing with, my name is Jared Mansell, Earl of Severn.'

He had remembered who he was! Amanda gave a gasp and took a step towards the two men, then stayed back: she could not risk Humphrey realising there was any mystery here. The Earl of Severn? The name meant little to Amanda, who had never mixed in such circles, but it appeared to mean something to Humphrey, who went even paler as he got unsteadily to his feet and stumbled out of the grove.

'Jay, oh, Jay!' Amanda ran across and caught his arm. 'You have remembered who you are!'

'Do you mind if I sit down?' Jay took at few steps to a fallen tree and collapsed on to it, pulling her gently down beside her. He twisted to look at her and smiled wryly at the expression on her face. 'It is all right, Amanda, truly. I just felt a little dazed, and I expect I will have the devil's own headache in a while.'

'And you remember everything, Jay—?' She broke off. 'I am sorry, my lord, I mean.'

'Jay will do very well.' He touched her face gently. 'I have grown accustomed to it on your lips.' He paused as she looked anxiously into his eyes, worried that she could still see some trace of that unfocussed look. 'And yes, I remember most things. Some are still a jumble, but I expect they will all come back in time. Did you recognise my name?'

'Not really,' she admitted. 'I was aware of it, of course, but I have hardly been in the position to mix with the peerage, and I rarely go to town. Humphrey appeared to know it.'

Jay smiled. 'I have a certain reputation.'

'As a duellist?'

'Amongst other things.' His smile deepened as he saw the apprehension in her eyes. 'There is nothing to worry about, Amanda, I am not in the habit of strewing the countryside with corpses. I prefer to fight with the rapier: one has more chance of ending things with a minor wound and honour satisfied on all sides.'

'But you fight many duels?' she persisted.

'I have to admit, Amanda, that my suspicion that I was a rake was quite correct. And as I am sure you will know from the cautionary warnings of your respectable relatives, rakes gamble, associate with ladies of, shall we say, flamboyant natures, and engage in gambling and sporting pursuits. And all of those things tend towards the occasional dispute and the need to defend one's honour.'

'Oh.' Amanda digested this. 'And the ladies to whom you refer?'

'I will not lie to you. There is one, very expensive, barque of frailty, who is unaware of the fact that she will shortly be leaving my protection.'

'Too expensive?' Amanda queried wickedly, suddenly aware of a great bubble of rising happiness inside her.

'No,' he said, his eyes reflecting back the mischief in hers. 'But inappropriate to my newly reformed lifestyle.' What did he mean by that? Her heart gave a little leap. 'And while we are on the subject, Amanda, I am not married, I have no fiancée and definitely no children.'

'I am glad to hear it, my lord,' she said primly.

'Why, Amanda?' He had captured her hand and his thumb was working its insidious magic on the inside of her wrist.

'I have been very concerned about the anxiety your unexplained absence would be causing them. And, given what you have just told me about the, er…barque of frailty, one can only be happy that they have not been deceived in you. If they existed, that is,' she finished, confused. If he did not stop what he was doing with her hand, she did not know what she would do. Thought was becoming very difficult.

'What else would you like to know at the moment?' he asked, watching the play of emotion on her face.

'Everything…no, nothing. You should not be forcing your memory. You will end up with brain fever.' Amanda reclaimed her hand with an effort of will and stood up abruptly. 'We will go back to the house. If we go in through one of the side entrances we should escape notice and comment and then I will find the housekeeper and request the use of a bedchamber for you. We can tell her you were struck by a falling branch, which is nothing less than the truth.'

Jay pulled her back down on to the tree trunk. 'There is no need. Unless things have gone very much awry, I only need to announce myself to be shown to my duly allotted chamber.'

'Your allotted chamber? You mean you are a *guest* here?' Amanda realised that her mouth was unbecomingly open and shut it hastily. 'So that was why you found the Clippings familiar! But what on earth has an, excuse me, rake got to do with agrarian reform?'

'Absolutely nothing,' he admitted. 'But as I told you just now, I am reforming my style of life. I have become aware that I have responsibilities to my estates and their people and, enjoyable as a life of pleasure is, there are other ways of finding it than in the clubs and haunts of fashionable London. It was becoming a bore.'

So, this 'reform' predated their meeting. It had nothing to do with her after all. Amanda lowered her lashes to hide the sudden hurt and said, 'Go on.'

'I was staying with my friend Oughton near Norwich. He is of a like mind, and had already done some reading and was in touch with Mr Coke. He has taken his estates in a firm hand and has thoroughly surprised himself by enjoying the experience.'

Jay leaned back against the tree stump and stretched his legs out in front of him. 'His friends were sceptical about this transformation and convinced there was some other reason for his absence from town, so he invited us down to demonstrate his new interests. I gather he mentioned to Mr Coke that he was being visited by

several reactionary landowners who needed a good example and the result was an invitation to all six of us
to come to the Clippings and stay at the Hall.'

Amanda was transfixed with curiosity. 'But how did
you get on the stagecoach with no cards and hardly any
money?'

'We were playing cards,' he began.

'Yes, you remembered that when Miss Porter spoke
about gambling.'

'Indeed. Well, we had been playing cards into the
small hours, and drinking too. Young Eden—do you
know him? Lands near Hunstanton, but a complete rip,
never there, always in town—was bemoaning the fact
that he was in debt again and his trustees were being
damnably unsympathetic. I am afraid I was equally so
and told him he would not be in such straits if he was
more moderate in his expenditure. As I had just won
two hundred guineas off him, he could hardly be expected to take the lecture in good grace.'

'I should think not,' Amanda said. 'There is nothing
more aggravating than being lectured by someone who
has all the faults you have.' She paused, thoughtfully.
'Unless it is being told off by one's man of business
for outrunning the bailiff and spending too much on
gowns, I suppose.'

Jay grinned. 'Yes, I am afraid I know all about the
cost of fashionable gowns—you see how honest I am
being with you, Mrs Clare? Anyway, Eden said that it
was all very well of me to lecture but he had never seen
any signs of my applying the slightest self-restraint or
economy and I would fail miserably if I did.'

'So you had a bet on it.' By this time Amanda had
curled up at the other end of the tree trunk, utterly engrossed in the unfolding tale. 'Go on!'

'We—or rather my loving friends—agreed that I should be cast out into the world with a change of linen, my razors and a few guineas in my pocket to survive until we met today at Holkham. I had every confidence that a fortnight of simple living would be no problem at all; they were all convinced I would be starving within the day.'

'You did look as though you were enjoying yourself when you boarded the coach,' Amanda remarked. 'Where were you bound for?'

'Wells. I thought as a small port it would have cheap lodgings in plenty which would allow me to live on as little as possible. And it is only a few miles from Holkham, so if I was penniless by this morning I could always walk here.'

'And what were you going to live on?' Amanda demanded. She could recall what had been in Jay's purse in the inn and even the cheapest lodgings would swallow that up in two weeks.

'Samphire off the marshes, crabs caught off the harbour wall, gulls' eggs from the dunes, and if all else failed, I would take to poaching and placate my landlady with a rabbit or two.'

Amanda laughed. 'Can you snare a rabbit?'

'Of course. Like all well brought-up young gentlemen, I ran away from my tutor at regular intervals and mixed with the riff and raff of the neighbourhood. I will have you know I can snare rabbits, tickle for trout, net pheasants and make a rook stew if I have to, all thanks to old Jensen, a smelly old man and a complete rogue.'

'Well, do not let the Holkham keepers hear you, that is all I can say!' The bubble of happiness inside her was rising and rising and any moment it would burst like champagne in a glass. Amanda looked at him, unaware of the feeling in her eyes, the tenderness of her slightly parted lips.

'Amanda, come here,' Jay said abruptly, holding out one arm to beckon her along the log.

Obediently she did as he asked, trustingly settling back into the curve of his arm against his chest. She could not see his face, but she could feel the rise and fall of his breathing and his breath disturbed the fine hairs on the back of her neck. She was conscious that she had lost her bonnet and that her hair was seriously disarrayed, but none of that mattered. The world might be going past just the other side of the protective wall of greenery, but she hardly gave them a thought. She was here in Jay's arms.

'Do you miss your husband?' he asked abruptly.

She did not pretend to misunderstand him. It was not Charles's conversation he was referring to. She thought for a moment, then answered him honestly. 'I was very young when Charles married me, and very innocent. I did not, from what Mama had told me, expect to find… some…parts of marriage enjoyable. I think he was very conscious that would be the case, and I sometimes wonder if his first wife was, perhaps, a somewhat nervous woman.' Jay sat very still, just the even rise and fall of his chest and the faint caress of his breath reminding her she was not simply recalling the past aloud to herself.

'He did everything to avoid alarming me. You said that surely I had seen a naked man before. Well, I never had, for we always…went to bed in the dark.'

Jay stirred at this, and murmured, 'I am sorry, I should have known better than to make assumptions.'

Amanda shook her head, dismissing the incident. 'He treated me as though I was made of glass. After the first time, it was no longer painful, and I gradually overcame the embarrassment, but I cannot say that I ever *enjoyed* it. But then, you see, I never expected to.

'But, I did enjoy the mornings.' Her voice brightened. 'He would come in in his long Indian-silk dressing gown and we would sit up in bed and drink our chocolate and plan the day, tell each other things. I learned so much from him, and he made me very happy.'

'But you are a very passionate woman,' Jay said, his arms finally closing around her waist.

'I do not know if I am. I did not know how I was meant to feel. You see, there was never another woman I could confide in about these things. I do not know now…'

'How do you feel in my arms?' Jay asked, his voice husky. 'How do you feel when I kiss you?' He turned her in his embrace until she was cradled on his knee, supported by one arm while the other caressed her face, trailed down the curve of her neck, caught her close to him.

'I feel—'

He kissed her, his lips covering hers gently. It was unthreatening, so very soft and undemanding, yet Amanda felt as though her entire body was on fire, that she would burn up if he did not stop, would fall to pieces in his hands if he did. Her body stirred against his and his lips hardened against hers until her mouth opened and she felt the startling intrusion of his tongue.

Greatly daring, she let her own flutter against the invading tip and was stunned by the heat of his mouth, by the sensation that lanced through her body. Her breasts suddenly seemed be too sensitive to touch even the fine lawn of her chemise, and as if he knew his hand caressed downwards to stroke over the curve as she arched instinctively against his palm.

Jay groaned deep in his throat and Amanda let the tide of heat wash over her. This was what passion was, this was what her body had been telling her she would experience with Jay if only she knew he was free and could surrender to him. And at that moment she had no doubt at all that love went hand in hand with passion.

Chapter Fourteen

What would have happened if things had continued uninterrupted Amanda had no idea. She was beyond thought, caught up in a torrent of physical sensation that drowned all of her thoughts except one great, overarching, feeling of happiness.

'Coom up, boy! In here, John, good deep shade by the looks of it.' The shout was echoed by another cry of 'Get on there!' and the barking of a dog, intermingling with the unmistakable sound of a flock of sheep approaching.

Amanda found herself swung neatly on to her feet with Jay's tall figure between her and the approaching shepherds. She scooped up her bonnet and attempted to cram her tumbled hair under it. Jay swung her round, put her hand on his arm and walked slowly, but directly, out of the other side of the grove as the hot sheep entered.

Amanda knew she was pink with embarrassment and the aftermath of his kisses, and try as she might she could not tie her bonnet strings without getting strands of loose hair caught in the knot.

'Jay,' she hissed. 'I cannot be seen like this.'

He cast her a concerned glance, which rapidly turned to one of amusement. 'Once again in our short acquaintance, Mrs Clare, you appear to have been dragged through a hedge backwards. Quickly, in here.' He sidestepped behind a tall bush, untied the much-abused ribbons, pulled off her hat and thrust it into her hands. 'Hold this, please.' Then with remarkable dexterity he smoothed back her hair, gathered up the loose weight of it and, using what few pins remained in the coiffure, secured it into a pleat. He whipped the hat out of her hands and placed it on her head before the hair could even think about escape again and ran the ribbons between his fingers to flatten them. With narrowed eyes he tied a neat bow to one side of her chin and stepped back to admire the effect. 'Perfect.'

'How on earth—?' Amanda caught the wicked twinkle and sighed. 'Practice, I suppose.'

'I am afraid so. I do not think there is much we can do about the marks on your skirt, which I think come from the tree your cousin pressed you against, but the housekeeper will doubtless be sorry to hear of your fall and will be able to brush away the worst.'

'She will think us a somewhat accident-prone couple, will she not?'

'It is not her place to speculate,' Jay remarked severely. 'Now, let us skirt our grove and its new occupants again and make our way back as quickly as possible.' He glanced down at her after they had covered some distance in silence. 'How do you feel now?'

'How do you think?' Amanda demanded. The few moments of walking, and the sensation of being surrounded by half the county, brought her back to reality with a jolt. 'I am delighted that you know who you are and that your friends will be here, but I have been assaulted by my cousin, watched a fist fight, confessed some of my most intimate secrets and been passionately kissed!'

She broke off as she realised an elderly gentleman had stopped and was bowing to her. 'Good day, Lord Matcham, yes, indeed, what lovely weather, but Mr Coke is always so fortunate in that respect, is he not. Oh, excuse me,' she added as the two gentlemen nodded at each other, 'Do you know Lord Severn?'

They assured her they had met, exchanged bows and Lord Matcham, after a few jovial remarks about the fame of their Norfolk event being able to attract the Pink of the *ton*, strolled off.

'Pompous old boy, but kindly,' Jay observed. 'Belonged to my father's clubs, I rarely come across him. Now, where were we? You were berating me for kissing you—was it for being too passionate or not passionate enough?'

'Oh, shh! I was not berating you. It was as much my fault as yours and I do not know what has come over me! Oh goodness, there is Mrs Ambrose, quickly, turn behind this wagon, she will prose on for hours.'

Jay obediently swerved to put the wagon between themselves and the overbearing matron and then resumed his path towards the house. 'Well, I know exactly what has come over me, but this is hardly the time and the place to tell you about it.'

Amanda glanced up at him, but his attention had been distracted by the group of young men walking across the grass towards them.

'Severn!' the one in the lead hailed him. 'Look, Eden, here he is, just as I said he would be. No signs of starvation and he hasn't even had to pawn his boots!'

'Your friends, I collect?' Amanda whispered.

'Indeed. Now, keep smiling and I'll introduce them.'

'But we have not even agreed a story—!' Amanda broke off and smiled as the gentlemen came to a halt in front of them, doffing their hats at the sight of a lady. They were obviously all agog to question Jay, but their good manners restrained them. Taking pity, she said, 'If you will excuse me, my lord, I will go and meet Miss Porter.'

'Not at all, Mrs Clare, I rely on you to uphold my account of my adventures, which these gentlemen will doubtless disbelieve without collaboration.' Jay held up a hand to silence their immediate protest and began to introduce them. 'Mrs Clare, may I present Lord Oughton, Mr Eden, Major Greene and Lord Witherington. Where is Hampton?'

The gentlemen bowed to Amanda in turn, then Lord Oughton remarked, 'Gone off to guess the weight of a pig, or some such frippery. Our friend Mr Hampton was convinced he had the eye for it, ma'am, so we left him to it.'

Amanda laughed. 'You do realise, gentlemen, that if he is the winner he will receive the pig itself as a prize?'

'My word! Well, let us go at once and bribe the good stallholder to amend our friend's guess. I cannot conceive what Hampton would do with a pig in his chambers in Albany!' Lord Oughton fell in beside Amanda and Jay and continued to chat as they made their way towards the cluster of sideshows, one of which was topped by a crude painting of an enormous pig. 'And you can vouch for Lord Severn's having abided by the terms of our challenge, can you, ma'am?'

'Yes indeed.' Jay said nothing to help, so she assumed he was happy for her to tell as much of the tale as she could. 'You should know that his lordship was involved in an accident to the stagecoach from Norwich and sustained a dislocated shoulder and a twisted ankle.'

She broke off while the news was absorbed and commented upon, then continued. 'I happened to be in a position to take up his lordship in my carriage and convey him to Holt where I recommended the Half Moon inn to him. Lord Severn—using an alias, of course— has remained at the inn for the past fortnight.'

'Living off what, might I ask?' Mr Eden demanded. 'If Mrs Clare has been kind enough to lend you your shot, or fed you every evening, then I call that cheating!'

Jay smiled at the indignant younger man. 'I have been earning my keep overhauling the landlord's chaotic books, and believe me, that was no easy task!'

Lord Oughton raised his eyebrow as he caught Amanda's eye. 'I cannot believe Lord Severn did not cause some speculation in the neighbourhood.'

'Indeed, yes, my lord. The general opinion, which I have to say he made no attempt to deny, is that he is indeed using an alias in order to view estates before making a large purchase at a keen price.'

This was greeted with some amusement, the view being expressed by his friends that the Earl of Severn had more land than was good for him already. Amanda watched Jay covertly from under her lashes. He was taking the teasing in good part, but she was conscious of a tension about him. She suspected that he could not remember everything yet and was treading carefully so as not to betray himself. If only they had not been together! She realised now that to tell the truth about his loss of memory would lay her open to speculation about exactly why she rescued this accident victim.

She decided she liked his friends. Lord Oughton was

amiable with charming manners and, she felt, a good mind behind a light-hearted manner. The Major was taciturn, somewhat correct, but obviously willing to take an interest in all around him and to be pleased with his company. Lord Witherington had the slight air of a dandy and made no secret of his alarm at finding himself in close contact with herds of beasts and their attendants. He was bewailing the coming together of one of his exquisite boots and the results of a herd of cattle being kept standing in one place, but Amanda guessed that this was more a pose than genuine disdain for his friends' interests. Mr Eden was much the junior of the group and they treated him like a younger brother: she suspected that he hero-worshipped Jay but would have died rather than admit it.

It appeared from their conversation that the missing Mr Hampton was the comedian of the party, apt to sudden enthusiasms and stumbling from one near-disaster to another, from which his long-suffering friends retrieved him. When they came upon him, leaning on the hurdle surrounding the pig pen holding the prize beast, he proved to be only a little older than Mr Eden, chubby-faced and very friendly.

The stall holder recognised her at once and hurried forward, doffing his hat and urging her to take a seat on a straw bale, the better to admire the animal. 'Mrs Clare, ma'am! What a pleasure to see you. And will you be investing your shilling on your estimation of this fine beast of mine?'

Amanda shook her head, laughing, but duly admired the enormous porker. Lord Oughton came and told her what his friend had guessed and she shook her head reassuringly. The gentlemen were in no danger of having to find a home for a pig that night.

She felt curiously light-headed to be sitting here, admiring a pig, in the middle of an agricultural gathering and surrounded by a cheerful group of town bucks she had only just met. She knew she should be feeling shocked by Humphrey's assault, ashamed of her own passionate response to Jay, but all she was feeling was anxiety over how rapidly he was recovering his memory and increasing apprehension about what would happen to them now. All her happiness seemed to have vanished and the cold, small knot of fear was back in her stomach.

Young Mr Eden's question shook her out of her reverie. 'And when do you expect to claim your winnings, Mansell?'

All eyes turned to Jay and Amanda could see from the faces of the men that this was the source of some amusement. And from the sudden blank look in Jay's eyes, that he had not the slightest recollection of what it was.

'Oh, do tell me what the wager was for!' she exclaimed brightly, looking directly at Lord Oughton.

He fell neatly into her trap and answered her at once. 'Well, ma'am, it is a horse of young Eden's. One that he bought last month.'

She saw Jay's eyes narrow in a secret smile directed just at her and felt encouraged to continue. 'But you gentlemen appear to find that amusing. Is a horse not something worth winning? I should think that Mr Eden is regretting his gesture.'

'Not if you saw the horse,' the Major remarked with a sudden grin. 'Eden here is possibly the worst judge of horseflesh you will ever have the misfortune to meet.' He ignored the indignant protest of his victim and explained. 'He was gulled into buying this beast by a Captain Sharp who knew a flat with a few guineas to waste when he saw one. It has the manners of a mule and the conformation of a coal heaver's cart horse.'

'Then why did Lord Severn accept such a wager?' Amanda demanded.

Jay smiled ruefully. 'I regret to say, ma'am, that I was drunk at the time.'

'Shocking,' she said, with a shudder which produced an answering twinkle from the Earl.

'I know, I am a sad rake, ma'am.'

There was no possible response to that and Amanda, feeling the conversation was slipping on to dangerous ground, stood up and dusted the hay off her skirts. 'It has been delightful meeting you gentlemen, and I thank you for your escort, but I really must go and find my companion before luncheon.' The parkland was dotted with stalls selling everything from fresh bread to flagons of ale and Amanda and Jane had intended to make some purchases and have an impromptu picnic.

Lord Oughton was gallantly stooping to remove a thistle that had caught in the hem of her walking dress when she heard the Major say to Jay, 'I knew there was a piece of news to tell you. The latest *on-dit* is that Lord Langham has offered for Diana Poste. Turn up for the book is it not, a man of that stamp offering for a girl hardly out of the schoolroom?'

'*What?*' Jay's voice was so sharp that Amanda jumped.

'Thought you would be surprised,' the Major continued. 'Some sort of cousin of yours, isn't she?'

'Distant,' was all that Jay said, but Amanda could see from the look in his eyes and the set of his jaw, that here was another area of his memory which had been lost until this moment.

'I have heard of Lord Langham,' Amanda said, low voiced, to Lord Oughton. 'He does not have a good reputation from what I can recall.'

'Dreadful,' his lordship agreed, one wary eye on Jay, who was looking more serious than Amanda had ever seen him. 'In his mid-forties now, but maturity has not put a stop to his, er…pleasures; in fact, they have become more scandalous.' He shot a quick glance at her face and added, 'Not the sort of thing I should be talking about to a lady. All you need to know about Langham, ma'am, is never to be alone in a room with him.'

'If you will not tell me about him, then tell me who this Diana Poste is.'

'Her mother was a cousin of Severn's—second cousin once removed or some such thing. Never met her, she died in childbirth, I believe. Miss Poste is scarce out of the schoolroom—not out until this coming Season, I imagine, although one has seen her at the occasional small party in town—' He broke off, a faint smile on his lips.

'And?' Amanda prompted with a growing sense that she did not want to hear his answer.

'Well, when she does come out there is going to be an uproar on the Marriage Mart—or at least, there would be if she wasn't already promised to Langham.'

'But why?' Amanda was watching Jay, who was in earnest conversation with the Major and Lord Witherington.

'Most beautiful female I have ever set eyes on,' Lord Oughton said simply. 'Absolute and utter perfection.'

Amanda felt a cold wave of apprehension come over her. Despite the sunshine she shivered. Knowing in her heart what the answer was going to be, she said, 'Indeed? Do describe her to me, my lord.'

He needed little persuasion. 'Blue eyes—that deep cornflower blue, and dark, curling lashes. Blonde hair, very long and absolutely straight. Thoroughly unfashionable, of course, but she makes no attempt to curl it and it is so fair, and so heavy and long, that one simply accepts it as beautiful. And the most lovely gentle smile: she smiles at you and you just want to—' He broke off in confusion. 'As I said, very, very lovely and with that wonderful fresh innocence one misses in so many débutantes who all think they must appear world-weary.'

Amanda blinked hard to keep back the tears that she felt gathering. It was the woman Jay had described when he had experienced that incredible flash of memory and emotion. But it did not all fit: he had known then that she was marrying an older man, and he described his own feelings of powerlessness to stop it. Perhaps it had been a premonition.

'The Earl appears to be highly concerned at this news,' she remarked. The entire party had begun to walk back to the Hall, Jay still apparently planning something with the Major. 'Was he not aware of Lord Langham's pretensions to his cousin's hand?'

'I am sure he was, there have been rumours. In fact, I believe he went to remonstrate with Sir James Poste about it, point out what an eminently unsuitable husband Langham would be. But, of course, he has no rights in the matter—it is not as though he were a trustee. I rather think Sir James told him to mind his own business in forthright terms.'

'If he has done his best, why should he feel the necessity to take some action now?' she pressed, for it was obvious that Jay was asking the Major to do several things for him: the military man was scribbling rapidly

on a piece of paper as they walked and breaking off to
fire questions.

'Oh, the general opinion is that Severn has been waiting for her to leave the schoolroom before he proposed
marriage to her himself. Once we had seen her, none of
us doubted that.'

Amanda had the sensation of a heavy door slamming
shut. It was impossible to speak and so she walked beside Lord Oughton, pretending to be engrossed in avoiding thistles and ruts.

Jay half-turned and caught her eye, a rather abstracted
expression on his face. 'Mrs Clare, I wonder if I could
presume upon your good nature to have your groom
take a message to Will Bream at the Half Moon?'

'Yes, of course,' she said as prosaically as she could.
'I assumed that would be necessary if you are to remain
here with your friends tonight. Will you be riding back
in a day or two?'

'No, I find I must go into Leicestershire urgently. I
intend offering to buy the horse, at whatever price Mr
Bream names, so I hope he will see no objection to that.
As for my few possessions there, and my portmanteau,
I will write again with instructions and money to have
it sent on.'

So he had no intention of returning. He was not even
going to leave via Holt and call to see her. 'Very well,'
she agreed. How could he make plans to walk away
from her so calmly after what had passed between
them? Was he going to make no effort to speak to her
alone? Or had it all been a rake's flirtation and, now he
recalled the beautiful girl he had decided to make his
wife, he would forget this Norfolk interval without a
qualm?

They had reached the foot of the sweep of steps up

to the front door. As they climbed Amanda heard the
Major saying, 'Yes, your curricle, horses and groom are
all safely established round at the stables. We came over
yesterday at an easy pace, so they will be quite fresh
for you tomorrow. If you are sure I've got a list of all
your obligations in town, I will cancel them for you as
soon as I get back. And I will drop this list in at the
house in Grosvenor Square and have your valet pack
for you and travel up.'

'Are you staying with friends, my lord?' Amanda enquired, desperately trying to keep up an appearance of
mild interest in front of these men.

'I have a hunting box there,' Jay answered. 'It is convenient for the call I have to make.'

He did not appear to wish to confide anything further,
but Lord Oughton hissed in her ear, 'Sir James Poste
lives about ten miles from the hunting box.'

At the top of the steps the party came face to face
with Miss Porter, Lady Grahame and half a dozen other
ladies, all apparently scanning the parkland. 'I cannot
think where she is,' Miss Porter was saying, then, 'Mrs
Clare! There you are, we were just hoping to see you.'

'Well, here I am indeed!' Amanda exchanged bows
with the other ladies and turned with a sense of mixed
misery and relief to the men. 'My lords, Major, gentlemen. As you see, I am claimed by my friends. Thank
you for your escort. Lord Severn, I trust you have a safe
journey into Leicestershire. If you ask a servant to take
your letter for Will Bream to my groom round at the
stables, I will make sure it is delivered.'

She kept her countenance friendly as she nodded politely to each man. Jay held her gaze with his for a long
moment, but she could not read his expression and he
said merely, 'Goodbye, Mrs Clare. I must thank you for

your unfailing kindness. Miss Porter, I hope your garden flourishes.'

The two parties separated. Amanda could see the intense speculation in Jane's eyes, but she whispered, 'I will tell you later.'

Lady Grahame smiled at her. She rather approved of the young widow. 'A dashing collection of blades you had collected as escorts, Mrs Clare, and the Earl of Severn too—a real feather in your cap!' She was not displeased by Amanda's blush, seeing it as charming modesty, and continued, 'I have a picnic all set out on the lower terrace where Mr Coke has kindly allowed us to establish ourselves and admire the grounds. Will you not join us?'

'Thank you, ma'am, I would be delighted.' Amanda fell in with the other ladies and followed Lady Grahame through the house and on to the terrace where a pair of footmen were setting up what appeared to be a full-scale luncheon party rather than a light alfresco meal.

Amanda swallowed hard. Just how long was she going to have to maintain a brave company face before they could go? To say nothing of the fact that leaving immediately after luncheon would cause comment from those who expected to speak to her during the course of the day. And even then, she would not be able to speak to Jane of anything but trivialities all the way home because of the groom perched up behind.

Jane caught her arm during a moment's disarray while the seating was sorted out. 'Is everything all right, dear?'

'Oh, yes,' Amanda said, managing to keep a bright smile on her face. 'Jay has recovered his memory, discovered that he is an Earl and is reunited with his friends. He is single, and not yet affianced.'

'But?' Jane could read Amanda's eyes despite what her lips seemed to be saying.

'But he is about to leave for Leicestershire where the lady he wishes to marry is about to be forced into marriage with an unsuitable man.'

'Oh, my goodness,' Jane whispered, appalled. 'Which means…' Her voice trailed away.

'Which means,' Amanda supplied, her voice hard with the effort not to cry, 'either he will return with a fiancée, or having been disappointed in his courtship of a girl I am informed is the most beautiful ever seen in Society. In either case, I imagine a flirtation with a Norfolk widow is unlikely to trouble his thoughts much.'

Chapter Fifteen

The picnic was long, lavish and extremely lively. The group of ladies who had gathered around Lady Grahame were all confident matrons from local society with much in common and plenty to talk about. Amanda knew many of them, if only slightly. At first she felt too bruised and shaken by her abrupt parting from Jay to do more than respond mechanically to any questions or observations directed at her, but after a while she found herself drawn into the wide-ranging discussions of everything from the use of laurels in shrubberies to the problems of keeping reliable servants.

The necessity to shield her feelings and to maintain a bright social front was surprisingly helpful, she realised. After a while it was as though what had happened was distanced, not quite real, and she could manage to exist on this level quite easily. She was aware of Jane's anxious glances, but smiled reassuringly. It would not do to worry Jane, and her own pride would not let her admit to anyone else that her heart was broken—if that indeed was what this incredible empty feeling was in her chest.

'Indeed, I do sympathise with you, Mrs Agnew,' she

responded to a worried young mother on her right who was bemoaning the loss of her children's excellent nurse to a position in a London household. 'I am about to lose my lady's maid, who is getting married. I am delighted for her, of course, but she will be hard to replace.'

Lady Grahame, who appeared capable of keeping an ear tuned to half a dozen conversations at once, inclined her elaborately coiffed head and remarked, 'I may be able to assist you, Mrs Clare. My sister-in-law writes to me to say that her own lady's maid—of whom she cannot speak too highly—has a younger sister who is wishful to follow in the same path. My sister-in-law knows the family and can recommend the girl for honesty, intelligence and good character. Would you wish me to say that you may be interested in seeing her?'

'Why, yes, that would be most welcome,' Amanda said gratefully. 'The thought of finding someone has been worrying me, I must confess. Where does the young woman live?'

'In London, I understand. I believe she is presently employed at home where her mother has been unwell, but she is now fully recovered so the daughter is released.' Lady Grahame reached into her reticule and scribbled on one of her tablets, which she passed to Amanda. 'There is my sister-in-law's direction, Mrs Clare. Please feel free to write.'

Amanda glanced at the note—a Mrs Thornton, in a most select part of town—and tucked it away with a word of thanks.

The party eventually broke up at three o'clock. Normally Amanda would have continued to stroll around the gathering for at least another two hours, meeting people and collecting information, but now she felt as though she had been up all night, or was about to come down with a cold. The thought of the drive home was tiring even to contemplate.

She turned to Jane, who was making her thanks to their hostess and when she was free said, 'I will walk around to the stables and find Ned. I hope you do not mind, but I am feeling quite worn out and would prefer to start home now. Will you wait for me at the front of the house?'

'Of course I do not mind,' Miss Porter assured her, with a covert glance of concern. 'I have had a delightful day. I will wait for you at the front of the house—the view of the entire scene is so stimulating from there. Would you like me to drive?'

'No…yes, please. I think I would, Jane,' Amanda agreed gratefully. Her companion was an excellent whip and the greys would be considerably subdued after their brisk drive in that morning.

Amanda walked round the side of the house, through a gate in the wall and made her way through a shrubbery towards the stableyard. As she rounded a corner she found herself face to face with Lord Severn. Jay was half-sitting on the balustrade, looking out over the plantings with a look on his face that suggested his thoughts were not pleasant.

His expression did not lighten noticeably at her approach, but he stood up and removed his hat. 'Amanda. I am sorry that we have had to part so suddenly.'

'I quite understand.' Her heart was beating so erratically that she wondered it was not visible through the thin lawn of her bodice, but by some miracle she found she could keep her voice light and cool and her face free of her betraying thoughts. 'Some family matter of urgency I understand from Lord Oughton.'

'Yes...of sorts,' he agreed. 'I have just given a message for Will Bream to your man. I regret having to leave without thanking him in person. He is a fine man, and deserves to do well at his new career.'

'Indeed, he is,' Amanda agreed. 'You set out tomorrow?' Sheer pride was keeping her here, calmly talking to him like this. The thought that he might suspect how she felt was appallingly humiliating.

'Yes—' He broke off, a sharp line furrowing his brow. 'Amanda, I cannot thank you enough for what you have done...'

'Oh, nonsense!' She was proud of the light laugh. 'Why, I told you I was incurably curious and managing. A mystery such as the one you presented does not come one's way every day!'

'It meant nothing more?'

What did he want from her? she thought, suddenly angry. *He goes off to another woman and he seems to expect that I will humiliate myself by admitting to an attachment!*

'Of course, I am greatly in your debt for dealing with Cousin Humphrey so effectively. I am sure I will have no further trouble with him. And I do not forget that if it had not been for you, I would have been far more seriously hurt in that accident.'

Jay moved closer and looked down into her eyes. His own were dark, but she kept her gaze steady. 'Earlier today you were in my arms, Amanda. The other night—'

'Was a dream,' she finished for him. 'And this morning...I am sorry I burdened you with my memories. I will not deny that you have...awakened part of me that was perhaps hidden. But one must be realistic about these things, my lord. Summer idylls come and go.'

'*My lord?* It was Jay this morning.'

'I did not know then who you were. But Jay does not exist, does he? And the Earl of Severn, who comes from a very different world, does.'

He moved away abruptly and she added, 'I told you I was a practical woman, my lord. And one with a life to be living, not spent on wakening dreams. This past fortnight has been an amusing interlude—if sometimes a worrying one on your behalf—but it is over and things move on.' She held out her hand to him. 'I will bid you goodbye, my lord, and good fortune.'

He took her proffered hand and held it while he looked at her. After a moment his thumb began to run gently over the swelling base of hers. Amanda snatched back her hand as though stung. 'Good day, my lord!' She swept round and stalked off towards the high wall that hid the stable yard. There was a crunch of gravel behind her, then it stopped as she vanished through the wicket gate and into the bustle and smells of the yard.

'...now pronounce you man and wife.' The Rector stopped speaking as Tom Green, blushing hotly, kissed an equally flushed Kate. An appreciative murmur of congratulation rose from the congregation and Miss Porter disappeared into a large lawn handkerchief, from which the occasional sentimental sniffle could be heard.

Amanda remained resolutely dry eyed, despite the swelling feeling of happiness for Kate and Tom that rose inside her. She had been telling herself 'You will not cry, you *will not* cry,' over and over again in the five days since she had parted from Jay at Holkham and it appeared to be working.

Not a drop had brightened her eye to betray her to her household or to Jane. Jane had been bitterly disap-

pointed to hear that Jay had gone, and that he had another attachment, and was extremely anxious about the
effect on Amanda. She had had no hesitation in saying
so.

'I had so hoped that the two of you would make a
match,' she said, when they were finally alone the next
day. 'My dear, this must make you very unhappy, I so
wish there was something I could do.'

'Nonsense,' Amanda had retorted briskly. 'I liked
him very much, and I will not deny I enjoyed flirting
with him, but that was all it was. And a good thing too,'
she added. 'An Earl is not the match for me!'

Jane had not looked in the least convinced, and had
said no more, but Amanda knew that she was watching
her closely. At first she resented it, then was grateful
that there was something else to bolster her pride and
stop her breaking down and giving in to grief. If Jane
guessed how she was feeling she would be even more
sorry for her, and Amanda hated the thought of being
pitied.

This frozen state was not comfortable, however. With
one part of her mind and heart rigidly disciplined not
to think of Jay, not to feel for him, the rest of her found
it hard to cope with the preparations for Kate's wedding
on the Monday following the third reading of the banns.

Thankfully Kate appeared to notice no restraint; if the
other servants thought their mistress more than usually
subdued, she assumed they put it down to her sorrow
at losing such a close attendant.

If she had heard the conversation in the servants' hall
after dinner every night, she would have been horrified.
'What does a town buck like that think he's about, coming down here and trifling with our lady?' Mrs Howlett

would demand indignantly, provoking a tumult of remarks from all around the long table.

'Pity she's no father to look after her', 'Needs a shot
gun taking to him!', 'That Humphrey Clare should be
doing something.' 'What, him? Useless slab of lard!'
'Poor lady, so white and all, he's broken her heart,
that's what he's done.'

Mr Howlett would wave a magisterial hand and qui-
eten the protests. 'All we can do is pretend we haven't
noticed. And if he does come back, he'll find the door
shut in his face,' he added viciously.

The congregation stood as the bride and groom
passed down the aisle together and out into the sunshine. Amanda and Jane followed them out to join the
rest of the guests throwing rice.

'Throw your flowers, throw your flowers!' the group
of single girls who gathered on the path in front of
Amanda called to Kate. She laughed and turned her
back on them, all the better to throw blind for the lucky
girl to catch.

'I do wonder where that superstition comes from,'
Jane remarked as the little flock of maidens jostled and
giggled.

'That the one who catches it will be the next bride?
I do not know either, but possibly the Rector does,'
Amanda suggested, twisting round to look for him. 'He
has a great interest in that sort of folklore.'

At that moment something struck her on the brim of
her bonnet. She put up her hands instinctively to find
them full of the posy of rosebuds and asparagus fern
which Miss Porter had so prettily assembled for Kate.

The guests turned to look at her, some of them calling
congratulations, some obviously wondering what to say.
Amanda flushed. 'I am sure that was an accident and

not what the Fates intended at all,' she said, trying to laugh it off. 'Will the charm work if Kate throws it again?'

But the wide-eyed girls all shook their heads and said, no, it must be true that Mrs Clare would be the next married. None of them dared tease her for the name of the lucky man. Flushed, Amanda returned the flowers to Kate, who took them without comment, knowing only too well that the mysterious Mr Jay had gone and her mistress had been sad ever since.

The big barn was hung with cloths and decorated with flowers for the wedding breakfast, with food spread out on big trestle tables and bales of straw set around for the guests to sit on. The sun shone, the ale flowed and soon a fiddler struck up and the dancing began.

Amanda danced with the bridegroom, the Rector, her butler, several local farmers and then found herself claimed for the next set by Will Bream, resplendent in his best waistcoat. By this time she was thoroughly enjoying herself and was surprised, when the music came to a halt, to find Will firmly steering her around the side of the barn away from prying eyes.

'What is the matter, Will?'

'That's what I was going to ask you, Mrs Clare, ma'am. I had a very civil letter from Mr Jay—his lordship, I should say—with more than enough to cover his expenses with me and a very fair price indeed for that hunter. Very civil indeed it was, but no word about coming back here and it seems like you aren't expecting to hear from him again, ma'am.'

'There is no reason why I should, Will,' Amanda said, shifting uneasily under his penetrating gaze. Will, fiercely protective of his late master's widow, took lib-

erties with his plain speaking that none of her servants—or even Miss Porter—would dream of. 'We
move in different worlds.'

'You don't fool me, Mrs Clare,' he stated, ignoring
her protest. 'He's been flirting with you, hasn't he, and
him going away has hurt you, hasn't it?'

'Oh dear, Will, I really don't want to talk about this.'
He regarded her stolidly until she admitted, 'Yes, we
flirted, and yes, I wish he had not gone away.'

'Was flirting all he did?' Will demanded.

'*Will!* You shouldn't be asking me something like
that!'

'You haven't got a brother or a father to ask it, and
that Mr Humphrey Clare is neither use nor ornament,
so it's up to someone like me who cares about you to
ask it,' he said.

Amanda knew she was blushing a deep, betraying
red. 'He kissed me, Will, but that is all, truly.'

'Humph. Well, if you say so, ma'am, then of course
it is so.' He looked slightly mollified, like a large dog
that has finally lowered its hackles after another dog has
walked past its gate.

'Will, what would you have done if I said he had…if
things had been…?'

'Made him do the right thing, of course,' Bream
looked astonished that she had needed to ask.

'My goodness.' Amanda regarded him wide-eyed, the
vision of the inn landlord marching up to the Earl of
Severn's front door armed with a shotgun rising in her
imagination. 'I do believe you would. I thank you, Will,
I could not hope for a stauncher defender, but believe
me, I do not need such extreme measures.'

It was his turn to look bashful. 'Promised Mr Charles

I'd look after you, best I could, and I will. But I can't stop you falling in love with a rake, can I?'

'No, Will, you cannot.' Amanda bent forward and kissed him on the cheek, causing him to blush hectically. 'I am afraid no one could have stopped that. Now come along, all the girls will be wondering where such an eligible partner has gone.'

That night Amanda dreamed that she was walking up the aisle towards the Rector, Kate's bouquet of flowers in her hands. The pews were packed with friends and neighbours, the church bells were ringing, but where the bridegroom should be standing there was simply a swirl of mist.

Then she was aware that she was escorted by Will Bream, his shotgun held in his other hand. As they reached the altar rail and the Rector the mist vanished, leaving nothing in its place and Will said, 'Now don't you fret, Mrs Clare, I'll fetch him back for you.'

Amanda sat bolt upright in bed, still shaking with reaction. It was as though everyone she knew had been in that congregation and now they were aware of her feelings for Jay and knew that he had left her—and were either pitying her or gloating, depending their point of view.

Of course, it was not true, she told herself fiercely, then started to think about it. Jane knew, Will knew, Kate doubtless guessed and Humphrey, once he stopped feeling sorry for himself, would also suspect. If he did, he would tell his mama, and she, no doubt, would thoroughly enjoy spreading the news of the young widow's humiliation around the district.

'But I cannot run away!' she whispered to herself, then, after a moment's reflection, 'Yes, of course I can—and I will.'

Next morning at breakfast she waited until Jane was sipping her second cup of coffee and enquired, almost casually, 'Would you find it very irksome if we were to go up to town for a few days?'

'London?' Jane put down her cup with a rattle and looked at Amanda in surprise. 'Is he...?' Then she caught herself up and said, 'I mean, whatever do you want to do in London at this time of year? The Season is over and it will be half-empty of society.'

'I want to take up the introduction Lady Grahame has given me to her sister-in-law. Do you recall she said she was able to recommend a new lady's maid? And I really must see about a new riding habit, my old one is quite beyond the pale. Have a fashionable new crop, perhaps.' She watched Jane's face. 'Would you be un-utterably bored?'

'Why, no, of course not. A change of scene would be delightful. When would you like to set out?'

'By the end of the week, I think. I will write to an hotel and bespeak two rooms and a parlour. We had better take a maid with us: who do you think? Maria, perhaps? She will not be able to dress our hair, but we can do each other's, I am sure. So that is the two of us and Maria. I must make sure the travelling carriage is cleaned and the traces checked over.' She reached for her tablets and jotted down *Hotel, carriage*. 'Is there anything else we need to do?'

'Which hotel?' Jane asked. 'Grillon's?'

'No, the Clarendon, the food is better.'

'How do you know that?' Jane looked puzzled. 'Have

you ever stayed there? I thought you always used Grillon's.'

'I have no idea…oh, yes, I do, someone recommended it to me.' And the sound of Jay's voice in the inn parlour in Saxthorpe came back to her. For a moment it was as though he was in the room with them. 'We will travel by easy stages, I think,' she said hastily. 'There is no need to rush.'

It was consequently a whole week later before the two ladies, and a maid rendered completely speechless by excitement, drew up in front of the Clarendon Hotel on the corner of Albermarle and Bond Street. Porters hurried out for their luggage and the doors were flung open wide to usher them in. At such an unfashionable time of year Amanda had had no trouble securing a fine suite of rooms and the sight of the two well-dressed ladies with their large train of luggage galvanised the hotel manager into obsequious welcome.

When they were finally settled in their rooms, Jane remarked, 'They certainly appeared impressed by our luggage. Are you sure you needed to bring so much, Amanda dear? I thought we were only going to stay for a week.'

Amanda stopped flitting about the private sitting room examining it. 'Oh, well, I am not sure. If we wanted to stay longer it seemed foolish not to have everything. Although I am sure we will want to make many purchases.'

Miss Porter grimaced. Shopping was not her favourite occupation. Still, if it took Amanda's mind off the Earl of Severn, she would gladly submit to an entire month of it.

She spied a London directory on the shelf. 'Do you

have the name and direction of Lady Grahame's sister-in-law to hand? It might be as well to call as soon as possible, for if the girl is already suited, or you do not like her, that will give you more time to try the domestic agencies.'

Amanda agreed and found the slip of paper. 'Here we are, Mrs Thornton, Upper Brook Street. Can you find it?'

Jane flicked through the pages. 'Yes, Number Four, almost on the corner with Grosvenor Square. Her eyes ran idly over the list of residents as she had the book open in her hands. A very distinguished company, and… Oh, my goodness!'

'What is the matter, Jane?' Amanda looked back from the window from where she had been surveying the street below.

'No…nothing, my dear,' Miss Porter said, hastily shutting the directory. After all, Lord Severn was safely about his courtship in Leicestershire, there was no risk of him being at home in his town house in Grosvenor Square. No, better not to mention it to Amanda at all.

Chapter Sixteen

Two days later Amanda set out for Mrs Thornton's house in Upper Brook Street, accompanied by Maria. She had received a most encouraging note in response to her own, assuring her that the young woman in question was indeed still free and about to seek employment, and inviting Mrs Clare to visit to interview her.

Susan Wilkes proved to be a neat little person with immaculate hair and well-kept hands and a great deal of shy reserve. Yes, she very much wanted to be a lady's maid. Yes, her sister had explained all the duties and had taught her how to mend and press and how to dress hair. Yes, she knew she had a lot to learn about caring for jewels and that sort of thing, but she was very willing to learn if only Mrs Clare would give her an opportunity.

Mrs Thornton, who had remained in the room during this conversation, suggested kindly, 'Why do you not retire to one of the bedrooms, Mrs Clare, and allow Susan to dress your hair? I always think there is no better way to judge if someone is careful and has potential.'

Nervously Susan followed the ladies to a small blue

bedchamber and hurried to pull out the chair before the dressing table. She took Amanda's hat and laid it carefully on the bed, smoothing the ribbons as she did so, then waited to be told what to do.

'Just unpin it, brush it through and put it up again, only this time, let a ringlet show on either side under the hat brim,' Amanda suggested.

Susan's hands shook, but she was confident with the brush and pins and soon had Amanda's hair just as she had requested. Amanda approved her clean, neat dress and apron, her short nails and the slight scent of lavender water.

'That is very good,' she remarked. 'Thank you.'

'Thank you, ma'am.' Susan bobbed a curtsy and waited, eyes downcast.

She was certainly a contrast to bubbly, noisy Kate, but perhaps she would come out of her shell with confidence and familiarity. Amanda asked her if she still wished to be considered for the position and mentioned the wage she had in mind.

'Oh, yes, ma'am!'

'And you realise it will be in the country? We are only a small household and although I entertain quite frequently, it will not be the same as being with a town household.'

Yes, Susan realised all that and confided that she would be frightened to start in a big town house. 'I'm used to the country, ma'am.'

She happily agreed to a month's trial, starting when Amanda returned to Norfolk, which would give her time to tell her family and collect up her belongings. Amanda took her direction and explained how she would be in touch.

As she went downstairs again to report success to her

hostess she heard the patter of feet as Susan ran along the landing, obviously seeking out her sister to tell her the good news.

Amanda felt happier than she had for days as she emerged on to the steps of Mrs Thornton's house a while after, Maria at her side. She had been dreading replacing Kate, for in their little household it was important to find someone who would fit in and contribute to the friendly atmosphere that Amanda found essential to her own contentment. Quiet Susan might be, and she would need training in many things, but Amanda felt confident that she was the right choice.

She was hesitating on the bottom step, wondering which way to take to Piccadilly and Hatchard's bookshop, when a figure, familiar from Holkham, approached from the direction of Grosvenor Square. Jay's friend Lord Oughton was strolling along, apparently in no hurry, and his face lit up when he saw her before him.

'Mrs Clare, ma'am! What an unexpected pleasure.'

'Lord Oughton, good afternoon. I am in London to engage a new lady's maid and for some shopping. I had not looked to find anyone I knew here at such a season.'

'I am waiting on my mama,' he explained, replacing his hat. 'May I escort you anywhere, ma'am?'

'I was just wondering which way to take to Hatchards, my lord, but I have no wish to turn you from your path.'

'It would be a pleasure, and you put me in mind that my sister wanted some novel or another collecting. I can combine duty with pleasure,' he added gallantly, offering her his arm.

'Thank you, my lord, in that case, I would be delighted.' Amanda took his arm and they strolled along,

Maria behind them, trying not to get lost or tread on their heels yet take in all the sights of the busy streets as she went.

Hatchard's proved a treasure trove and Amanda had soon found two new novels and an account of travels to the East, which Jane had thought sounded interesting. Lord Oughton, who had collected his sister's package, proved more than willing to browse amongst the shelves and tables loaded with new publications and to tempt her with more suggestions.

Amanda found him very good company, and was soon laughing with him over his teasing suggestions of which frivolous novels might appeal to a lady with time on her hands.

'With London so thin of company,' he was saying as they walked out on to the pavement again, 'you will need at least one book a day to keep you entertained. Will you not allow me to take you driving to fill some of these long hours while your tailor stitches your new habit?'

'That would be delightful, thank you, my lord. But will Lady Oughton be able to spare you?'

'Mama is happily occupied with her plans to move to Brighton for the summer. She has been much put out because not all of them are falling into place... My goodness, see who is there, ma'am, the young lady in the barouche.'

Obediently Amanda looked at the vehicle, which was pulled up a little further along Piccadilly. It was facing towards them, its occupant leaning out to speak to someone who appeared to have walked across the street to speak to her, for he was standing on the road side of the vehicle, obscured from their view and all Amanda could see was the lower part of a pair of boots.

'Is it someone you know, my lord?'

'That is Miss Poste, the young lady I was telling you about at Holkham.' Lord Oughton tucked Amanda's hand under the crook of his elbow and began to stroll along the street towards the carriage.

'Oh!' was all Amanda could manage. She had no wish to meet the youthful object of Jay's affections, yet she felt extremely curious to see her. She rallied slightly. 'Are you acquainted with the lady, or do you simply know her by sight?' That was as near as she could venture to demanding whether she was about to be introduced to Miss Poste, and she soon received her answer.

As they came up to the barouche its occupant looked across and saw them. 'Lord Oughton, good morning.'

His lordship stopped and doffed his hat. 'Miss Poste, how do you do. I believe you will not have met Mrs Clare.'

He moved forward and Miss Poste moved to lean out and shake hands. Amanda, who was taking in the fact that Lord Oughton had not exaggerated one whit in describing Miss Poste's extraordinary beauty, was conscious of a hastily suppressed exclamation from the other side of the carriage. Good breeding stopped her glancing in that direction while she shook hands in turn with Miss Poste and with the thin lady introduced as 'Miss Woodley, my companion', who occupied the forward seat.

Only then did she turn her head to look at the gentleman standing on the far side of the barouche, and, with a sinking sense of inevitability, saw it was Lord Severn.

'Mrs Clare,' he said formally, raising his hat and making her a slight bow.

'Lord Severn,' she acknowledged him coolly. Her heart seemed to be in her mouth and she wondered if she had gone as white as she felt. She was conscious of Miss Poste's gaze on her as Jay made his way around the carriage to join her and Lord Oughton on the pavement and schooled her expression to one of polite indifference. Those huge blue eyes had sharpened at the greeting and Amanda was careful to maintain a light flow of chit-chat with the ladies in the carriage while Jay greeted Lord Oughton.

'I had no idea you were in town,' she heard Jay remark to his friend. She longed to look at him, but did not dare risk her face betraying her. All she wanted was to be close to him, to look into his eyes and read how he felt, how he was. In that first glimpse he had seemed thinner, as though his features had sharpened, but perhaps that was just her imagination.

'Summoned by my mother,' Lord Oughton replied. 'Heard that you were here, though—in fact, I was just returning from a fruitless visit to you in Grosvenor Square when I was fortunate enough to meet Mrs Clare.'

This was enough to focus attention on Amanda and she said, smiling, 'And poor Lord Oughton has paid for his kind offer of escort by being dragged into Hatchard's and then burdened with books for his pains.'

There was general laughter at his lordship's gallant attempts to protest that it was no burden at all and Jay enquired, 'Do you make a long stay in town, Mrs Clare?'

'I have not yet decided,' she said calmly. How could she stand there like this, in the middle of bustling Piccadilly, when she wanted to run to his side, trace the lines of his face with her fingers, reassure herself that he was well? 'Possibly.' She had no intention of explaining herself or her presence.

Was it her imagination or was the atmosphere prickling as though at the onset of a thunderstorm? She glanced around the group: the chaperon was sitting poker-faced and silent. She did not appear either welcoming or disapproving of the group gathered around her charge, but it was not she who was contributing to Amanda's feeling of discomfort.

Being close to Jay was, of course, very uncomfortable. She felt embarrassed, which was hardly surprising, but she also sensed that he was angry about something. Nothing showed on his face and his eyes were unreadable. In any case, she mused as she chatted lightly about the prospects for the weather, what on earth could he feel angry *about*?

The she saw his glance flicker towards Lord Oughton, who was certainly taking his role squiring her seriously, As well as patiently carrying her books, he had twice moved to protect her from any risk of jostling from passers-by on the bustling pavement and was standing very close, one hand at her elbow. Surely Jay could not be feeling jealous of his old friend? Could he be such a dog in the manger when the very lovely object of his own attentions was sitting so close?

She had tried hard not to appear to stare at Miss Poste, who might well be thoroughly weary of people gawping at her quite astonishing looks. Now, she caught her eye and, under cover of discussing the theatrical entertainments that would be available at that season, took the opportunity of studying her more closely.

Diana was patently very young—just seventeen, if Amanda was any judge—and her skin had the bloom of a fresh apricot, completely without blemish. Her eyes

were as Lord Oughton had described them: huge, cornflower blue and expressively fringed with long dark
lashes, which caressed her high cheekbones as she modestly lowered them. Her nose was small and straight,
her mouth sweetly curved and her chin had a little dim-
ple. Despite her youth, her figure was well formed and
her simple muslin gown modestly displayed a curva-
ceous form.

The wave of dislike that swept over Amanda was so
violent that she almost gasped. How could she react like
that to a young woman she had scarcely met? *And I was
thinking Jay was jealous*, she chastised herself furiously, forcing a smile. The poor child cannot help being
born so lovely, nor could she help the attentions of men
who found her so. Diana tossed her head slightly and
the heavy mass of straight hair, which hung so grace-
fully down her back, rippled slightly. Amanda found
herself looking for the men's reactions.

Jay's mouth tightened and she caught just the flash
of appreciation in Lord Oughton's eyes, then both men
were speaking of something together and the moment
passed. But she also caught the look in Miss Poste's
eyes and realised that the girl was not as unaware of
the effect she was having as she first appeared. As soon
as the men's attention was turned from her Amanda
caught her glancing from one to the other with an as-
sessing look. *She knows what effect she has*, Amanda
thought. *She knows and she is toying with them, seeing
how well she scores in gaining their attention and playing one off against the other*.

Well, could she blame the girl? It was not her fault
if her perfection of looks led others to expect her character to be as perfect. In a young woman with less an-

gelic features, perhaps, one would not think twice about that look of calculation.

Then, out of the corner of her eye, she saw the glance Diana was directing at her. That, too, was calculating, and it was exactly the look that she had last seen on the face of a society lady about to unsheathe her talons and set about dealing with a rival. *She suspects something between Jay and I*, Amanda thought, and ridiculously felt a tiny twist of fear. What was there to fear from this child? She was just rather spoilt.

'Are you out yet, Miss Poste?' she enquired, knowing the answer, but thinking it a question she might be expected to ask.

'No, not until next Season,' the girl replied. 'Although Papa allows me to attend country dances and the theatre and so on. In fact...' and her glance slid sidelong to see the effect of her words on Jay '...in fact, I may be married before next Season.'

'I must felicitate you,' Amanda said, with all the warmth she could muster. 'I had not seen the announcement.'

'No, nothing has yet been announced.' Diana said this with a strange smile, as though at a secret she was not going to share.

Amanda was aware of Jay's back stiffening, and could feel, as strongly as though he had spoken the words, that he was willing her to drop the subject. She ignored the sensation and said, knowing she sounded patronising, but almost hoping to goad the girl, 'Perhaps your papa might wish you to wait a little. After all, you are *very* young and it would be a pity not to enjoy your first Season as a débutante.'

There was a flash of anger in the blue eyes. Obviously Miss Poste did not relish advice from older ladies.

'Oh,' she said sweetly, 'do you recall your first Season so clearly after so long?'

Why, you little cat! Amanda thought. 'I recall it vividly,' she replied, maintaining her smile. 'I met my husband then, so it has happy memories for me.'

'And is he in town?' Diana enquired.

'I am a widow,' Amanda told her and watched the calculation in the cornflower gaze. *I am obviously past my first youth, and of no more than passable looks compared to her, so can be discounted on those grounds*, she thought, interpreting the look. *But as a widow I have more freedom than most married ladies, and certainly more than a single girl. And 'widow' has certain connotations if combined with an independence and passable looks. Oh, yes, she has seen me as a rival.*

The atmosphere had lost none of its charge, despite the polite interchanges between all those gathered around the carriage. Amanda felt that Jay's hackles were rising, that Lord Oughton was uneasy and that Miss Poste was definitely hostile. She felt ashamed of herself for goading Diana into exposing herself, although she very much doubted if either man had noticed anything amiss with the exchanges between the two ladies.

'I really must be going, it was delightful to meet you, Miss Poste, Miss Woodley. Good day, Lord Severn. No, no, Lord Oughton, I have presumed on your time far too long and those books are hardly any weight at all.'

His lordship, however, was not to be deprived of his burden and, promising to call on Jay later, he raised his hat to the ladies and steered Amanda back along Piccadilly, Maria following at a discreet distance.

Despite her feelings, Amanda was conscious of a little amusement. He was obviously dying to comment on the encounter, but was in difficulties, for his good manners forbade him to enthuse about the beauty of one woman to another. Kindly, Amanda put him out of his misery.

'What a very lovely young lady,' she commented. 'You did not exaggerate in the slightest. No wonder Lord Severn is enamoured.'

She was so convinced that she had read Lord Oughton's mood accurately that his answer took her aback. 'I cannot say I approve.'

'Really? It is not a brilliant match, I will grant you, but respectable.'

'She is too young.' He broke off to guide Amanda round a barrow, which had become wedged against the kerb, then appeared to be unable to continue.

'Well, I expect her father will postpone the actual wedding until later.'

They turned into the comparative quiet of Albermarle Street and he finally said, 'It makes me uneasy. Miss Poste is almost exactly the same age as my sister Lizzie and yet she seems ten years older in many ways. I know how I would feel if men admired Lizzie the same way as they do Miss Poste—and I would not feel happy if she received their attentions with so much—' He broke off, obviously lost for the right word.

'Aplomb?' Amanda suggested. 'She does seem very mature for her age, I will grant you. But girls all mature differently. Your sister will amaze you by growing up all of a sudden.' She fell silent, working out her own impressions. 'I may be wrong, but I am not sure she knows her own mind about either man: doubtless she is flattered by being the focus of admiration.'

'Yes.' He seemed happier for a few minutes, then said, 'Forgive me for being so frank, ma'am, but I feel

I can confide in you. I am just uneasy that my friend Severn should show such attention to her. It is unlike him.'

'Surely you do not doubt his good intentions towards her?' Amanda asked, shocked, but was reassured by Lord Oughton's expression of horror. 'No, I can see that you do not. It is unusual in him to pay court to débutantes? He normally prefers more…mature ladies?'

Lulled by the calm way she expressed this outrageous question, Lord Oughton agreed that that was exactly the case, then blushed scarlet at what he had implied.

Amanda took pity on him. 'Then perhaps he has decided it is time to settle down and he feels that a very young bride will suit him better.' They had arrived at the steps of the hotel at this point and Lord Oughton was saved from considering this tricky question further. He handed her parcel of books to the doorman and asked, 'At what time may I collect you tomorrow for our drive? Will two-thirty suit?'

The time agreed, he took himself off, leaving Amanda to climb the stairs slowly, her mind a whirl of jostling emotions. She had seen Jay and had managed to behave with calm dignity, despite how she had felt inside, but now reaction was setting in and she realised that her feelings for him had not abated one jot for all the days they had been apart. But then, how could she expect them to? Surely love did not change like that. If he was besotted by Diana Poste, then her opinion of his judgement had undergone a change, that was all.

'*Love is not love which alters when it alteration finds,*' she was saying to herself as she opened the door of their sitting room.

'What did you say, dear?' Miss Porter glanced up from her sewing. 'Is that Shakespeare you are quoting?

How very literary of you!' She saw the pile of books in Amanda's hands and exclaimed, 'Ah! That explains it, you have been browsing in a bookshop.'

Amanda was tempted to let it go at that, but she felt the need to confide. 'Yes, I have been in Hatchard's, Jane. But that is not why I am quoting Shakespearian sonnets, I am afraid. Lord Severn is in town.'

'Lord Severn! Oh, my goodness! Did you meet him in Grosvenor Square?'

'No.' Amanda looked puzzled, not knowing of Jane's unsettling discovery of his address. 'No, I was fortunate enough to secure Lord Oughton's escort to the bookseller's and we met with Jay and his cousin Miss Poste and her companion. The ladies were in their barouche and he was on foot.'

Miss Porter blinked as she tried to assimilate so much information. 'Lord Oughton? Oh, yes, you spoke of him. How very kind of him. And this Miss Poste, is she as beautiful as you were led to believe?'

'Even more so,' Amanda admitted.

'And Mr Jay…Lord Severn, I should say?'

'Very attentive to Miss Poste and not best pleased to see me, I suspect.' Amanda cast off her bonnet and began to unbutton her pelisse.

'Oh, dear.' Jane sighed. 'And I suppose a cool reception has done nothing to change your feelings for him, hence your quotation?'

'I am afraid not.' Amanda sank down in the window seat.

'Do you…do you *love* him, dear?'

'Yes.'

'Oh.' The ladies sat in silence for a while, then Miss Porter said, with the air of someone who knew they should not ask, but could not restrain themselves. 'And what did you think of Miss Poste? Will she make him a suitable wife, do you think?'

Amanda took a long, considering breath. 'Miss Poste is beautiful, spoilt and I think will prove to be a complete little madam. I pity any man who takes her to wife.'

'Oh, my! I do not recall you saying that Lord Oughton made any such judgement on her character, although I suppose he hardly would.'

'I do not think that gentlemen perceive her real nature: she is too stunning, and so very young. And she takes more care about how she presents herself to men than to women. But, interestingly, Lord Oughton did express doubts about the wisdom of the match to me. She makes him feel uneasy, I think, and not just because he finds her so beautiful.'

Jane cheered up slightly. 'Lord Oughton appears to be taking an interest in you: first he escorts you, then he shows a flattering degree of confidence in confiding in you. What do you know of him? I do wish I had met him.'

'Well, you will tomorrow afternoon, for he is engaged to take me driving. All I know is that he is in London waiting on his mama's pleasure while she makes plans to go to Brighton for the summer, and he has a young sister of about seventeen called Lizzie.'

Miss Porter had jumped to her feet and was thumbing through a rather worn *Peerage* which was on the shelf. 'Here we are. James Henry, third Baron Oughton. Hmm, twenty-eight, single, son of…sister Elizabeth Georgina…principal seat…' She put the book down. 'Do you like him? He seems extremely eligible.'

'Well, yes, I like him very well, Jane. But however eligible he is, he is not courting me—why, we have only met twice, and in any case, I am not looking for another suitor. He is simply a very friendly, personable man who enjoys company.'

'What a pity,' replied Miss Porter with a sigh. 'Well, tell me about your visit to Mrs Thornton. Is the young woman she recommends a suitable lady's maid?'

Chapter Seventeen

Amanda enjoyed driving in Hyde Park with James Oughton and had no hesitation in accepting a second invitation for the following day, once she was sure Miss Porter would not be neglected by her absence.

Over the tea that she was pouring for Lord Oughton and Amanda on their return from the park, she assured them that she was more than occupied. 'Providing Mrs Clare does not require me.' She had a wide circle of friends in town and had also promised herself visits to a number of libraries, so was perfectly happy to be left to her own devices, especially—although naturally she did not express the thought—if it allowed Amanda more time to spend with her pleasant new friend.

She was convinced, whatever Amanda might say, that Lord Oughton was courting her, and thoroughly approved. She admitted to herself that she had quite lost her own heart to Jay's dangerous charm, and knew it would take Amanda a long time to recover, but Lord Oughton struck her as a decent and a patient man and not someone who would be rebuffed by a first refusal.

Amanda therefore found herself collected at half past two the next afternoon. James Oughton helped her up into his curricle and began to guide his team of striking Welsh bays through the narrow streets towards the park. 'Will you forgive Hyde Park for a second time, Mrs Clare? I had promised my mother that I would pass on her invitation to take tea with her this afternoon, and if we go any further afield that would cut down on our time driving.'

'How kind of Lady Oughton, I would be delighted to take tea with her, and of course I do not mind Hyde Park. It is very lovely at this time of year, is it not?' Whatever Jane said, Amanda had no stirring of doubt over whether Lord Oughton was courting her. There was nothing in the slightest bit lover-like in his demeanour, he simply appeared to enjoy her company. Or perhaps he was simply taking the opportunity to introduce a new face to his mother, at a time when London was thin of society. She resolved to stay alert, though, for she had no wish to trifle with his affections.

Once within the park boundaries, he offered her the reins. 'I gather you had driven yourself to Holkham in very dashing style, Mrs Clare. Would you care to try my bays?'

'I would be delighted!' she replied with real pleasure. 'I have been admiring them almost to the point of jealousy. But are you sure? You have no idea of my skill and I might jab their mouths for all you know.'

'I have every confidence,' he said with a smile, handing her the reins, and then, once she had arranged them in her gloved hands, the whip. He sat back as she gathered the team confidently, letting them feel the bits and then giving them enough rein to trot out along the tan carriageway. 'Severn told me you were a notable whip and I see he was correct.'

Her start of surprise must have communicated itself to the horses, for the leaders tossed their heads and she had to give them all her attention. 'Really?' she asked with a light laugh after a moment. 'Do tell me what he said.'

'He said that he had never seen such a combination of courage and light hands, and he wished he might see you with a team instead of just a pair.' Amanda blinked back a tear of sheer pleasure. That was a compliment indeed, and she could just hear the warmth in Jay's voice as he said it. Lord Oughton added, 'He is about to have his wish fulfilled.'

It was all Amanda could do to keep her hands steady on the reins, for Jay was indeed riding towards them at a controlled canter, the hunter he had bought from Will Bream showing every sign of disapproving of this restraint.

He reined in by the side of the track and Amanda felt she could do nothing else but pull up as well as the team came alongside. The day before yesterday she had been too conscious of Miss Poste's sharp eyes to do more than throw the most indifferent and fleeting of glances towards Jay. Now, with every excuse to keep a sharp eye on the horse and rider so closely to her team, she reflected once again what a very striking figure he cut on horseback. His riding attire showed no exaggeration of cut; in fact, it was elegantly simple, but it showed off his long, well-muscled legs and the width of his shoulders to perfection and Amanda had to take herself severely to task for the sudden stab of desire that shot through her. Fine behaviour for a respectable drive in the park!

'Good afternoon, Mrs Clare.' He removed his hat. 'Oughton.'

'Is that the beast you bought in Norfolk, Mansell?' Lord Oughton regarded it with some doubt. 'Very big, isn't it?'

'Too big for the Shires, possibly,' Jay admitted, cursing the animal softly under his breath as it sidled and fretted at having to stand. 'But it can jump a hedge bank from a standing start and will go all day. No manners yet, but that will come with work.'

'You observe that Lord Oughton has kindly allowed me to drive his team?' Amanda asked, for Jay appeared set on exchanging the merest commonplaces with her, if that, and she wanted so much to provoke him. 'I understand I owe this honour to you.'

'To me?' His eyes narrowed and he looked from one to the other.

'Well, Lord Oughton tells me you remarked kindly upon my driving skill, so he feels able to risk his team with me.'

'No risk at all,' retorted his lordship cheerfully. 'I have never seen a lady better able to balance a team—and not many men either, come to that. You were quite right in your praise, Mansell.'

Amanda shot him a glance of glowing appreciation at the generous tribute, then caught Jay's eye. He looked furious. Suddenly she felt angry: what did he think she should do with herself? Take her bruised feelings and stay modestly in her Norfolk backwater, being grateful that she had attracted the attention of such a well-known rake? Or, having ventured out, go scuttling back again once she realised he was in town, just in case she embarrassed him by her presence?

'Are you jealous, my lord?' she enquired sweetly.

'Jealous?' The reaction was all she could have hoped for. His brows drew together sharply and the look he gave her would have sparked tinder. She felt her heart beat faster and a warm glow spread through her. This was a foolish and dangerous game, but to know she had the power to force a reaction from him still, even one of anger, was balm to her wounded feelings.

'Why, yes. Jealous that Lord Oughton should have the confidence to allow me to drive, when you did not have the courage to let me ride your new hunter.'

Unfortunately, for it seemed that she had finally provoked him to the point of incandescence, Lord Oughton broke in. 'Ride that animal? Why, I should think not, Mrs Clare! You might be a notable horsewoman, but that beast would be too much for you.'

'If you say so, my lord,' she responded meekly, then hated herself. She had no right to involve James Oughton in her conflict with Jay: why, she was behaving no better than Miss Poste. 'You are quite right,' she said with a laugh, 'and I am very wrong to tease both of you. That horse would cart me from one end of the park to the other—if it did not have me off its back in three seconds—and I know it quite well.'

This frank admission, however, did nothing but bring a glow of admiration to Lord Oughton's grey eyes, which caused her to blush, more at her own foolishness, than for any fluttering the look produced in her heart.

'When do you return to Norfolk?' Jay asked her abruptly.

'As I believe I said before, my lord, I am not certain.' There was no doubt about it, he wanted her gone, and she was not going to give him the satisfaction of meekly telling him her plans.

'Do you stay long in town?' Lord Oughton asked Jay. 'I wonder if there are enough of us to make up a party one evening.'

Jay was as curt as she had been. 'I expect to leave within the next few days.'

'And Miss Poste?' Amanda could not resist it, then was so flustered at having asked such a stupid question that she dropped the long whip, making the bays snort and back nervously.

'Are you all right, Mrs Clare?' Lord Oughton asked anxiously, earning her abiding gratitude for not taking the reins from her. 'Can you hold them while I jump down and get it?'

'Yes, of course, I am sorry to have been so clumsy.' She steadied the animals, but they had already moved on several paces and Lord Oughton had to walk back to pick up the whip.

Jay edged the big hunter closer to the box and said, low voiced, 'I suggest, Mrs Clare, that you stay away from Miss Poste.'

Amanda stared at him, too taken aback for a moment to reply. His eyes were hard and his mouth a thin line. Whatever had prompted such a remark? 'You *suggest* I stay away from her?' she asked in a puzzled voice, unable to quite comprehend such an abrupt order.

'Very well, ma'am, if that is not clear enough, I *insist* that you stay away from her.'

Then, as she was gathering breath to retort, he raised his voice and said, 'Good day to you. Good day, Oughton.' And was gone, turning the hunter off the track and cantering away into the trees.

Lord Oughton climbed back to his seat and handed her the whip. 'Where on earth has Lord Severn gone to in such a hurry?' he enquired. It was obvious that the hissed exchange had gone unheard.

'Insufferable man!' Amanda exclaimed, suddenly too angry to watch her tongue. She caught a glimpse of

Lord Oughton's face and hastily added, 'Lord Severn, I mean.'

'Well, it did seem an abrupt departure,' James Oughton began, then, seeing Amanda's stormy expression, added, 'But I can see it is more than that! Tell me, Mrs Clare, has Lord Severn done anything to distress you? I would not have it for the world, and you have only to say for me to take him to account.'

'Oh, my goodness, no! The merest irritation of the nerves on my part…you must excuse such an intemperate remark.' It seemed that she was doing nothing but stopping men stalking off to challenge others on her behalf—first Jay with Humphrey, now James Oughton looking darkly serious about how Jay had upset her. She could hardly tell him what had annoyed her so much, especially as it was quite inexplicable why Jay had spoken as he had.

Lord Oughton still looked concerned, so she added, 'It is merely something we cannot agree about and Lord Severn lays down the law about it somewhat.' She made herself laugh lightly. 'I cannot imagine why he takes such a dogmatic line over nothing.'

Even as the words left her lips, she realised exactly why Jay had wanted to stop her speaking to Diana Poste: he thought she would be indiscreet enough to let slip something which might disclose their…flirtation. She felt injured that he would so misjudge her tact. Surely he knew her better? Then she realised the full explanation, and a shock of hot embarrassment seemed to surge right through her. He thought she would *deliberately* say something! He thought that because he had left her so abruptly and with hardly any explanation she would behave like a scorned woman and spitefully meddle to turn the girl he wanted to marry away from him!

The thought was so embarrassing that she almost let go of the reins and had to exercise every bit of self-control to continue driving steadily. Surely she must be blushing scarlet? She felt as though she had been dipped in hot water from head to toe. The thought that anyone at all, let alone Jay, should glimpse her broken heart and could think that she would behave in such a way as a result was deeply shaming.

Amanda doubted she would feel worse if she was driving along with a placard on the carriage telling the world that she had been foolish enough to fall for a rake, to almost succumb to his lovemaking—and was now behaving like an embittered gossip as a result.

The carriage reached the end of the driveway and she asked, 'Which way, my lord? Or would you like to take the reins again? The traffic is rather heavy here.' It was incredible how calm her voice sounded, how steady her hands were, as she handed the reins and whip to him and sat back while he turned the team neatly out of the gate by the Tyburn turnpike and began to drive down Oxford Street.

'Is Lady Oughton accompanied by any of your family?' she asked. It would not do to sit like a dummy beside him.

'My sister Elizabeth—Lizzie to the family—is with her. She is just seventeen and Mama intends for her to make her come-out next Season. She is taking her about a good deal to give her a little confidence before she is officially out.'

'How very wise,' Amanda remarked. 'I wish I had had the opportunity to find my feet a little before my first Season! One feels such a green goose: one minute half in the schoolroom, the next with one's hair up and skirts down, expected to behave like a young lady of fashion.'

'And all the gentlemen surveying this year's débutantes through their quizzing glasses?' James Oughton said teasingly.

'Oh, the gentlemen were no problem at all,' Amanda smiled, thinking back. 'It was all the mamas, and the dowagers and the matchmakers. They look and criticise and demolish any poor girl they take a dislike to: one can be quite crushed by their unkindness. In fact, I had nothing to compare it to until I began to go to market and watched the farmers leaning on the sale ring fence, criticising the unfortunate beasts up for auction.'

This made Lord Oughton laugh so much he was still chuckling when they turned into Holles Street and then into Cavendish Square. They drew up in front of one of the impressive corner houses and the door opened even before he could jump down.

Amanda, ushered in by an imposing butler and two footmen, reflected that, despite his easy-going demeanour, Lord Oughton kept a very fine establishment indeed. 'Mama insists on bringing Hodgkins and a good two-thirds of the country staff up to town with her. It sets up the back of the steward here, and half the footmen have nothing to do, but there's no arguing with her.'

This disclosure did nothing to make Amanda feel any easier: by the sound of it, the Dowager Lady Oughton was going to prove every bit as formidable as the matrons who had turned her knees to jelly at her come-out.

Lord Oughton ushered her up the stairs and threw open the door into what was obviously the principle salon to be greeted with a shriek, a cry of pain and a fleeting glimpse of what appeared to Amanda's startled gaze to be a large, highly coloured feather duster.

'Peters, for heavens sake stop leaping around like the village idiot and seize the thing!' an imperious feminine voice demanded.

'It's bitten me, my lady!' The anguished cry came from a very young footman who was shaking his bleeding right hand and ducking as a large blue and scarlet parrot flapped around the room.

Lord Oughton hastily shut the door behind them and the scene of chaos resolved into two footmen, a young lady helpless with laughter on a sofa and a small, but elegant, grey-headed lady who was attempting to organise her deeply reluctant staff into catching the bird.

Amanda instinctively put out a hand to catch James's arm and the parrot landed on her forearm with a painful thump. There was silence and a sudden stillness as everyone observed the bird. It sidled up Amanda's arm, not hesitating to dig in its claws at every step, eyeing her sideways with an expression of sly calculation as it went.

'Pretty Polly,' she ventured, receiving a black look of contempt for her pains.

'Be damned to the French!' it announced loudly and settled on her shoulder. Amanda felt a twinge of alarm for both her ear and her bonnet trimmings.

'I am so sorry, my dear,' the lady declared. 'You must be Mrs Clare—what an introduction to our house! Lizzie, get up off the sofa and see if you can persuade Nelson to come down off Mrs Clare's shoulder before he eats her ribbons. Peters, wrap my handkerchief around your finger and go straight down to Mrs Doughty and have it bandaged. Watkins, if you will pick up the perch…'

Lizzie coaxed, Amanda stood very still, the second footman advanced stealthily with the perch and, with the air of a bird who had no intention of doing anything but behave in the most obliging manner, Nelson sidled on to it and permitted a chain to be clipped to his leg ring. 'Keelhaul the bastards!' it announced, causing the younger ladies to cover their ears and Lady Oughton to declare.

'Take him straight down to the scullery, Watkins, with my apologies to Mrs Doughty. The Admiral will just have to take him back, I do not care what he says about the inconvenience.' She turned to Amanda with an impish smile, which took thirty years off her age. 'He belongs to my brother, Admiral Fitch, who begged me to take him while he is in the West Indies. He is home now, and the wretched bird can go back to him directly.' She gestured towards the girl who had conquered her giggles and was now waiting to be introduced. 'My daughter Elizabeth. Do, please, sit down, Mrs Clare. I will ring for tea and we can all relax after that imbroglio.'

Amanda liked the Oughton ladies at once. They were charmingly informal, made her instantly at home, and managed to make her feel as though she had known them for years. The ludicrous incident with the parrot quite banished the encounter with Jay in the park from her mind and, with the ice broken so thoroughly, Amanda was relaxed and, had she known it, at her most endearing.

Lady Oughton shot a grateful glance at her son. He had suggested that she might like to meet Mrs Clare, knowing that she was finding London short of company and that she was disappointed with part of her plans for their stay in Brighton. She had discriminating tastes in her confidantes, but if she was going to take a liking to someone it was almost always at first sight.

With the apparent impetuosity that characterised her, she asked, 'Do you intend to remove to Brighton this summer, Mrs Clare?'

'Why, no, ma'am, I had not thought of it. In fact,' Amanda confessed, 'I have never been. Living beside the sea as I do, I suppose it does not occur to me to travel to another coast for relaxation.'

Lady Oughton laughed. 'But, my dear, delightful as I am sure it is, the north Norfolk coast is hardly Brighton!'

The words chimed strangely in Amanda's head and she seemed to hear an echo of her own voice saying, 'This is hardly Brighton!' *Déjà vu*, it had to be. 'Why, no, ma'am, I am sure it is not. I had merely planned to come up to town to engage a new lady's maid, which I have done, and to have a new habit tailored. When that is ready, in a day or so, I suppose I will return to Norfolk.'

'But you have no pressing commitments at home?' her ladyship persisted.

The vision of Cousin Humphrey filled her mind unpleasantly. 'No, I confess I have not.'

'Then why not remove to Brighton? It is charming at this time of year.'

'Yes, do come,' Elizabeth chimed in eagerly. 'We are going at the end of the week, Mama has secured such a charming villa.'

'It is very tempting,' Amanda agreed. 'But I am sure that such accommodation must be engaged well in advance of the summer and I would not care to stay in an hotel.'

'Indeed, normally all the best places have long been

booked, but by a happy chance I have the option upon
two properties. I thought my sister and her younger children were going to join us and I took a smaller villa
next to ours for them. The children have now got mea-
sles, of all the maddening things—'

'Chicken pox, Mama,' Lizzie corrected.

'Maddening,' Lady Oughton persisted, 'and I was
about to write to the agent to cancel it. But you can
take it instead.' She smiled round the room triumphantly. 'There, is that not a good idea?'

'Splendid, Mama,' her son agreed, looking enquir-
ingly at Amanda. 'But Mrs Clare must be feeling quite
breathless at such a sudden suggestion. And perhaps we
have put her off with our lunatic parrot!'

'Why…' Amanda looked at the three friendly, pleasant faces and thought of parties and dances and a fashionable promenade. 'Why, I would be delighted! So
long, that is, as my companion Miss Porter does not
object.'

'Then that is settled.' Lady Oughton clapped her
hands in delight. 'Lizzie dear, ring the bell and have
the particulars fetched, for Mrs Clare must approve
them before she commits herself.'

'Oh, I am sure that if they were your selection they
will delightful,' Amanda demurred. Yes, she and Jane
would have a holiday, far from Norfolk, far from London. And if Jared Mansell, Lord Severn, thought that
he could send her packing off home with one arrogant
word, then he had better think again. She looked around
the room again, her eyes sparkling with a delight tinged
with anger. 'I am sure I must replenish my wardrobe. I
do hope you can advise me on what will be suitable,
Lady Oughton.'

'We will go shopping!' Lizzie crowed, her delight
overriding her brother's faint protest and earned a smile
from her new friend.

Chapter Eighteen

The ladies did indeed go shopping. Even Miss Porter, intrigued by the novelty of a seaside holiday, purchased three new gowns and a smart new parasol. Her luggage was also weighed down by the addition of the latest guidebook to the resort, which she had been persuaded to pack rather than to put in her reticule to con upon the journey.

'I am afraid we will seem very provincial, never having been to Brighton before,' she confessed, as their carriage rattled over the cobbles, heading south. 'I should be reading the guide in advance.'

'Nonsense,' said Amanda bracingly. 'Lady Oughton will tell us how to go on, never fear.'

Jane cheered up at this. She thoroughly approved of Amanda's new acquaintances, although at first she had been amazed at the speed with which they had taken up the young widow. But having met them, and seen Lady Oughton for herself and even heard the story of the parrot, her mind was set at rest. She was still curious about Lord Oughton: Amanda was adamant that he was not courting her, and there was nothing of the lover in his open, friendly manner, but Jane tried a little fishing as the hired chaise left the outskirts of town.

'I must say I like the Oughtons very much,' she remarked. 'Lady Oughton is quite an original, is she not? Few ladies would take such an instant liking as she did to you, and then manage to whisk their new friend off on a holiday at such speed.'

'Yes, as you say, an original,' Amanda agreed, laughing. 'And Miss Elizabeth is a charming girl.' Her face clouded slightly. 'Very unlike the beautiful Miss Poste I told you about. Lizzie is so unaffected and enthusiastic.'

'And Lord Oughton,' Miss Porter persisted. 'Very attentive, is he not?'

'I agree, a very good son, and yet not at all tied to his mama's apron strings,' was all Amanda could be led to remark upon.

Oh, well, Miss Porter thought, as the chaise rattled over the cobbles. *Time will tell. She fell for Lord Severn too hard and too fast, perhaps if this young man is interested he will have the sense to court her more steadily.*

The journey down passed uneventfully, although the impressive train of vehicles, consisting of Lady Oughton's travelling coach, Amanda's chaise, the two carriages with luggage and servants, Lord Oughton's curricle, the groom driving his phaeton and the second groom leading two riding horses, caused not a little comment in the villages they passed through.

'I feel as if we are a travelling circus,' Amanda giggled at one point as they descended at an inn to change horses and take refreshments. The ostlers were too busy to stare, but several yokels paused to gawp and the maids hung out of the upper windows to assess the arrivals' fashions and carriages.

'Well, we are not the only cavalcade of such a size,' Jane pointed out as another party clattered past, obviously heading for a change at an inn further along the street. 'They should be used to it on this road.'

'What…?' Amanda shook her head. No, the glimpse through the inn yard arch of carriages and horses in a cloud of dust was too indistinct. There must be any number of large, raw-boned bay hunters on the roads. She was imagining things again. Ever since that encounter in Hyde Park she had been seeing Jay wherever she went—and always finding her eyes, or imagination, were playing her false. She firmly stamped down the humiliating memories of that brief exchange and concentrated on what Lady Oughton was calling as she descended from her carriage.

'My dear, I swear I have been jolted half out of my senses! Never mind, let us see what refreshment we can find within.'

The two villas on Marine Street were every bit as delightful as Lady Oughton's agent had promised. Amanda and Jane, accompanied by both Maria and Susan Wilkes, could find nothing at all to criticise in a pretty house of three stories with a parlour overlooking the bustling street and with tantalising glimpses of the sea, four small but elegant bedrooms to choose from and a resident cook-housekeeper whose first dinner boded well for the remainder of their stay.

The only fly in the ointment of their holiday was Susan. Almost vibrating with nerves, she was trying too hard to be the perfect lady's maid and Amanda found herself spending more time reassuring her than she had expected to spend instructing her.

The next morning Susan became hopelessly muddled and laid out a combination of riding habit, half-boots and a straw bonnet when requested to get ready Amanda's new promenade dress. When the mistakes were gently pointed out, she burst into tears and sobbed inconsolably, convinced she was about to be sent back to London in disgrace.

Amanda was consequently somewhat late in setting out for her walk, perforce accompanied by Maria. Miss Porter had pushed her firmly out of the house saying, 'Get out in the sunshine, dearest, I will calm Susan down.'

Calling first next door to enquire if either of the Oughton ladies wished to accompany her, or had any commissions for her, Amanda was amused to discover that her idea of a late start to the day did not agree with theirs, especially on the morning after a long journey.

So she and Maria went off alone to explore. 'Where shall we go first?' she asked the maid.

'The Pavilion, please, ma'am,' Maria announced, eyes shining at the treat. 'They were telling me all about it last night in the servants' hall, like a fairy tale it is, they say.'

'Then that is where we will go. It will be as well to find it early on so we can take our bearings from it.'

Progress proved slow for there were many things to distract them, from a glimpse of bathing machines—'Ooh, ma'am, you wouldn't, would you? Doesn't seem decent somehow'—to the shop windows, including Donaldson's book shop, which seemed certain to meet with Miss Porter's approval.

Amanda was quietly pleased to see that her own new promenade gown of fawn twill with a trimming of ribbed silk ribbon in a darker shade, a bonnet to match with one small ostrich feather curling under the brim and a particularly frivolous parasol in deep pink were every bit as fashionable as any she saw on her walk. It was doubtless a lowering thought that one's spirits could be so much elevated by a new gown, but she refused to feel guilty about it.

The Pavilion took their breath away, although Amanda suspected that her feelings were not quite those of her maid. After standing speechless for a full minute Maria announced, 'It's even better than the circus!'

Amanda could admire the sheer enormity of the confection, the wild imagination behind it and even some of the details, but the entire building seemed so bizarre, sitting here in an English seaside resort, she could not take it seriously.

'It looks as though a magic carpet has set it down here, all the way from India,' she said at last, still not quite able to make up her mind about it.

'Look, ma'am,' Maria pointed. 'There is a gate and we could walk in the gardens.' Indeed, it did appear that the public might approach right up to the walls of the Pavilion, and there was nothing to prevent the vulgarly curious from peering in at the windows.

Amanda opened the gate and they began to stroll through the gardens, stopping every so often to marvel at some conceit of plasterwork, filigree or gilding. The plantings were quite thick in places and Amanda was walking around one large shrub, craning to make out the detail on a minaret, when she walked into a gentleman striding briskly in the opposite direction.

'I beg your pardon, ma'am.' Jay had lifted his hat

from his head before he recognised her, then the expression of concerned apology on his face turned to anger. 'Amanda! What the devil are you doing here?'

'Will you kindly mind your language, my lord?' she snapped in return, glancing round for Maria. The wretched girl was nowhere to be seen.

Jay made no attempt to acknowledge her reproof. 'Are you following me?'

'*Following you?*' Amanda gasped. Of all the arrogant, impertinent... She searched frantically for an adequate response. 'I would not follow you, my lord, if you had the last loaf of bread on this earth!'

Jay flushed angrily. He was rather too close for comfort and Amanda stepped back, away from the cold green eyes, to find she had backed herself into a holly bush. 'Ouch!' An equally hasty step forward and she was close enough, should she be so foolish, to touch him.

'Then what are you doing in Brighton, might I ask?' He sounded not just irritated with her, but downright furious, and Amanda could only assume that finding her here had only added to his assumption that she was an angry, jealous woman pursuing her former lover, intent in placing a spoke in the wheel of his new courtship.

'I can see no reason why I need explain myself to you, Lord Severn, but as *I* have no need for secrecy, I am doing what hundreds of other people are doing and spending a few days at the seaside.' She was pleased with the cool indifference of her tone .

'Are you telling me that you secured lodgings at this short notice? You had no intention of coming here a few days ago.' He had been holding his tan gloves in one hand and Amanda was pleased to see that he was now wringing them tight in both fists. She was certainly succeeding in provoking him, and for some reason that was producing a fizzing feeling of exhilaration in her.

'I can see no reason why I should have shared my plans with you,' she observed, twirling her parasol nonchalantly. 'However, although at first I had no intention of coming down here, Lady Oughton suggested it and was able to put me in the way of a very eligible lodging next to hers.'

'Lady Oughton?' His brows drew together darkly. 'She is very busy about her son's affairs.'

'I have no notion what you mean by that remark, but it would become you to speak with more respect of the mother of a close friend.' Amanda had a sinking feeling she knew exactly what Jay meant and that he had concluded that James Oughton was paying court to her. She did not want to be the source of friction between the two men, even less did she want to give Lord Oughton the wrong impression of her feelings, but the discovery that Jay was jealous was intoxicating.

That feeling lasted for only a few seconds. Jay ignored her last remark and said, 'I trust you remember what I said to you on the subject of Miss Poste?'

Of course: Diana Poste. He might indeed be jealous, but only because he expected her to be pining for him, not because he wanted her rather than Miss Poste. Insufferable, arrogant man! Amanda regarded him with lips compressed, searching for something sufficiently cutting to say. Insufferable, arrogant…exciting…The man who had saved her on the stagecoach, rescued her from Cousin Humphrey, the man who could ride like the devil and make love like…

'I remember your impertinent orders, my lord. I assume from you having the ill grace to repeat them that Miss Poste is in Brighton. Let me make myself clear: I had no intention of obeying you then, and I have none now.' With her chin up, she confronted him. 'Now, if you will kindly step out of my way...'

He did not move. He stared down into her defiant eyes and said slowly, 'You are the most infuriating, aggravating, provoking, troublesome woman I have ever encountered, and if you were not such a little innocent...'

'I am not a little innocent!' Amanda protested, ridiculously affronted.

'No?' His voice was suddenly soft, but under it she could read a throb of anger, and something else.

'No!'

He took her in his arms with such suddenness that Amanda dropped her parasol, stepped back into the prickly shrub and then recoiled, only to find herself locked in the embrace. Jay's hands were hard on her arms and his mouth, when it captured hers, was equally unyielding. He had kissed her before with passion, he had kissed her teasingly, sleepily and formally, but he had never kissed her like this, in anger.

His mouth plundered hers despite her reaction, despite her attempts to bite and kick. She had never been so aware of his size and his strength and the sheer power of him. Unbidden, the memory of him walking naked out of the sea came into her mind and a wave of sheer desire came over her. It made her angrier, both at him and at herself, more determined to break free before she made any more shaming discoveries about her responses to him.

Jay let her go as abruptly as he had taken her. Amanda took a long, shuddering breath, raised her right hand and hit out. He parried the blow with insulting ease on the flat of his palm and they stood for a moment, frozen in a pose of arrested violence. Then Lord Severn turned on his heel and walked back the way he had come.

Amanda stood staring at the point where he disappeared from view, then shakily looked around. No one, thank goodness, was in sight although she could hear Maria calling, 'Mrs Clare, ma'am!'

What on earth did she look like? Amanda straightened her bonnet and dabbed her flushed face with her pocket handkerchief. Her mouth felt tender, swollen, and she pressed the back of her hand against it, shutting her eyes as she struggled with the memory of that furious kiss. Her feelings were too confused to allow her to think straight, and as to what had prompted Jay, she did not like to contemplate.

'Maria!' she called at last and was rewarded by the sight of her errant handmaiden, running around the side of the shrubbery.

'Oh, ma'am, I am that sorry…'

'Where have you been?' Amanda demanded angrily. 'All I ask is that you stay with me, and you vanish into the gardens—whatever might have happened to you, wandering about on your own?'

That was the pot calling the kettle black with a vengeance. Amanda felt a twinge of guilt, but the girl had been at fault and her mistress's irritation did at least provide an excuse for Amanda's flushed face and agitation.

'I'm sorry, ma'am, I only looked in a window for a moment, and you were gone.'

'Looked in a window! I am ashamed of you, Maria! This is a private house and regard for other people's privacy, let alone your respect for his Royal Highness, should have told you better.'

'Yes, ma'am.' She hung her head. 'Oh, your parasol, Mrs Clare!'

The beautiful pink parasol was indeed on the ground and covered in dust. It also, Amanda realised, snatching it up, bore the imprint of a large, masculine boot. Amanda flapped at it with her handkerchief and turned on her heel. 'We are going home directly,' she announced. 'Now, this time, do try to pay attention and stay close!'

To walk through the streets, thronged with fashionable visitors, with a flushed face, disarranged hair and a crushed and dirty parasol was salt in the wounds Amanda felt she had just received. She took a chance on remembering the map in Jane's guidebook and took Edward Street rather than hazard the crowds on Marine Parade. After one or two false turns they found themselves back at Marine Street and Amanda sent a chastened Maria off to the kitchens.

She walked slowly upstairs, untying her bonnet strings and trying to sort out just how she felt. It was surprisingly difficult to formulate a coherent thought. She met Jane on the landing and saw in her face confirmation of her dishevelled looks.

'My dear Amanda! Whatever is the matter?' Miss Porter hustled Amanda through her bedchamber door, took her bonnet and gloves and pressed her down into a chair. 'My love, you look positively distracted.'

Amanda looked back into her kind, anxious eyes and all her confusion and desire welled up inside her. 'I met Jay at the Pavilion, and he kissed me, and I hate him!'

And she burst into a storm of angry tears.

Miss Porter patted and clucked and produced clean handkerchiefs, *sal volatile* and sympathy until Amanda calmed down. She emerged from the depths of a handkerchief and remarked, with a brave attempt at a watery smile, 'I'm as bad as Kate.'

'What!' Miss Porter dropped the bottle of smelling salts. 'You are not—'

'No, no! Good heavens, Jane, of course I am not, er…with child.' She blew her nose firmly. 'All I meant was that I have just made as much of a noisy exhibition of myself as Kate did. I am amazed it has not fetched the servants up from the kitchens!'

'Shall I ring for a cup of tea?' Jane enquired anxiously. Taking Amanda's rather distracted nod for assent, she did so, intercepting Susan on the landing and telling her that Mrs Clare had a severe headache and she was to leave the tea tray on the landing table and not disturb her by knocking.

'You told her no untruth,' Amanda admitted ten minutes later as she wanly sipped at the tea. 'I feel as though my head is in a vice. What a perfectly horrible morning.'

'Can you tell me about it yet, dear?'

'Maria and I managed to become separated in the Pavilion gardens and I bumped—quite literally—into Lord Severn. He and Miss Poste must be staying here too. He was furious that I was here, angry to discover that Lord Oughton had had a hand in it and ordered me not to have anything to do with Miss Poste.'

Jane, who had been listening with rapt attention, had no difficulty in reaching the same conclusion that Amanda had. 'Why, that is outrageous!' she exclaimed. 'Does he think you would deliberately say something to that child out of spite?'

'I can think of no other explanation. Humiliating, is it not, to be thought of by the man you love as a jealous, spiteful woman?'

'You still love him? You said you hated him.'

'Love him…hate him…I do not know, Jane.' Amanda looked down at her clasped hands. 'He kissed me, Jane. He was so angry…it was a horrible experience, and yet…oh, Jane, I *wanted* him so much!'

Miss Porter turned a rosy shade of pink. 'Oh.' She thought a moment, then bravely asked, 'I do not know about this sort of thing, of course, but do you think it is because it is rather a long time since your poor husband died and you…that is…?'

'No, I do not.' Amanda considered her feelings as objectively as she could. 'I think I desire him because I love him. And I am well aware that no well-bred lady would express such a sentiment, but I am not going to start lying to myself, or to you. And, yes, I know what you are going to ask: why do I still love him when he is being so horrible?'

Miss Porter agreed that, yes, that was exactly what she was wondering.

'I have no idea Jane, unless that is how I know it truly *is* love.'

'And what will you do if you meet Miss Poste?'

'Be as pleasant as I can be to her. She might be a spoiled young beauty, but she is very young and it sounds as though she is in the middle of a tug of war between her father, Lord Severn and this man with the horrible reputation.'

'Lord Langham?'

'Yes. It must be a horrible position to be in, especially if her father really does favour Lord Langham's suit. The poor child needs all the friends she can muster.'

'But if by befriending her you assist her in marrying Lord Severn?' Jane ventured. 'What then?'

Amanda bit her lip. 'He is not going to marry me, that is for certain, so it will be better all round if he marries the girl he loves.'

Miss Porter reached over and took her hand. 'That is very noble, dear, but is it really what you want?'

Amanda gave a dry sob. 'No, of course it is not what I want, but I think it is what is right.'

Chapter Nineteen

After luncheon Amanda did her best to put on a brave face, but Lady Oughton, calling round to thank her for her earlier offer, took one look at her and declared that she should rest.

'You look worn to the bone, my dear Mrs Clare. The journey must have taken more out of you than you thought and going out so early this morning did not allow you the rest you needed. Lizzie is just the same—she bounced out of bed at seven of the clock and now is yawning her head off.'

Amanda agreed that, yes, she did not feel quite herself.

'I find the sea air often has that effect on new arrivals. After a day you will feel thoroughly invigorated, I promise. Now, I intend going and writing our names in the book at the Pavilion—not that I expect any receptions there just at the moment, but we must not neglect any attention due to his Royal Highness—and also at the Assembly Rooms. The Master of Ceremonies will then be certain to inform us of all the dances and card parties at the Old Ship and the Castle inns…'

'Is there much regular entertainment, then?' Amanda

asked. She had never felt less like dancing, but this might be the place to begin her campaign to propel Miss Poste into Jay's arms.

'Indeed, yes. Nothing to compare with Almack's, as you would expect,' Lady Oughton said somewhat dismissively. 'But the refreshments are infinitely more acceptable—not that that would be difficult! The society varies a great deal, depending on who is in town, of course. One has to resign oneself to a more limited circle of acquaintance, but one doesn't regard that too much when one is away for a relatively short time.'

The next day the ladies spent in strolling around Brighton and window shopping. Lady Oughton dealt firmly with Miss Elizabeth's pleas to try sea bathing, but encouraged Amanda to try it. Amanda was equally firm in denying all desire to venture out into the waves, even from the sanctuary of a bathing machine under the supervision of one of the formidable bathing women.

'Look how public it is,' she protested, waving a hand towards the young gentlemen who were casually strolling along, pretending not to ogle the distant bathers.

'They cannot see anything.' Lizzie laughed, then stopped abruptly as her attention was drawn to a telescope, which could be seen protruding from an upper window on Marine Parade. 'Men are *beasts*!' she announced, just as her brother joined them.

'In that case, I shall turn on my heel and go straight back to our lodgings,' he said in a wounded tone. 'I had only sought you out in case I could assist with any parcels, but if my entire sex is repugnant to you…'

'Not you, James!' Lizzie lowered her voice. 'But all these men positively ogling the bathers. Is it not deplorable?'

'Deplorable,' he agreed solemnly, catching Amanda's eye. 'There is no justification for it, however attractive the ankle glimpsed might be.'

Amanda repressed a giggle and accepted his proffered arm, his mama and sister having announced that they wanted to sit upon one of the benches and admire the prospect for a while.

'Dear Lizzie,' he chuckled. 'She is very young, and still not at all up to snuff. I am afraid the wicked flirtations of the gentlemen she will soon be encountering will be a shock to her.'

'She is very charming, and I do not think she will have trouble dealing with rakes. One scandalised look from those innocent big eyes and they will retreat in disorder.'

'Speaking of rakes—' Lord Oughton waved a hand in greeting. '—here comes Severn.' He felt the involuntary stiffening of Amanda's arm and glanced down. 'Are you and he still at odds?'

'No, not in the slightest,' she managed to say.

Jay crossed the road in response to his friend's signal. Amanda scanned his face anxiously as he approached them. What would his mood be? She struggled to compose her face into an expression of amiable disinterest, which she felt was the most socially acceptable response in the situation, and was amazed to see that he appeared not only friendly, but positively pleased to see her. She felt her eyes narrow suspiciously and forced a smile.

'My lord.'

'A happy coincidence,' he remarked after greeting Lord Oughton. 'I was coming to call upon you, Mrs Clare.'

'Indeed?'

'I was going to invite you to drive with me on the Downs.'

'I am afraid I am engaged.'

'Not every day, surely, Mrs Clare?'

She kept her gaze firmly to the front as she walked slowly between James Oughton on one side and Jay on the other. All she could see of him was the flash of polished leather and the swing of the tassels on his Hessian boots at each step, but the warmth of his shoulder and arm, so close to hers, seemed to burn in a way that the touch of Lord Oughton's forearm under her hand did not.

'I thank you, my lord, but I do expect to be engaged every day.'

She expected him to show some anger at this snub, especially after his reaction to her defiance the day before, but when he replied she could hear the smile in his voice. 'And will you be attending dances while you are here?'

'I will be guided by Lady Oughton,' Amanda replied. 'I have no plans of my own.'

'Running scared, Amanda?' Jay enquired wickedly.

Her frosty, 'I *beg* your pardon?' coincided with Lord Oughton's 'What do you mean, Severn?'

'Merely that I wished to tease Mrs Clare for pretending to be a country mouse and not daring to venture out except under the guidance of Lady Oughton,' Jay answered placidly.

Wretched man! He appeared to have smoothed down his friend's hackles, for James Oughton laughed and enquired, 'Is your cousin Miss Poste in Brighton?'

'Yes, her father has taken a house along the Old Steyne. I believe they intend to make a long stay.' Jay's voice was perfectly indifferent and Amanda risked a glance at him. He was looking relaxed, tanned and fit and perfectly at harmony with all around him. Amanda longed to puncture what she was certain was a front.

'And is Lord Langham also in Brighton?' she asked. 'Miss Poste is engaged to be married to him, is she not? I have heard so much about him that I long to see this notorious rake for myself.'

'He has no need to take lodgings,' Jay said, with, she was interested to note, the first hint of reticence in his voice. 'His country seat is not far out of Brighton. I believe he stays at the Castle inn on occasion.' He met Amanda's gaze and there was a hint of a challenge in his. She smiled into his eyes, then swallowed at the sudden flash of fire in their green depths.

Being with him was painfully pleasurable, like eating a delicious sweetmeat when one had a bad tooth and having the pain lance through the delight when one least expected it.

'If you will not drive with me and cannot tell me where you may be found in the evening, I am at a loss, Mrs Clare.'

'Why is that, my lord? Oh, look, Lord Oughton, there is Lady Oughton and Miss Elizabeth, we should rejoin them.'

'Excuse me one moment, Mrs Clare.' Lord Oughton freed her arm and strode across the road to join his family. Amanda could see an earnest discussion was starting, with each of them apparently having a different view on where to go next.

Jay paused for a moment, then answered her question. 'I need to speak to you.'

'Is that necessary? A note of apology for your behaviour yesterday would be acceptable—in fact, more so than your presence.'

'You made me very angry, Amanda.' He took her arm and steered her slightly away from the passing pedestrians.

'And that is your excuse for…for *assaulting* me?'

'No, not an excuse.' He hesitated and for the first time Amanda guessed that he was genuinely uncertain how to proceed. No doubt it was difficult to tell a lady just how poorly you feared she would behave towards the new object of your affections, but she was certainly going to give him no help. 'I need to explain something to you.'

Amanda regarded him with eyes that sparkled with angry, unshed tears. If the Earl of Severn thought she was going accept his explanation, he was seriously mistaken. She had a sinking feeling that if she stayed close to him a moment longer she was going to cry, and that if he touched her she would humiliate herself by throwing herself into his arms and telling him she loved him whatever he did.

Help was at hand. Lady Oughton, her children behind her, swept out into the road with a sublime disregard for the traffic and bore down upon them. 'Lord Severn! How well you look. Is Brighton not charming at this time of year?'

The five of them lingered for a few moments together exchanging pleasantries. Amanda, distracted though she was, had a feeling that the dowager was well aware of the tension between herself and Jay.

Her parting shot filled Amanda with dread. 'It is Thursday today, is it not? Ah, yes, then tonight is the dance at the Ship. Will we see you there, Lord Severn?'

'I hope so,' he responded with a polite bow. 'Does all your party attend?'

'If Mrs Clare and Miss Porter are willing, then certainly we will all be there.'

In the face of this Amanda could do no more than reply that she would be delighted and had no doubt that dear Jane would be too.

Indeed Miss Porter was only too happy to display her new gown and indulge, as she put it, in a little 'raking'. 'We do not have many opportunities to dance at more than small gatherings,' she explained to Lady Oughton. 'Why, I cannot recall the last one. It is several weeks even since the dinner at the Hall, is it not, Mrs Clare?'

Amanda hoped that no one had noticed the blush that rose to her cheeks at the reminder. She had no idea how she would react if Jay asked her to dance this evening: her only consolation was that there was no moonlit garden, no classical temple, to be alone with him in. There would be no opportunity for either lovemaking or quarrelling in such a public place.

Almost defiantly she dressed in exactly the gown and jewels she had worn for the dinner at Glaven Hall. She did not know whether it was because she wished to rekindle the memory of that night in Jay's heart or because she wished to demonstrate to him that she did not care whether he remembered or not.

Lord Oughton collected the ladies and had secured chairs for them for the comparatively short distance to the Ship inn. 'Mama felt it would be better than all of you risking crushing your skirts in the carriage,' he explained as he marshalled his little flotilla of chairs and their bearers.

When he helped them out, he remarked to Amanda, 'I think you will be impressed by the ballroom here,' and indeed she was startled into admiration by the great classical chamber with its rows of columns and painted freeze.

'It is not at all what I expected in an inn,' she admitted. A rapid glance around had revealed some faces that were familiar to her, but there was no sign of Jay or of Diana Poste.

'Eighty feet long, I believe.' James Oughton sounded somewhat distracted. Amanda realised that the Oughton ladies had disappeared into the throng. 'Mrs Clare, could I beg the indulgence of a few words alone?'

'Why, yes,' Amanda agreed, her heart sinking. Had she been wrong and Jane right and he was about to make her a declaration?

He drew her aside into a curtained alcove and said, 'I hope you will forgive me if this is an impertinent question, but I feel you are under my protection at the moment.'

Not a proposal of marriage, she thought with relief. But what on earth was he about to ask? 'Please, ask whatever you wish my lord.'

'It is simply that I fear there is something very amiss between you and Lord Severn, and if he is causing you any distress, you have only to say the word and I will speak to him.'

Amanda stared at him, too taken aback by this very frank query to produce an instant, light response to dismiss it.

'I see there is something,' he said slowly, a frown marring his normally amiable expression.

'Yes…but there is nothing you can do or say. And please do not think that Jay…that Lord Severn is in any way making, er…unwelcome advances or anything of that sort. We have disagreed about something and I am too stubborn, and he is too autocratic, to settle our quarrel easily.'

If Lord Oughton picked up her slip over Jay's name, he said nothing of it. 'Very well, but do tell me if there is any way in which I can assist you.'

'I will, and thank you,' Amanda replied with genuine warmth. 'I think I had better return to the ballroom or Lady Oughton will be wondering what has become of me.'

'Yes, I will follow in a moment.' Lord Oughton took her hand and kissed her fingertips. Amanda could not help remembering Jay's lips on her hand, his thumb tracing erotic havoc in her palm.

She parted the curtains and left him, stepping rather blindly out into the bright lights of ballroom. The place was becoming thronged and it took her a few moments to make her way more than a few steps forward. Glancing around, her eyes met Jay's across the dance floor and she saw his eyes narrow suddenly. His gaze was focused over her shoulder and she realised that Lord Oughton had emerged from the curtains behind her.

Unable to cope with facing either of them, Amanda began to weave her way through the throng. At length she emerged towards the back of the ballroom into a slightly quieter area and saw Miss Poste standing with her companion Miss Woodley and chatting to two other young ladies. She saw Amanda and her remarkable blue eyes widened, but she did not seem unfriendly and Amanda walked towards her, a smile firmly on her lips.

The other girls faded away at the sight of an unknown matron and Miss Woodley effaced herself, leaving Amanda and Diana Poste effectively alone amid the crowded room.

'Good evening, Mrs Clare.' As befitted a much younger woman she curtsied neatly.

'You remembered me, then,' Amanda said pleasantly. 'I was not sure that you would.'

There was none of the sharp, watchful expression on the girl's face this time and she murmured. 'You were very kind when we met, ma'am. I am afraid I was not polite.'

'It is not always easy when one is just out to always strike the right tone,' Amanda said conciliatingly, wondering if she had misjudged the child. It had been a frank apology. She tried to respond in kind. 'And perhaps one's elders can seem just a little patronising?'

Diana flashed her a grateful look, then bit her lip. 'Might I...might I confide in you, Mrs Clare?'

'Why, of course, anything which it is proper for you to discuss with a stranger.' Amanda was taken quite aback by this sudden question. It was what she had been hoping for, but the speed of the girl's approach startled her. 'After all, you have your companion...'

'She has not been married.' Diana cast down her eyes and blushed, managing to look, if anything, even prettier.

'Oh.' Amanda stepped back into a embrasure with an unoccupied sofa. 'Well, you may ask me what you wish, but I cannot promise that I will answer everything!'

'Thank you, ma'am.' Diana clasped her hands in her lap and burst out, 'Should I be guided absolutely by what Papa wishes?'

'You mean in marriage? Well, you should listen most carefully to his advice; after all, he will be trying to do his best for your future.'

'He wants me to marry Lord Langham,' Diana whispered. 'He is much older than I am.'

'I do not know his lordship,' Amanda temporised, wondering if she really should pursue this conversation.

'He is over there. See.' Diana made a little gesture. 'The tall, slender man talking to the lady in the puce toque.'

One look at Lord Langham and Amanda felt she could not, under any circumstances, do anything but oppose such a match. His lordship was certainly an elegant figure, but his face was alive with a hard, wicked, satirical intelligence and a lifetime of experience and dissipation seemed to speak from every feature.

'He is much older than you,' Amanda said, shaken. *I would not like to find myself alone with him*, she thought and an involuntary shiver ran through her.

'He is forty-five, I think,' Diana confessed. 'I am a little afraid of him.' She flushed delicately.

'I am not surprised,' said Amanda, nailing her colours to the mast. 'I do not think you should marry him at all!'

'Oh.' Diana gave a little breathy sob. 'You see, there is someone else.' She was obviously overwrought, for her voice quivered with what Amanda could have sworn, under other circumstances, was laughter.

'Who?' she prompted gently, patting the girl's hand. It tensed under hers, curling into a little claw, then relaxed. Poor child, she thought, forgetting her own pain, she is a mass of nerves.

'The Earl of Severn,' Diana whispered. 'You know him, of course. He is a distant cousin of mine.'

'You love him?' *You see*, her inner voice told Amanda, *it is perfectly possible to do the right thing.*

She loves him, he loves her. What does your breaking heart matter?

'Yes.' Diana buried her face in a lace handkerchief, her shoulders shaking.

'Try not to cry, dear, you might be observed,' Amanda said gently, wishing she could burst into sobs herself.

'Of course.' The perfect little face emerged from the lace, not a tear in sight. 'I must control myself, I know. Do you think there is any hope for me?'

'You must explain to your papa, Miss Poste. Surely he would consider a match with an Earl more than eligible?'

'Under normal circumstances, yes.' Miss Poste lowered her voice and added, 'But I think Lord Langham has a *hold* on Papa. And darling Jared has done something to annoy him, so Papa will not listen to him. They had the most awful row only the other week.'

Darling Jared… 'You must be strong,' Amanda counselled, wishing she could follow her own advice. 'Explain to your papa respectfully, but firmly. He can hardly force you to the altar.'

'If only I knew where my duty lay.'

Really, Amanda thought, *she has been reading too many novels!*

'I cannot believe that any young lady's duty lies in sacrificing herself to a hardened rake,' she was saying tartly when Miss Poste's lips parted in a little sigh, showing two rows of perfect white teeth.

'Oh, here he is!'

Amanda looked up, bracing herself for a confrontation with the sinister Lord Langham, only to find Jay approaching them, an expression of considerable displeasure on his face.

'Cousin Jared!'

The name rang uncomfortably in Amanda's ears. *He's not your Jared*, she longed to protest, *he is my Jay!*

'Diana, my dear, surely you should be with your companion and not talking to strangers? Mrs Clare, may I have the pleasure of this dance?'

Amanda swallowed. Beside her she could feel Diana, almost vibrating with emotion at this comprehensive snub. She wanted to say, *He is angry with me, not with you*, but that was impossible, so she stood up and said, 'Good evening, Miss Poste, it was delightful to meet you again. I am sorry, my lord, I do not dance this evening.'

She began to walk past him, but somehow Jay was standing in her way, quite uncaring that Diana was right beside them.

'Oh, I think that you do ma'am,' he said with a chilly calm and with a quick movement had encircled her waist, taken her right hand and whirled her into the waltz, which was just striking up.

Chapter Twenty

Amanda was forced by Jay's peremptory move to take several rapid steps to keep her balance and to scoop up her trailing skirts with her free hand. By that time they were on the floor and, short of wrenching herself free and storming off, she had no option but to dance with him.

'How dare you!' she hissed while keeping a fixed smile on her lips. Her fingers quivered against his palm, his other hand seemed to burn through the thin fabric at her waist.

'I told you, Amanda, do not talk to Diana Poste.' He was smiling too, a smile that did not reach his eyes.

'You have certainly snubbed the poor child comprehensively.'

'She needs to learn discretion,' Jay replied coldly. 'If it is not too late.'

'She may well attend to your instructions, but how do you intend to enforce your demands on me in the middle of the dance floor?' Amanda enquired sarcastically. 'You can hardly kiss me into silence here, can you?'

'Believe me, the temptation is considerable.' His

smile this time was genuine, but the quality of it made her shiver. 'On this occasion, my intention is simply to remove you from that end of the ballroom and to deliver you to your suitor and his family at the other.'

'He is...' Amanda choked back the words. She had no intention of telling Jay that she and James Oughton were friends and no more. He had forfeited all rights to ask her about anything in her private life. If he wanted to raise it with Lord Oughton, then let him see where that got him!

'So you do not deny it, then. You have done well to secure his regard, Amanda, he is a good man.'

'I am well aware of that,' she snapped, then hastily refixed her social smile.

'So we are in agreement on something,' Jay said, almost pacifically. 'Then why do you not relax and enjoy this dance?'

Everything she could think of to say was either spiteful, petty or exposed her broken heart. Amanda shut her lips and tried to do as Jay told her. They danced in rigid silence for a long minute, then the music claimed her and she let herself go with it, go with his lead. It was as though they had been made to dance together, she realised hazily. His long, fit body guided her without effort, without any compulsion. He appeared to have an innate sense of rhythm and balance, weaving her between the other dancers until she felt they were in a world of their own.

She was not aware that her eyes were closed, that her lips were parted in a tender, sensual smile. Across the dance floor James Oughton swore softly under his breath and his mother said, 'I thought that was how the land lay.' She shot her son a sharp glance. 'Had you any thought of...?'

'No. I think that if I allowed myself to, I would be very attached to Amanda Clare. But almost from the start I have sensed something between them.' He frowned, watching the circling couple. 'I wonder if I said something tactless at Holkham. I mentioned an attachment I thought Mansell had made, but I think now I was wrong.' He thought for a while longer. 'No, I could only make things worse if I try and interfere now. Those two have got their problems to resolve and I do not think that my well-intentioned meddling is going to help!'

'No,' Lady Oughton agreed thoughtfully. 'Best to leave well alone. They are two grown people, after all.'

The music ended with a flourish, depositing Amanda and Jay neatly in front of the Oughtons. Amanda reluctantly opened her eyes and met the somewhat quizzical gaze of Lady Oughton. She blushed and curtsied to Jay. 'Thank you, my lord.'

He bowed to her and the dowager and directed a somewhat ironical smile towards Lord Oughton, then walked away around the edge of the ballroom.

Amanda looked round to find that James had vanished and that the dowager was regarding her with a raised brow.

'Ma'am—' she began.

'What a good dancer the Earl is,' Lady Oughton remarked blandly. 'I understand you have known him for rather longer than you have been acquainted with James?'

She began to stroll along the room, exchanging nods and greetings with other matrons, and Amanda could do nothing but follow.

'Yes, ma'am. Lord Severn introduced us at Holkham.'

'Hmm. About time that young man settled down.'

'Er…which one, Lady Oughton?'

The dowager laughed. 'Why, both of them, my dear! Now, where has Lizzie got to? I am being a very lax chaperon.'

Amanda scanned the room, looking for the errant debutante. James she could see on the other side of the floor, dancing a country measure with an attractive red-head. She looked further along and saw a very dark head close to a striking blonde one and realised that Jay had made his way back to Diana Poste. Amanda knew she should not stare, but she could not help herself. They seemed deep in serious conversation: she could not see Jay's face, but Diana's was turned up to his, a look of earnest attention on her features. As Amanda watched she nodded and Jay took her arm and steered her back towards the chaperons.

Some instinct made Amanda look in the other direction and there was Lord Langham watching them, his face very still. As if he felt her gaze on him, his eyes turned and met Amanda's. Even across the room she could see them widen in a look of blatant appraisal. She felt as though he had stripped off her dress and she hastily turned her head and hurried after Lady Oughton. Ugh! Awful man! The thought of him touching that pretty child…

Lady Oughton had found her daughter, who was sitting on a sofa beside Miss Porter, sniffing miserably at a vinaigrette.

'Oh, Lady Oughton!' Jane got to her feet and drew the dowager and Amanda closer to the seat. 'Poor Miss Oughton has the most afflicting migraine. I was about to seek you out: I really feel she should go home at once and rest.'

'Indeed she must! I must thank you for looking after her, Miss Porter. Excitement sometimes has this effect. There, there, Lizzie dear, we will soon be home.'

With a word, Amanda slipped away to find James Oughton. Luckily his dance partner's red head was visible amidst the throng and Amanda caught him as he escorted her off the dance floor. 'My lord, please excuse me, but your sister is feeling unwell and your mama thinks she should be taken home at once.'

Lord Oughton soon returned with the news that chairs had been called. As his mother and Miss Porter shepherded the wan figure of Lizzie towards the door, he stopped and took Amanda's hand. 'There is no need for you and Miss Porter to spoil your evening. Why do you not remain and I will return to escort you home later?'

'I would not dream of it,' Amanda protested. 'To stay here while poor Miss Elizabeth is feeling so unwell! No, we will return with you in case there is anything we can do to assist your mother.'

'You are very good,' he said warmly, raising her hand to his lips.

'Nonsense.' Amanda smiled back, then saw Jay watching her over James's shoulder. It seemed he had been walking towards them; now he turned on his heel and vanished into the card room.

Amanda left the Castle inn in a state of inner turmoil which she congratulated herself was not visible to her friends. However, she had underestimated Jane's powers of observation, although, as so often, Miss Porter favoured the oblique approach.

Back in their little villa she perched on the edge of Amanda's bed and remarked, 'I saw Lord Severn there this evening.'

'Really? So did I. In fact, we had one dance together.' Amanda unclasped her necklace and handed it to Susan. 'That is right, the blue box, with the earrings.'

'He was entering the card room,' Jane continued. 'Something had obviously annoyed him: his face was like thunder.'

'Indeed? Thank you, Susan, if you will just help me out of this gown and into my robe, you may go to bed. I will manage my own hair.'

She waited while Susan shut the door behind her and then began to sweep the brush through her loosened hair. 'I spoke for some time to Miss Poste and he was annoyed by that.'

Miss Porter got up and came to take the hair brush, smoothing the tangles at the back of Amanda's head. 'And what was your opinion of Miss Poste on closer acquaintance? Do you still think her spoilt?'

Amanda wrinkled her nose thoughtfully. 'I am not sure. She is very young, and at times her conversation was positively banal—almost too predictable. Which is odd, because I do not think her unintelligent. But she showed none of that sharp, unbecoming, edge I noticed in London. I think it may have been nerves and gaucheness.'

'And did she speak about Lord Severn?' Jane prompted.

'Oh, yes,' Amanda said with a short laugh. 'She informed me that she loved him, but that she thought she should do what her father wanted and marry Lord Langham.'

'That seems very strange,' Jane mused. 'Why should anyone prefer a middle-aged rake of the lesser nobility to an Earl for their daughter?'

'Diana maintains that Langham has a hold of some

kind on her father. I thought it melodramatic, but having seen the man I can believe he might well stoop to black-mail to get what he wants.'

'What is he like?' Jane put down the brush and sat down on the bed again. 'Come, get into bed and tell me all about it.'

'There is not much to tell,' Amanda admitted, snuff-ing out the dressing table candles and climbing into bed. She plumped up the pillows behind her and settled back. 'Are you warm enough, Jane? There is a rug on the chair. Diana tells me he is forty-five, and he certainly looks every one of his years. I did not speak to him, I am glad to say, but he struck me as…oh, reptilian.'

'It is you who are being melodramatic now, surely!' Jane hooked the rug off the chair, wrapped it around her shoulders and settled back against the post at the foot of the bed.

'Indeed I am not! The man gave me the shivers, even across the width of the dance floor. He caught my eye, Jane, and the look he gave me! Why, I felt besmirched.'

'Then it is easy to understand why Miss Poste prefers her cousin Severn. Surely she only has to tell her father so?'

'She appears to be torn between her duty to her papa, fear that he will make her marry Langham whatever she says, and adoration for Jay.'

'Have you seen them together?'

'Yes.' Amanda cocked her head on one side in thought. 'He snubbed her thoroughly for talking to me, but a while later I saw them together and he appears deeply concerned for her. I think the way he spoke to her was simply over-protectiveness and he does indeed care for her.'

'Then you are determined on this course of bringing them together?'

'I could not, in all conscience, do anything to obstruct it, that is for sure.' Amanda sighed. 'It is every bit as difficult as I thought it would be. It would be even worse if Lord Langham was not so dreadful: how can I not make a push to at least try and help her avoid his clutches?'

Miss Porter looked worried. 'You know, my dear, you have often owned to me that you are constitutionally inquisitive, managing and—'

'Interfering?' Amanda finished for her. 'Well, and so I am!'

'Yes, dear, and that is all very well about your own affairs and with our own people in Norfolk. But here you are meddling with the affairs of two prominent men. And one of them, by all accounts, is a very unsavoury character.'

'And the other is autocratic, insufferable, arrogant and determined to get his own way,' Amanda finished for her. 'I know that, and I have no hope at all that I am going to emerge from this without suffering, at the very least, some knocks to my self-esteem.'

Shaking her head at this obstinacy Jane folded the rug and made her way to her own bedchamber. Amanda, left alone in the darkness, drifted off to sleep, a sleep filled with the whirling images of the dance floor as she spun round and round in Jay's arms.

'I love you,' she murmured against the pillow and in her sleep tears rolled gently down her cheeks and soaked into the linen.

The next morning dawned bright and warm. Lady Oughton sent round a message asking if Jane and

Amanda would care to join her and Lizzie in a carriage expedition along the coast road.

It will blow away the remains of her migraine, she wrote, *and a change of pace from the hustle of the town will calm her. I am sure you will enjoy the scenery and I know of a charming inn where we may take luncheon in a private parlour. Dear James has to go back to town on a matter of business for two days, but we will take a footman with us.*

'That does sound tempting,' Jane remarked when Amanda passed her the note over breakfast. 'The scenery is so different from what we are used to, I would enjoy seeing more of it. What do you think, my love?'

'You go, Jane. I have so many letters I must write, and there is a very complicated one from my steward that I have been putting off wrestling with for three days! It seems hard to think about a dispute over drainage rights here, but I cannot leave it any longer.'

'You will not be writing letters all day, surely,' Jane protested. 'To miss out on such a lovely day as this seems a shame.'

'I will take a walk later,' Amanda promised. 'You go, or I will feel guilty.'

It was almost eleven when she sealed the letter to Mr Pococke and her head was spinning from studying his minute drawings of ditches and boundaries. In the end she had to agree with his proposed course of action and she was rather mutinously thinking that she need not have expended so much effort at all when a guilty pang reminded her that she had never spent so much time away from the estate before. There was something to be said about a subject as prosaic as drains, she mused, ringing for Susan, it most certainly took one's mind off other troubles.

'Susan, these letters are to go in the hall to be collected for the next post to London. Now, if you will fetch our bonnets and my parasol, we will go for a walk.'

The new maid hurried off, leaving Amanda reflecting how much she had improved with the short time they had spent in Brighton. She was still not exactly chatty, but she had calmed down and proved herself a very competent young woman once her nerves were under control.

They set off along Marine Parade, stopping at Royal Crescent to admire the fine new houses with their facing of black mathematical tiles, and the rather less impressive statue of the Prince Regent, which was already crumbling badly under the force of the sea winds and spray.

They had turned back and began to retrace their steps when Amanda saw a smart carriage with a crest on the door forced to halt on the other side of the road by a child chasing its hoop into the roadway. There was a flurry of activity with the panicking nursemaid, the crying child and the coachman expressing his views on 'Wimmin wot can't look after so much as one brat!'

The hubbub was cut short by a cold voice from the carriage enquiring whether the coachman intended to sit there all day?

Amanda, who had been watching the child with some concern, looked at the carriage properly for the first time. The speaker, a man, had obviously let down the window on the far side from her and was leaning out, but looking out of the near side window was Diana Poste.

She met Amanda's eyes and immediately her face became twisted into an expression of imploring despair. Her lips moved, soundless, but Amanda thought she had mouthed, 'Help me!'

The man sat back next to her and Amanda realised that the profile, sharp against the blue sky, was Lord Langham's. With the light bright on the carriage it was quite plain that there was no one else in it—no companion, no chaperon. The child and its hoop were removed from the road to the accompaniment of loud wails and the carriage moved off. Behind it, strapped on, was a pile of expensive luggage.

'Mrs Clare, ma'am?' Susan was at her side, obviously wondering why her mistress was standing stock still, staring at the vanishing carriage.

'One moment, Susan, I must think.' What could this mean? There was no respectable reason Amanda could imagine why a young lady should be alone, unchaperoned, in a closed carriage with a man who was not her father or her brother. Yet there was Miss Poste, obviously in distress, with the notorious libertine her father was attempting to force on her. And the pile of luggage gave the impression that this was not simply an imprudent drive, but a journey with a destination other than Brighton.

Try as she might, Amanda could come to no conclusion other than that Lord Langham, wearied by Diana's prevarication and Jay's interference, had simply snatched the girl, knowing that her father was likely to turn a blind eye and countenance a marriage after, rather than before, its consummation.

Blindly she began to walk again. Who could she ask for advice? Jane and Lady Oughton were gone for the day, James Oughton was away for two days. That only left Jay and she had no idea of his direction. She stopped again, making Susan hop sideways to avoid running into her.

'Who would know?' she said out loud.

'Ma'am?'

Of course! The Master of Ceremonies would have every visitor of the *ton* in his famous Book. She would have thought of it earlier if Lady Oughton had not undertaken the task of inscribing the names of her entire party herself. 'Come along, Susan, we must go to the Assembly Rooms at once!'

If the Master of Ceremonies, a portly and stately functionary, was surprised to be summoned from his offices to attend a breathless lady enquiring about one of the most eligible bachelors in town, he did not allow it to shown on his face.

'Please take a seat, Mrs Clare, ma'am, may I offer you refreshments?' Mr Yardley said, pulling out a chair. 'I do hope you are having a pleasant stay in Brighton. If there is anything, anything at all—'

'Indeed there is,' Amanda interrupted, as calmly as she could. 'I require Lord Severn's direction as I find I have something of his that he dropped when we were speaking yesterday and I have no idea how to return it.'

'Of course, ma'am. Or I can have a porter take it round for you now?'

'No, I thank you, I would welcome the walk. If you would just…'

With a maddeningly stately bow the Master of Ceremonies dipped his quill in the standish and wrote an address. 'There you are, ma'am. And I wish you good day.'

This was said to the tail of Amanda's skirts as she whisked out of the door and away. Mr Yardley raised an eyebrow. Over the years in his exalted position he had seen many a scandal, all of which were locked discreetly in his breast, not even to be shared with Mrs Yardley. This appeared to be yet another developing. How very interesting.

Susan, hurrying in the wake of her mistress, was equally intrigued. She had heard from her sister that the Quality were given to queer starts, and also that she must expect to observe many a flirtation and even illicit goings-on. Still, Mrs Clare had not seemed that sort of lady at all. It just went to show! Calling at a gentleman's lodgings, even with a maid in attendance, was fast indeed.

Amanda, with a hasty glance at the paper in her hand, was conning the numbers of the houses along St James Street, just off the Steyne. She found the one she wanted and hurried up the steps to rap the knocker.

The door was answered by a smartly liveried footman who managed to restrain his surprise at the sight of a lady on the doorstep. 'Madam?'

'Is Lord Severn in?' Amanda demanded.

'His lordship is not at home, ma'am.'

'Do you mean he is in but not receiving, or out?' Amanda demanded. 'This is a family matter of the utmost urgency.'

The footman bowed. 'I regret that his lordship is away, I believe for the rest of the day, ma'am. Would you care to leave a message?'

'Yes…no.' What on earth could she write? She needed to speak to Jay, and in any case, every minute's delay could be fatal to Diana's reputation and well being. 'Do you know where his lordship has gone?'

'His lordship has not confided that, ma'am.' The man

was obviously becoming embarrassed by her persistence.

'Thank you.' Defeated, Amanda turned and walked down the steps. What now? She had counted on finding Jay at home, which was foolishly optimistic, she now realised. She had felt absolute trust that he would cope with the situation, now she was on her own again.

Well, Amanda Clare, she chided herself, beginning to walk back to Marine Street. *You pride yourself on your common sense and practicality. Now deal with this yourself.*

Lord Langham had a house near Brighton, Jay had told her that, she recalled. That must be where he was taking Diana: surely any further with a reluctant girl would be out of the question.

She hurried through the door, calling for the landlady. 'Mrs Charles! Mrs Charles, are you at home?'

The landlady was and able at Amanda's request to name a convenient and reliable livery stables. She was also happy to send off her maid to engage a gig for Amanda's immediate use.

With a breathless Susan on her heels, Amanda swept into her bedchamber. 'My riding habit and gloves,' she ordered. 'Oh, and Susan, find me the *Peerage*.'

She opened the book on the dressing table and flicked through it. Here it was: Langham…principal seat Downsmore House near Steyning.

Susan helped her out of her promenade dress and into her habit. Amanda sat down while the maid unpinned her hair and dressed it more simply to go under her riding hat and veil. Suddenly she pulled open a drawer and fetched out notepaper and a quill. The standish was to hand as well and she began to write, her hand shaking slightly as she attempted to put the facts into the briefest and most coherent form.

But halfway down the note she stopped and read it through again. No, it was hopeless. What was the point of sending this to Jay's lodgings? By the time he returned it would be too late in any case. Amanda screwed up the note and tossed it aside.

'I can hear the gig, I think,' Susan announced, running to peer out of the window. 'Yes, here it is, ma'am. I will fetch my bonnet.'

Amanda nodded, then called, 'No, I will go alone, Susan.'

'But, ma'am, will you not then take a groom?'

'No…no. Susan, this is a matter of some delicacy. It may be that I will be returning with a young lady and in that case there will be no room for three of us. And I do not want a groom standing up behind—it is not as though we have any of our own people here who I can rely on absolutely. No, I will go alone, but I will be back before dinner time, never fear.'

The clock struck twelve. 'Ma'am, will you not take luncheon first?' Susan did not have the confidence, as Kate would have done, to argue further.

'No, no time.' Amanda ran down the steps and was helped up into the gig by the groom from the stables. The horse, she was relieved to see, looked a quality animal, fit to go to Steyning and back without any problem. She adjusted her veil, took the whip with a word of thanks and, urging the animal to a trot, took the road out of town.

Chapter Twenty-One

Amanda had conned the guidebooks often enough during her short stay in Brighton to know which road to take for Steyning and she made good time. Once closer to the town, however, she found she had to stop several times to ask the way to Downsmore House.

She received several knowing looks and one landlord, when she stopped at his inn to enquire the way, was almost insolent. The flash of angry eyes behind the veil made him alter his tone, but Amanda was heartily glad she would have no cause to revisit the area. Lord Langham's reputation was obviously widespread.

It was three o'clock, she estimated, by the time she turned the now somewhat weary horse into the carriage-way leading to Downsmore House. The gatekeeper agreed that yes, his lordship had arrived back that day, although whether he was receiving, he could not say.

Amanda, who had no intention of asking for his lordship, thanked the man and drove on, feeling uncomfortable. The unwisdom of calling alone on such a man was beginning to oppress her. Still, she was not going to turn back now.

A groom came out to hold her horse as she pulled

up by the front door, and led the gig away before she could protest that this was just a short visit. However, the butler who opened the door to her was an eminently respectable-looking upper servant and her confidence rose again.

'I understand that Miss Poste is staying here? I would appreciate the favour of a few words with her on a matter of urgency. Here is my card. There is no need to disturb his lordship.'

To her surprise the man opened the door wide without further ado and ushered her in. 'If you would wait here, ma'am.' He showed her into a small retiring room and closed the door. He was back in a few minutes. 'Miss Poste asks if you would attend her in her chamber, madam.'

Amanda followed him up the long sweep of double staircase, which rose on either side of the hallway. The whole house seemed dark and hushed as though holding its breath. She shook herself for being so fanciful and was led down a corridor to a panelled door. The butler knocked, opened it, announced 'Mrs Clare, Miss Poste,' and went out, leaving her in a big, shadowy room.

The furniture seemed to loom over the figure of Diana Poste who stood up as Amanda came in. She was smiling, but Amanda stopped dead as she registered the expression. This was not a smile of relief, but one of malicious triumph.

'Why, this is famous!' The girl laughed, clapping her hands. 'I was sure you would fall for it, although Robert said no one would take meddling so far as to *follow* us.'

'Miss Poste, Diana…I gather that you are not here against your will and that you are congratulating yourself on having played a trick on me, which I must tell you is both cruel and foolish.' Diana merely pouted at the reproof. Amanda choked down her rising anger and persisted. 'But however ill judged your sense of humour, I beg you to consider your position. You told me you were in love with Lord Severn...'

'Well, I am not, although it was fun to tease you. He only cares because of my mother. I am tired of his lectures. I want to marry Robert.'

'Are you certain?' Amanda demanded anxiously. 'There is still time to go back, you know, you can come with me. Do consider, leaving aside his reputation, you are so very young to be thinking of marriage to a man of his age.' Getting no response, she struggled to find other arguments.

'You cannot have considered. He may be very indulgent now, but there are other things in marriage, things you are too innocent to know about yet. You will find that intimacy with someone of his sophistication, his age—'

She broke off in confusion at Diana's peal of laughter. 'But I know all about that,' she scoffed. 'Robert is a wonderful lover.' The knowing caress in her voice left Amanda in absolutely no doubt that the girl was not referring to flirtation.

'You mean that you and he...that already...'

'Oh, yes.' Diana's smile made Amanda go cold all over. 'A *wonderful* lover,' she repeated.

Amanda tried one last desperate throw. 'But in a few years,' she stammered, 'he is so much older than you...'

'He does not mind sharing me with his friends,' Diana said, running the tip of her tongue around her lips. 'Some of them are quite young enough. And so many of them...' She broke off, laughing at the sight of Amanda's horrified face. 'Oh, yes, Mrs Prim and Proper. *Orgies*. Just like all the tittle-tattle says.'

There was the sound of carriage wheels on the drive below. Diana flitted across to look out of the window. 'The first guests are arriving now. Soon the house will be full. We will be having such a wonderful party to-morrow night.'

Amanda felt frozen as though her feet had taken root to the floor. She could not believe that this beautiful girl had been so corrupted, so debased. Surely she was parroting the words of Lord Langham, making up these shocking things to hurt the woman she saw as interfering in her life.

Then a smooth, silky voice behind her spoke and Amanda knew it was all true. 'Yes, a wonderful party tomorrow night, and you, Mrs Clare, appear to have invited yourself.'

She spun round. Lord Langham lounged elegantly in the doorway, his smile saturnine as he watched her face. 'Come here, my love.' Diana ran to his side and he put an arm around her, caressingly. 'Such a clever girl. Such a fast learner, Mrs Clare.'

'Stand aside, my lord,' Amanda said, trying to keep her voice steady and confident.

'But no, you are our guest. I insist,' he said with an emphasis on the last word. 'You invited yourself here, you will participate—fully—in our revels tomorrow night.'

'You mean...' Amanda could hardly believe the nightmare she had stumbled into.

'Exactly. There are never enough young ladies to go around for try as one might, one simply cannot get the quality one's friends require.' He smiled at her as though asking her to share in his difficulty over recruiting domestic staff.

'That would be rape!'

'That all depends on you my dear.'

'I will have the law on you! You cannot abduct respectable women off the streets!'

'Abduct? But my dear—Amanda, is it not? You came here of your own free will. I have no doubt you enquired the way along your route, and enquired it of people of the first respectability who will all testify that you were alone and under no duress. You asked for me at the gate house, and you walked in here quite willingly, as my butler will testify. Where is the abduction? And before you advance any other arguments, I think a married lady is going to have a problem proving rape, is she not? Always assuming you have the courage to expose yourself to the resulting notoriety attendant on making a fuss about this.'

'I would rather die!' Amanda spat at him.

'They all say that,' he remarked languidly. 'They never mean it, you know. Now, I have guests to receive. Food and hot water will be brought up to you. Until tomorrow night, I bid you farewell.'

The door shut and the key turned. Through the heavy panels Amanda could hear the faint sounds of Diana's laughter. She stood in the middle of the room, fighting down her fear and nausea, until things stopped spinning around her and her breathing calmed.

'I must not panic!' Amanda said out loud and the sound of her own voice in the stillness steadied her. She had walked into this nightmare and it was up to her to get herself out. She had told no one where she was going or why, so there could be no hope of rescue. She almost gave way to self-recrimination, then shook herself out of it. How could any sane person have imagined such a situation or have guarded against it?

The door was indeed locked and none of the other

doors in the room led to anything but the most shallow
closets. The chimney was wide, but as she peered up
she saw there was a heavy iron smoke baffle across it:
doubtless it could be removed to admit a chimney boy,
but it was too heavy for her to shift.

That left the window. It was locked shut and the
panes were firmly bedded in their leading. It might be
possible to smash it open, but only by creating the most
incredible amount of noise, and once open there would
be no escape. The brickwork seemed to fall straight to
the ground with nothing, not even ivy, to offer a hand-
hold.

It did, however, offer a fine viewpoint, for it appeared
to be the window over the front door. Amanda observed
a number of carriages pull up, exclusively with male
occupants, and shuddered. If she could not get out, was
there any weapon to be had? A search of every drawer
and closet produced only a long silver skewer, possibly
pressed into service at some time as a letter opener. It
was not very sharp, but Amanda did not want to kill
anyone, simply make her escape, and it made her feel
a little more secure.

With the skewer clasped in her hand, she resumed
her post at the window and tried to see who was arriving. Perhaps six carriages came, and then there was a
lull. Despite her fear and horror, Amanda realised she
was very hungry and thirsty. When would a servant
come with the promised food and water? Would there
be any chance of making her escape then?

Someone on foot appeared from the direction of the
stables. Amanda frowned, she did not think she had
missed anyone arriving. Then she saw it was Jay, strolling up to the front door in his riding dress.

'Oh, thank God!' Amanda pressed her face to the

glass, terrified that this was simply a vision brought on
by her mental state. Then, as he vanished under the door
canopy, she realised that he could not be here for her,
for he did not know where she was.

'No!' The single despairing whisper seemed to fill
the room. If he was not here for her, then he was a
guest... The implications were so awful that all her
courage, all her self-control, ebbed away, leaving her
huddled on the window seat, too devastated even to cry.

There was a noise at the door. Amanda lifted her head
and listened. Yes, unmistakably the key was being
turned. Suddenly she did not care what she had to do
to get out of this place. With the skewer held like a
dagger in her fist, she flew across the room and stood
behind the door as it swung open.

A man walked in and shut the door behind him and
with a sob of determination she lunged at the unpro-
tected back. The little noise gave her away. He spun
round, catching her upraised hand, then pulling her to
him in a smothering embrace. His fingers round her
wrist were so tight she dropped the skewer with a cry
of pain, then she realised who was holding her.

'You!'

Jay held on to her out of sheer self-defence, for her
eyes were spitting fury, her teeth were bared and her
fingers curled into talons. 'Amanda, stop it! You are
safe now!'

'Safe! What are you doing here?'

'Looking for you.' Then her meaning must have sunk
in and he stared down into her anguished face. 'Looking
for you, Amanda,' he repeated.

'How did you know I was here?' she demanded.
'You are a guest here, are you not? Tell me the truth,
I am sick of these hideous games.'

'No! My footman described you. He said a lady had called and was anxious and distressed. I went to your lodgings and your maid—Susan, is it?—told me you had gone out in the gig and that you were upset. She let me into your room when I asked her what you had been doing. I found the *Peerage* open as you had left it and your note, screwed up on the dressing table.'

'Oh! Oh, Jay, I am so sorry.' Amanda collapsed shaking against his chest. 'I saw you walk in here so calmly and openly, and everything else had turned into such a nightmare, I—'

'You did not know who to trust,' he finished for her. 'The easiest way to get into somewhere where you should not be is to act as though you had every right to be there. My face is not unfamiliar to Langham's servants: I just walked in and airily announced that I had ridden on ahead and my carriage was half an hour behind me. They were in such a flurry that I was able to slip upstairs. Luckily your door was the only one I could see with the key on the outside.'

Amanda clung to him, hardly understanding the words, just drawing comfort and strength from the feel of him, the warm, familiar scent of him. Jay pressed her down into a chair.

'Now tell me, has he touched you?'

'No! No…just words. Just the promise that I would be forced to join his…party tomorrow night.'

'My God!' Jay spun away from her and took two rapid paces across the room. He took his hand from his pocket and Amanda saw he was holding a slender, long-barrelled pistol. 'I am going to kill him,' he said, quite calmly.

'No!' Amanda got to her feet and clung to his arm.

'Please, Jay, the scandal! Too many people know I am here. And then there is Diana.'

She saw his lips tighten. 'Oh, Jay, I am so sorry to have to tell you this, but she is already his mistress.' He said nothing. 'And not only that. Jay, I cannot repeat what she said, but I am afraid he has utterly corrupted her.'

'Her upbringing had already done that,' he said at last. 'Langham has merely finished the process.'

'You knew, then?'

'Oh, yes, for many months now. But because of her mother, I felt I had to keep trying.'

'Her mother?' Amanda was completely confused. 'Lord Oughton told me at Holkham that you intended to marry Diana. What has her mother got to do with it?'

'Oughton!' Jay looked at her, then slowly shook his head. 'So that was why you were suddenly so cool towards me!'

'But of course.' She walked away from him and took the chair again. Her legs were too shaky to stand.

'I will have words to say with James Oughton when I can find him,' Jay said grimly. 'I had not expected an old friend to play me such a trick for his own ends.'

'Oh, no.' Amanda could almost see the humour in the situation. 'He is not courting me, we are only friends. And he honestly believes you to be in love with Diana—he is quite worried about it.'

Jay shook his head, his face suddenly alight with laughter. 'What a tangle! Now, we must get out of here.'

'Not before you promise me that you will not call out Lord Langham,' Amanda said fiercely. 'It will compromise me, and whatever Diana is, you could be ruining any chance of her at least marrying the man.' And you could get killed, she thought, but did not say it. Jay was too angry to be prudent on his own behalf, she could only hope he would be careful on hers.

'If you can swear to me he has not laid a finger on you.' She nodded and Jay shrugged. 'Very well, Miss Prudence, if that is your wish.' He looked out of the window. 'Damn it, there are more guests. We had better stay here until they have been received.'

'Tell me about Diana's mother,' Amanda prompted. 'Is she anything to do with that strange flash of memory you had? Do you recall when you were so angry to discover that I had married an older man?'

'Yes, how could I forget it?' There was no other chair in the room, so he came and sat on the floor beside hers, his back against it, his eyes on the door, the elegantly lethal pistol in one hand. 'Clarissa was my second cousin, and four years older than me. She was the happiest, sweetest person you could ever meet. She was a cross between an angel and an older sister, and as I grew older she became, I suppose, my first glimpse of what else a woman could be. Not that I understood that, I was only thirteen when she married: all I knew was that I worshipped her.

'Her father fell into debt and, quite literally, sold her off to Poste who was a libertine even then. His first wife was dead, no one quite seemed to know how, and within a year, so was Clarissa, giving birth to Diana.'

He fell silent. His dark head was resting against the arm of the chair, his hair just out of touch of Amanda's fingertips. She longed to touch it, caress it, but she did not dare break the mood. 'Poor lady. And poor Diana,' she said after a moment. 'No mother and a father like that.'

Jay got to his feet, his eyes shadowed. 'Enough ancient history,' he said briskly. 'Time to get out of here.'

'We are surely not going to walk out of the front door?'

'No, not this time. Come, and stay behind me.' Jay checked the corridor and gestured for her to come out, turning the key in the lock and leaving it there. 'They will give themselves a headache wondering how you escaped,' he whispered as they trod softly to the head of the stairs.

There was noise from the rooms at the rear of the hall, but no servants in sight. Jay hissed, 'Follow me,' and they descended the stairs to the point where a tapestry cloaked the wall. 'Wait,' and he was across the hall and trying the door opposite. After a moment he gestured to her and she ran, whisking in after him as another door opened and the sound of voices swelled.

Then it was the work of a moment to open a window, climb out and run across the grass to the concealing shrubs. 'My gig,' she whispered.

'Is it hired?' She nodded. 'I'll compensate the stables, forget it now. I have a chaise on the other side of the park. Can you manage?'

'Yes, of course,' said Amanda stoutly, and promptly fainted.

Chapter Twenty-Two

Amanda came round to find herself being handed up into the grasp of a burly stranger and tried to struggle.

'It is all right, Amanda, this is my groom, John,' said a voice in her ear and she realised that Jay was holding her. She stopped fighting and was soon seated in the curricle with Jay beside her and the groom tucking a rug around her knees.

'She looks in a poor way, Mr Jared,' he observed gruffly.

'Mrs Clare has had an unpleasant experience, John, and the sooner we can get her away safe the better.' He saw Amanda's expression at the free use of her name and added, as the man swung up behind them, 'John has been my groom since I was a boy—as you can tell by the disrespectful way he addresses me. You may trust him as you would trust me.'

There was a chuckle from behind. 'Can't be doing with all this "me lording."'

'He is fierce enough of my dignity in front of others, though,' Jay remarked, giving his team their head now they were out onto the road.

'Yes, well, I'm an Earl's head groom, and they had better not forget it,' John muttered.

Amanda managed a small smile. 'It is his dignity he is defending, my lord, not your own.'

'I fear so. Amanda, you need to sleep, but I do not think it is safe for you to do so while we are driving at this pace. Can you hold on for a few miles? I know of a respectable inn, off this road a way. I cannot believe Langham will attempt to follow you, and he has no way of knowing you can get far away: I think we can be assured of some peace and rest there.'

Amanda murmured that she was quite all right, and set herself to prove it. It was no easy task, although the fresh air and the swaying of the curricle provided some counter to the wave of exhausted lethargy that was sweeping over her.

She was safe. Jay did not love Diana Poste. Those two facts kept whirling in her brain until she was dizzy. But did he still have any feelings for her? He had said nothing of love: she could place no reliance on his desire to challenge Lord Langham. Any gentleman confronted with that libertine's actions towards a lady would have done just the same. And she had—if only for a moment—believed he was part of Langham's infamous circle. Could he forgive her that?

Jay was setting a killing pace and the curricle swayed and lurched along the post road. John's muttered commentary from behind her provided a bizarre chorus to the entire ghastly experience. 'You'll break our necks, that's what you'll do, Mr Jared...watch that leader... there now, look at the way you caught that whip point, taught you well, I did... Damn it, sir, you'll have the wheel off!'

Jay appeared to ignore him completely until after one

particularly vehement protest he said, 'Be quiet, do, John. Mrs Clare does not need to hear you complaining about your rheumatism!' This effectively silenced the groom, who subsided muttering.

At last Jay slowed and turned the team into a side road. A mile further on at a crossroads he pulled up in front of a substantial and well-kept inn. 'It looks as though the recommendation for this place was correct, John,' he remarked as the groom jumped down to fetch the landlord.

'Lord Witherington is rarely out when it comes to good food,' the groom agreed. 'House, there!'

The landlord hurried out and Amanda noticed the inn sign. 'Two Magpies,' she murmured. 'Two for joy…' Everything was slipping away again, but she was just conscious of Jay's voice as he lifted her down into John's arms.

'We have had an accident on the road, landlord. My wife is very shaken up and all our luggage lost. Do you have a room and a private parlour where we can rest while my man goes…?' His voice faded away and Amanda circled down into darkness.

She came to herself to find she was sitting in a comfortable wing chair in a cosy parlour, her feet on a stool and a rug over her knees. A respectable-looking woman in a vast white apron was setting a tray down on the table and exclaimed, 'There now, sir, she is opening her eyes, poor lady!'

Amanda blinked, tried to focus and realised Jay was at her side. 'What you need, my dear, is a glass of wine and some food. Mrs Brownsmith has not eaten since this morning,' he added to the landlady, who went out clucking and saying that if they wanted anything at all, he only had to ring, otherwise she'd leave the poor lady to rest and not disturb them until the morning.

'Mrs Brownsmith?' Her mouth seemed to be full of flannel and it was an effort to speak.

'Convenient, is it not, that we have an alias ready to hand?' Jay was pouring wine, ruby red, into a glass and holding it for her. 'Here, try this. Although I seem to recall being mortified by you telling Mrs Clay at the Lamb and Flag that my given name was Augustus. I think I will stick with Jared—or Jay, it is your choice.' He pushed the glass back towards her lips when she tried to reject it after only one sip. 'No, you are as weak as a kitten with shock and exhaustion. Another sip and I will give you some of our hostess's vegetable broth.'

He patiently spoon-fed her the warm, savoury soup and gradually the mists seemed to clear and some strength come back into her limbs. It had seemed that they were back in the inn after the stagecoach accident and that everything in between was simply a nightmare, but now reality came back.

'Thank you,' she said. 'I feel much better now.'

'The wine is by your side, try and drink a little more.' Jay looked at her closely, seemed satisfied with what he saw, and took a chair at the table. He began to eat soup, bread and cheese, washed down with a tankard of ale and let her sit quietly, nodding approvingly when she sipped a little of the claret.

'What has happened?' she asked at length.

'Since we arrived here? John has borrowed a hack and has ridden into Brighton with a note from me to Miss Porter, assuring her of your safety and promising you will be returned to her tomorrow. Meanwhile the Brownsmiths, who you must agree are a well-travelled, if adventure-prone, couple, are settled here for the night.

Mrs Whiteleaf the landlady has assured me that she has set out for you a nightgown, a brush, a comb and you have only to ring for whatever else you might require.'

Amanda felt the strength gradually flowing back into her body. Her mind, too, seemed much clearer and she was no longer getting flashes of Lord Langham's face or memories of the absolute despair she had fallen into.

'And where are we sleeping?' she asked. She saw Jay's eyes narrow in amusement at the sharp edge to her voice.

'There are two bedchambers,' he said equably. 'You have only to choose.'

'Oh.' She had expected to have to be firm with him, to insist on a separate bedchamber, to explain that whatever the situation in the past, she could not carry on with the dangerously passionate relationship they had had. Yet, even though the ambiguities and mysteries were all swept away, he had said nothing of his feelings for her, which meant, as one realised if one was sensible about it, that he had none deeper than attraction and friendship.

'Unless,' his voice said softly in her ear, 'unless of course you wish to economise on our shot and share a room, my darling.'

Amanda twisted round in her chair, her heart leaping. He had moved so silently she had not realised he was there.

'Ja…Jared…what did you call me?'

'My darling. Do you dislike it? I must say that I like the sound of my real name on your lips. I had grown used to Jay, but the way you say Jared…say it again.'

'Jared,' she said and his lips covered hers.

She found herself lifted and carried across the room, through a door and into a bedchamber. Jay…Jared laid her down on it and stepped back. 'You are tired, I should not have said anything.'

'No!' Amanda struggled to sit up in the enveloping feather bed and held out her arms. 'Jared, I am feeling much better, I promise you. You called me your darling.'

He sat on the edge of the bed, just out of her reach, looking at her. His mouth twisted wryly. 'I dare not touch you. You look so white, so fragile. My God, Amanda, when I think of you in that house, in Langham's power…'

'It is over,' she said gently. 'A bad dream.'

'I wanted to tell you I loved you, but to even speak of it in that place, let alone kiss you, that would make everything I felt seem smirched. And you thought that I was part of that group—' He broke off.

'No, stop! I am so sorry,' she cried. 'I knew almost at once it couldn't be so, my heart could not believe what my eyes were telling me. Jared, please forgive me!'

'I would forgive you anything Amanda,' Jared said simply. 'Anything. The question is, can you forgive me for my arrogance?'

'Which particular incidence of arrogance?' Amanda enquired wickedly, suddenly realising that against all the odds, the dream was coming true, that surely everything was going to be all right.

Jared shot her a gleaming look. 'Minx,' he said appreciatively. 'I should have told you about Diana, told you what I was about. But it was going to be a squalid affair, however things came out. I had no confidence that I could extricate her—at that point, remember I had no notion of just how mired in this she had become. I feared I would end up calling out Langham and that alone would have created a mighty scandal. I thought I could go and deal with it as best I could, make one last throw to help Clarissa's daughter, then come back to you.'

'And at Holkham I was cold?'

'And I was too worried to realise what you might be thinking. And of course, I had no knowledge that my helpful friend was convincing you that I had fallen for a beautiful schoolroom miss!'

'And in London?' Amanda prompted.

'By then I had a good idea of exactly what that young woman was about. The last thing I wanted was you going anywhere near her poisonous tongue, her evil little manipulative schemes.'

'But why did you not tell me?' Amanda demanded. 'Have you any idea what I thought you were so anxious about?'

'No, I just thought you were angry with me and that you had found a much more satisfactory admirer in Oughton!'

'I thought you were afraid that I would behave like a spiteful, rejected woman and poison Diana against you. I did not relish being portrayed as the cast-off, bitter lover, believe me.'

Jared looked at her aghast. 'I would never…no wonder you were so angry with me. But why on earth were you so anxious to try and save Diana from Langham? You did not know the girl, you did not know her story, you had no reason to help any connection of mine.'

'I thought you were in love with her,' Amanda said simply. 'She told me she was in love with you, but had to obey her father. Besides trying to help any girl in such a position, I thought it would be best for you.'

He looked down at his clasped hands for a long moment, then looked up and met her eyes. 'I thought…I hoped that you were in love with me. Was I wrong?'

'No, Jared.'

'But you were prepared to do that because you thought I loved her?'

'Yes.'

'My God, Amanda!' He was on his feet, one fist thudding into the bedpost, his face dark with an emotion she had never seen before.

'I am sorry if my feelings embarrass you, I do not have any claim on you, I am going away…' she began to stammer, appalled at what she had unleashed, her happiness replaced by an aching void of hurt.

'Embarrass me!' He swung round to face her, green eyes gleaming, face alive with a sort of astounded wonder. 'I am just wondering what I have done to deserve you, how I can ever be worthy of you.' He came to her side and fell on one knee, catching up her hands in his. 'Amanda, I love you to distraction. I've loved you since that moment in the field just outside Holt when you looked up at me and said that one should make every effort to help one's friends. Do you remember? You said it with such a mischievous twinkle in your eye, and off you went to do battle on my behalf, risking reputation and peace of mind without a qualm.'

'I had qualms,' Amanda admitted. 'I was finding you dangerously attractive even then and repeated daily the reminder that you probably had a wife and four children!'

'Those children!' He was laughing now. 'How I came to dread the look that came over your face. I knew I was about to be reminded of them yet again, poor little devils.'

'Why poor little devils?'

'Because I assumed I was a dreadful father—you were making me certain I was a dreadful husband.'

'I am sure you would make an excellent father and husband,' Amanda said, keeping her voice absolutely neutral.

'Really?' He carried her hands to his lips. 'Do you think four is a good number of children, my love? Perhaps three, or six?'

'Is that a proposal, my lord?' It was curiously hard to speak.

'It is, madam. Will you do me the honour of becoming my wife?'

'Oh, yes, Jared! With all my heart.' And then she was in his arms and he did not seem worried any longer that she was too fragile to touch. His mouth roved from her lips to her throat, to the swell of her breast then back to her mouth until she was whimpering with desire, her fingers moving from his hair to the fastenings of his shirt, never still.

Somehow all her clothes were gone and he was looking down at her stretched beneath him on the big soft bed. She had expected to feel shy, but all she could do was glory in the look in his eyes.

'Jared!'

He smiled at her and began to pull off his own clothes and she could, at last, run her hands down the hard muscles of his back, flatten her palm against the smooth planes of chest and thigh, find her eyes widening at the aroused strength of him.

She had been so used to the gentle, almost apologetic lovemaking that was all she had experienced before. Jared's strength, his certainty that she could feel as powerfully as he, was utterly intoxicating. Each touch was a new sensation as his hands roved where they wanted, making her gasp and arch against him. His mouth lingered on the apex of each breast in turn, sending slivers of delight from each taut nipple and the stubble on his unshaven chin sent a delicious *frisson* through her as it touched her sensitised skin.

When she thought she could bear no more, that she was going to shatter into a thousand pieces of sensation, he paused, looking down into her wide gaze with eyes dark with passion. 'Yes, Amanda?'

'Oh, yes, Jared.' Then agreement turned to exultant delight. 'Oh, yes, oh, Jared, oh, yes...'

'I love you, I love you...'

Mrs Clare floated gently up into a delicious state of half-sleep, half-waking and hovered there for a few moments, lulled by the reassuring sound of deep, regular, male breathing from the other side of the bed.

Her hand touched a warm, naked flank and her body sank into the central dip of the bed, to touch his lightly.

Amanda Clare moaned gently, wriggling closer to the long form beside her, then sighed as a strong arm gathered her close in a comforting, sleepy embrace. She began to wake again, to become conscious of his nearness and her own pleasurable anticipation.

Very cautiously Amanda opened her eyes and found herself looking into the sleepy green gaze of her bedmate. He was so close that their noses were almost touching. Amanda realised that she was holding her breath and that her heart was banging so hard against her ribs that they felt bruised.

The man's eyes widened slightly, then crinkled into a smile as he leaned forward and kissed her firmly on the lips. 'Good morning, my love.'

'This time you remember where you are?' she teased.

'Oh, yes,' replied Jared Mansell, Earl of Severn. 'I recall exactly where I am, who I am and most definitely who you are, my love. But should you have any difficulty recalling it, I intend to remind you all over again.'

And he did, to such effect that Mrs Whiteleaf, knocking on the door with the breakfast tray, gave up and went away again. 'Poor things,' she muttered as she went down the stairs. 'I do hope they slept well.'

*   *   *   *   *

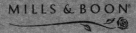

2 FREE

books and a surprise gift!

We would like to take this opportunity to thank you for reading this Mills & Boon® book by offering you the chance to take TWO more specially selected titles from the Historical Romance™ series absolutely FREE! We're also making this offer to introduce you to the benefits of the Reader Service™—

- ★ FREE home delivery
- ★ FREE gifts and competitions
- ★ FREE monthly Newsletter
- ★ Exclusive Reader Service discount
- ★ Books available before they're in the shops

Accepting these FREE books and gift places you under no obligation to buy, you may cancel at any time, even after receiving your free shipment. Simply complete your details below and return the entire page to the address below. *You don't even need a stamp!*

YES! Please send me 2 free Historical Romance books and a surprise gift. I understand that unless you hear from me, I will receive 4 superb new titles every month for just £3.49 each, postage and packing free. I am under no obligation to purchase any books and may cancel my subscription at any time. The free books and gift will be mine to keep in any case.

H3ZEA

Ms/Mrs/Miss/Mr ....Initials...................................
BLOCK CAPITALS PLEASE

Surname ....

Address ....

....

....Postcode ....

Send this whole page to:
UK: FREEPOST CN81, Croydon, CR9 3WZ
EIRE: PO Box 4546, Kilcock, County Kildare (stamp required)